Copyright © 2023 Fred Charles

First published August, 2023

Cover Design by Fred Charles

Dark Confessions

"The Beast of Birkenshaw."

The Peter Manuel Story

Author

Freds Henry Charles

Introduction

The Shadows of Infamy

In the annals of criminal history, there exists a chilling and sinister tale that transcends the boundaries of the macabre, a story that continues to haunt the collective memory of Scotland and beyond. It is a tale of malevolence that strikes at the very heart of our darkest fears, a narrative where the boundaries between humanity and monstrosity blur, and the fragility of our existence stands starkly illuminated. This is the story of Peter Manuel, a name synonymous with terror, an embodiment of evil that defied the norms of sanity, and a man whose gruesome deeds etched an indelible mark upon the pages of true crime lore.

In the realm of criminal psychopathy, Peter Manuel occupies a realm of infamy all his own. His life and crimes are a grotesque tapestry woven from the darkest threads of human behaviour, a mosaic of malevolence that bewildered even the most seasoned investigators and sent shockwaves through the tranquil landscapes of post-war Scotland. The haunting enigma of Peter Manuel is a saga that has both repulsed and captivated the human imagination for decades, leaving us to grapple with the timeless questions of morality, justice, and the depths of human depravity.

The Fascination of the Macabre

Why, one might wonder, do we find ourselves irresistibly drawn to the darkest corners of human existence, to stories that chill our bones and send shivers down our spines? Perhaps it is because we, as a species, are innately wired to seek out and confront our deepest fears. In the dimly lit corridors of our psyche, there exists a curiosity that compels us to gaze into the abyss, to peer into the minds of those who have willingly abandoned the moral compass that guides the rest of us. It is a fascination with the macabre, a morbid curiosity that demands satisfaction, even as it threatens to consume us.

Peter Manuel's story encapsulates this very fascination with the dark and the demented. His crimes were so heinous, so unfathomable, that they seemed to transcend the bounds of reality. The newspapers of the time, with their sensational headlines and gruesome descriptions, painted a picture of a fiendish murderer who revelled in the suffering of others. The very mention of his name sent shivers down the spines of Scotland's citizens, and his reign of terror left an indelible scar on the national psyche.

But it is not just the horror of his crimes that captivates us; it is the enigma of the man himself. What drove Peter Manuel to commit such unspeakable acts? How did he elude capture for so long, taunting the authorities with his brazen audacity? And what inner demons led him down the twisted path of violence and death? These are questions that have gnawed at the curiosity of generations, questions that demand answers, and it is the quest for these answers that propels us forward into the heart of darkness.

The Genesis of this Journey

As an author, I too have been inexorably drawn into this abyss, compelled by an unrelenting desire to uncover the truth behind the enigma of Peter Manuel. This journey into the depths of his life and crimes is not undertaken lightly, for it is a journey that forces us to confront the very essence of evil. It is a journey that challenges our perceptions of justice, morality, and the human capacity for malevolence.

My motivation in embarking on this odyssey is twofold. First and foremost, it is a solemn duty to ensure that the memory of Peter Manuel's victims is preserved, their stories told, and their voices heard. In the midst of the lurid headlines and sensationalism that surrounded Manuel's reign of terror, it is all too easy to forget that his victims were real people with families, dreams, and aspirations. They deserve to be more than mere footnotes in the chronicle of a serial killer's infamy.

Secondly, it is an opportunity to delve deep into the psyche of a killer, to explore the complexities of human behaviour and the factors that can transform an individual into a harbinger of death. It is a chance to shed light on the darkest recesses of the human soul and, in doing so, to gain a deeper understanding of the fragility of our own humanity.

The Structure of This Narrative

This narrative is not merely a recollection of events; it is an immersive exploration of the life and times of Peter Manuel. We will journey through the annals of history, from his early years and the shadows that cast their ominous presence, to the murder spree that shook a nation, and finally to the courtroom drama that would decide his fate. We will delve into the lives of his victims, the terror they endured, and the impact his actions had on their families and communities.

We will dissect the investigative efforts that sought to unmask the killer and the legal battles that would ultimately determine his destiny. We will confront the moral and ethical questions surrounding the death penalty and the enduring legacy of Peter Manuel's crimes. We will, in essence, peer into the abyss and seek to understand what lies within.

As we embark on this harrowing journey, I invite you, dear reader, to prepare yourself for a descent into the darkest recesses of the human soul. Together, we will unravel the enigma of Peter Manuel, confront the horrors he unleashed, and attempt to fathom the unfathomable. In doing so, we may emerge with a greater understanding of the fragile threads that bind us to our own humanity, and the eternal struggle between good and evil that defines the human experience.

Welcome to the chilling world of Peter Manuel, a world where the shadows of infamy loom large, and where the pursuit of truth may lead us to the very precipice of darkness.

Dark Confessions   " The Beast of Birkenshaw "

Chapter 1

The Early Years

Childhood and Background

In the quiet, unassuming town of Newarthill, nestled in the heart of Lanarkshire, Scotland, a darkness was born. It was in this unremarkable setting, amidst the rolling hills and the comforting embrace of a close-knit community, that Peter Manuel took his first breath on March 13, 1927. To understand the genesis of a killer, we must first peer into the seemingly innocuous beginnings of his life.

The Humble Roots: The Manuel Family's Journey

Peter Manuel's early life was deeply rooted in the humble beginnings of his family. The Manuels, like many immigrants of their era, sought a new life in Scotland, leaving behind their native Spain in search of opportunities in the industrial landscape of Newarthill. However, even as they pursued their dreams in this new land, they were confronted with the stark reality of poverty that persisted in their lives.

1. The Immigrant Experience

Peter Manuel's parents, Peter Sr. and Bridget Manuel, embodied the immigrant experience of their time. Leaving their homeland behind, they embarked on a journey to a foreign land, driven by the hope of creating a better life for themselves and their family. Their pursuit of the "American Dream" in the Scottish context mirrored the aspirations of countless others who sought refuge and opportunity in new lands.

2. The Toil of the Coal Miner

Peter Sr., by profession a coal miner, represented the working-class backbone of the industrialized society. His days were marked by gruelling labour beneath the earth's surface, where he endured the harsh conditions of the mining profession. The ceaseless grind of the mines, with its physical demands and safety hazards, was a testament to the sacrifices made by labourers like Peter Sr. in pursuit of a livelihood.

3. Bridget's Role: The Family's Backbone

Bridget Manuel, on the other hand, played a vital role in the family's humble household. Devout in her Catholic faith, she dedicated herself to the domestic sphere, nurturing and caring for her children. In an era when traditional gender roles were often rigidly defined, Bridget's commitment to her family's well-being underscored her role as the family's backbone.

4. Modesty and Resilience

The Manuel family's life was characterized by modesty, resilience, and a deep sense of community. They lived in an environment where hard work was a daily reality, faith provided solace and guidance, and the bonds of community were essential for support and mutual assistance.

5. The Siblings: Martin and Annie

Peter Manuel had two siblings, a brother named Martin and a sister named Annie. Their lives were intertwined by the shared experiences of growing up in a working-class immigrant family. Together, they navigated the challenges of their environment, forming enduring familial bonds that would shape their individual journeys.

Conclusion: The Foundation of Peter Manuel's Story

Understanding the humble roots of Peter Manuel provides essential context for comprehending the complex narrative of his life. The Manuels' immigrant experience, marked by hard work, faith, and community ties, laid the foundation for the journey that Peter would ultimately undertake—one that would lead him down a path of darkness, crime, and infamy. The contrast between his modest beginnings and his later life as a notorious serial killer adds depth to the tragic tale of Peter Manuel.

The Early Years of Peter Manuel: Shadows of Deceit

Peter Manuel's childhood, though seemingly uneventful on the surface, held within it subtle hints of the darkness that would come to define his later life. These formative years, marked by education and the development of his personality, revealed early signs of his penchant for lies and deceit.

1. A Facade of Normalcy

Peter Manuel's early years were outwardly unremarkable. He attended local schools, engaging in the typical activities of childhood. To those around him, he appeared reasonably intelligent and capable, blending into the fabric of the community. Yet, beneath this facade of normalcy, a troubling undercurrent was beginning to emerge.

2. The Seeds of Deceit

It was during these formative years that the seeds of deceit were sown. Peter exhibited a propensity for dishonesty and manipulation that would become increasingly pronounced as he grew older. This behaviour, often dismissed as childhood mischief, foreshadowed the manipulative tendencies that would later come to define his criminal career.

3. Fabrications and Manipulation

Peter's willingness to fabricate stories and manipulate those around him set him apart from his peers. Whether it was bending the truth to avoid trouble or crafting elaborate falsehoods to gain an advantage, his early proclivity for deceit marked him as someone who was willing to blur the boundaries of honesty to achieve his goals.

4. The Early Warning Signs

In hindsight, these early warning signs take on a chilling significance. While many children engage in imaginative storytelling and minor deceptions, Peter Manuel's behaviour hinted at a deeper and more troubling inclination. His ability to manipulate emotions and perceptions was an early indicator of the cunning and manipulation he would later employ in his criminal activities.

5. The Intersection of Nature and Nurture

The origins of Peter Manuel's deceitful tendencies are complex and likely a result of both nature and nurture. It is difficult to pinpoint the exact causes of his behaviour, but a combination of genetic predisposition and environmental factors may have contributed to the development of his dark personality traits.

Conclusion: The Growing Darkness

The early years of Peter Manuel's life provide a window into the gradual unfolding of his sinister tendencies. While the community may have seen a seemingly ordinary child, beneath the surface, a complex and troubled individual was emerging. These formative experiences, marked by deception and manipulation, would lay the foundation for the darkness that would ultimately consume him and lead him down a path of crime and infamy.

The Roots of Alienation: Unravelling Peter Manuel's Deviance

1. A Sense of Otherness

Peter Manuel's early years were marked by a profound sense of otherness. His Spanish heritage set him apart in the predominantly Scottish community in which he grew up. This marked difference in ethnicity often left him on the fringes of acceptance, contributing to a growing sense of alienation. The experience of being an outsider, of not quite belonging, could have been a crucial factor in his detachment from societal norms.

2. The Burden of Being Different

Being a member of an ethnic minority in a predominantly homogenous society can be challenging for anyone, especially a child. Manuel likely grappled with questions of identity and struggled to reconcile his Spanish heritage with his Scottish surroundings. This internal conflict may have manifested itself in various ways, including a growing sense of alienation and a desire to assert his identity, even if it meant doing so through deviant behaviour.

3. Family Dynamics and Emotional Neglect

The role of family dynamics in Manuel's upbringing cannot be underestimated. While his parents, Peter Sr. and Bridget, worked tirelessly to provide for their children, their efforts may have inadvertently left emotional voids within the family unit. The long hours Peter Sr. spent toiling in the mines and Bridget's dedication to domestic chores left little room for nurturing emotional connections with their children.

4. The Emotional Fallout

The emotional fallout of this dynamic may have contributed to Manuel's sense of alienation. The absence of emotional support and nurturance within the family may have left him seeking fulfilment and validation elsewhere, potentially leading him down a path of seeking recognition through negative means, such as criminal behaviour.

5. The Intersection of Factors

It is essential to recognize that Peter Manuel's deviance likely resulted from the intersection of various factors. His sense of otherness, coupled with potential emotional neglect, may have created a fertile ground for the development of deviant tendencies. These early experiences could have set in motion a series of events that ultimately led him to commit heinous crimes.

Conclusion: A Complex Tapestry of Alienation

The roots of Peter Manuel's deviance are woven into a complex tapestry of factors, including his sense of otherness due to his Spanish heritage and potential emotional neglect within his family. These early experiences of alienation and detachment from societal norms may have played a pivotal role in shaping his criminal path. Understanding the profound impact of these formative years is essential to comprehending the intricate web of factors that led to one of Scotland's most notorious criminal careers.

The Making of a Killer: Unravelling the Complex Interplay

To truly understand the making of a killer, we must embark on a journey into the intricate interplay of nature and nurture that shaped Peter Manuel's life. His early years were indeed marked by a toxic combination of alienation, deception, and emotional detachment, but these factors alone do not provide a complete explanation for the dark path he would eventually tread.

1. Nature vs. Nurture: A Complex Dichotomy

The age-old debate of nature versus nurture surfaces prominently when examining the life of Peter Manuel. It asks whether a person's inherent traits and genetic predispositions (nature) or their environment and upbringing (nurture) play a more significant role in determining their behaviour. In Manuel's case, both sides of this dichotomy appear to have contributed to his transformation into a killer.

2. The Nature Component: Genetic Predisposition

While not all individuals with difficult childhoods become killers, some research suggests that genetic predispositions may make certain individuals more susceptible to deviant behaviour. Factors such as personality traits, neurological conditions, and even the potential presence of mental illness can be influenced by one's genetic makeup. These factors might have played a role in shaping Manuel's propensity for violence and manipulation.

3. The Nurture Component: Environmental Influences

On the nurture side of the equation, we must consider the environmental factors that surrounded Manuel during his formative years. The toxic brew of alienation, deception, and emotional neglect created a challenging backdrop for his development. The sense of otherness he felt due to his Spanish heritage, coupled with his early proclivity for deceit, may have laid the groundwork for a distorted sense of identity and a detachment from societal norms.

4. The Complex Interplay

It's crucial to recognize that it's not a straightforward case of either nature or nurture but rather the complex interplay between the two that shaped Manuel's path. His genetic predispositions may have made him more susceptible to certain behaviours, while his challenging environment fuelled his descent into criminality.

5. Unravelling the Mystery

Unravelling the mystery of how an individual becomes a killer involves peering into the deepest recesses of psychology, genetics, and environmental influences. While we can identify factors that contributed to Manuel's criminality, the precise sequence of events that led to his transformation into a serial killer remains elusive.

Conclusion: A Puzzle Beyond Comprehension

The making of a killer is a puzzle that often defies complete comprehension. In Peter Manuel's case, it's a blend of genetic predispositions and environmental factors that contributed to his deviant path. To understand it fully, we must acknowledge the complexity of human behaviour, recognizing that the causes of criminality can be as multifaceted and elusive as the human psyche itself. The story of Peter Manuel underscores the intricate tapestry of influences that can lead an individual down a dark and destructive path.

The Role of Psychopathy: Unveiling the Dark Complexities

In the intricate narrative of Peter Manuel's journey towards becoming a serial killer, the presence of psychopathy emerges as a pivotal element.

Psychopathy is a complex and deeply unsettling personality disorder characterized by a disturbing array of traits, including a profound absence of empathy, manipulative behaviour, and a disturbing propensity for violence. To fathom how psychopathy influenced Manuel's descent into criminality, we must explore the multifaceted interplay between genetic predisposition and environmental factors.

1. The Nature of Psychopathy: Genetic Component

Psychopathy has long been a subject of fascination and scrutiny within the realm of psychology. While the exact origins of psychopathy remain elusive, it is widely acknowledged that there is a genetic component at play. Some individuals may carry specific genetic markers or variations that render them more susceptible to developing the traits associated with psychopathy.

2. Early Signs of Psychopathy

From an early age, the ominous shadows of psychopathy cast their presence over Peter Manuel. His readiness to lie, manipulate, and deceive bore witness to a fundamental absence of empathy for the feelings and well-being of others. These traits stand as poignant indicators of psychopathy and manifested themselves prominently in Manuel's actions and interactions with those in his sphere.

3. The Charming Facade of Manipulation

Perhaps one of the most unsettling facets of psychopathy is the ability of individuals like Peter Manuel to don a charming facade, concealing their darker proclivities beneath a veneer of affability. Psychopaths are adept at projecting an image of charm, which allows them to manipulate others with disconcerting effectiveness. This charm serves as a mask, obscuring their true nature and rendering it challenging for those in their orbit to discern the depth of their deceit.

4. The Intersection of Environmental Factors

While genetic predispositions lay a foundational framework for psychopathy, environmental factors wield considerable influence in its development. In the case of Peter Manuel, the toxic amalgamation of alienation, deception, and emotional neglect in his upbringing likely exacerbated his psychopathic tendencies. These environmental stressors may have served to nurture the growth of his manipulative and callous traits.

5. The Confluence of Factors

The confluence of genetic predisposition and environmental influences resulted in a perfect storm within Peter Manuel. His psychopathic traits found fertile soil in an environment characterized by deception, emotional voids, and a profound sense of alienation. These elements intermingled, propelling him further down the harrowing and destructive path that culminated in his reign of terror as a serial killer.

Conclusion: The Ominous Presence of Psychopathy

The role of psychopathy in Peter Manuel's progression towards becoming a serial killer is undeniably ominous and far-reaching. It serves as a stark reminder that individuals harbouring psychopathic traits can navigate the world with a facade of charm and manipulate those in their orbit with chilling precision. While genetics play a part, the intricate dance between nature and nurture in the formation of psychopathy remains a deeply complex and ongoing area of exploration, offering both insight and disquiet as we continue to grapple with the enigmatic facets of the human psyche.

The Erosion of Morality: Unveiling the Descent into Darkness

In the intricate tapestry of human psychology, it is crucial to recognize that psychopathy alone does not solely forge a path towards becoming a killer. Rather, it is the gradual erosion of moral boundaries, often influenced by a complex interplay of genetic predisposition and environmental factors, that propels an individual into the abyss of violence.

1. Beyond Psychopathy: The Moral Abyss

While psychopathy lays a foundation for certain traits and behaviours, it is the unravelling of one's moral compass that allows the journey towards violence to commence. Psychopathy may provide a fertile ground for the absence of empathy and manipulative tendencies, but it is the erosion of moral boundaries that gives these traits a direction towards malevolence.

2. Early Signs of Moral Erosion

For Peter Manuel, the erosion of morality began early in his life. His capacity for deception allowed him to engage in increasingly deviant behaviour without arousing suspicion. It was a gradual process, starting with petty thefts and vandalism, but these acts of transgression against societal norms became stepping stones on the dark path toward more heinous crimes.

3. The Progression of Deviance

The progression of deviance in Manuel's life is a harrowing illustration of how moral erosion takes hold. The initial, seemingly minor transgressions served as a gateway to more severe offenses. Acts of cruelty toward animals, a known precursor to violent behaviour in some individuals, further indicated his growing detachment from empathy and morality.

4. The Alarming Normalization

One of the most alarming aspects of moral erosion is how deviant behaviour can become normalized in the individual's mind. As Peter Manuel continued down his path, the boundaries of what was acceptable shifted for him. What might have initially been perceived as morally reprehensible gradually became a part of his new normal.

5. The Role of Environmental Reinforcement

While Manuel's psychopathic traits played a role in his moral erosion, the environment in which he operated reinforced his deviant behaviour. The lack of oversight, coupled with a lack of meaningful consequences for his actions, allowed him to descend further into the abyss.

The Disturbing Progression

The erosion of morality is a disturbing process that occurs at the intersection of psychopathy, environmental influences, and the individual's choices. It is a gradual descent into darkness, where the boundaries between right and wrong become increasingly blurred. In Peter Manuel's case, the early signs of moral erosion evolved into a chilling journey towards heinous crimes, highlighting the profound impact of both nature and nurture in shaping the moral compass of an individual. Understanding this process is essential in unravelling the complexities of criminal behaviour and the tragic transformation of an individual into a killer.

The Early Shadows

The early years of Peter Manuel's life provide a glimpse into the complex interplay of factors that would ultimately shape the mind of a killer. It was a life marked by alienation, deception, and a gradual erosion of moral boundaries. Yet, these elements alone cannot fully explain the horrors that lay ahead.

As we delve deeper into the twisted psyche of Peter Manuel, we will uncover the chilling progression of his crimes, each step leading him further into the abyss of depravity. In the chapters that follow, we will explore the murders, the investigations, and the courtroom dramas that would come to define this infamous serial killer. But always, in the background, the spectre of his early years will linger—a dark shadow that serves as a constant reminder of the intricate tapestry of factors that forge the path of a murderer.

In the next chapter, we will step into the chilling world of Peter Manuel's murders, where the first seeds of his murderous desires would bloom into full-blown horror.

Chapter 2

Peter Manuel's early criminal activities

Early Criminal Activities: Peter Manuel's descent into criminality began at a young age. He was involved in various thefts and burglaries during his teenage years. His criminal activities escalated over time, setting the stage for his later, more heinous crimes.

Early Crimes:

Housebreaking and Theft: Manuel's criminal career began with a series of housebreakings and thefts in the 1940s. These crimes primarily involved breaking into homes and stealing valuables. His skills as a housebreaker would later become instrumental in his more violent crimes.

Sexual Assault: As a teenager, Manuel escalated his criminal activities to include sexual assault. His early victims were often women he encountered while breaking into homes. These assaults foreshadowed the more heinous crimes he would commit in the future.

Car Theft: Manuel was also involved in car thefts during his youth. He exhibited a propensity for criminal activities that ranged from property crimes to violent offenses.

Arrest and Sentencing:

Manuel's criminal activities did not go unnoticed, and he was eventually arrested for his actions:

Juvenile Offender: Manuel was a juvenile when he began his criminal career, which led to his arrest as a minor offender. The legal system treated him as a young offender, and he faced sentencing in Borstal institutions.

Borstal Sentencing: Borstal institutions were intended for the rehabilitation of young offenders. Manuel was sentenced to serve time in these institutions, where he received a mix of educational and vocational training, as well as discipline aimed at reforming his behaviour.

Life in Borstal:

Life in Borstal: Shaping the Criminal Mind of Peter Manuel

The early experiences of a young offender can profoundly influence their future path in life. For Peter Manuel, his time spent in Borstal institutions during his formative years played a significant role in shaping the criminal mindset that would eventually lead him down a path of heinous crimes. In this exploration, we delve into the conditions, influences, and experiences that Manuel encountered in Borstals, shedding light on the factors that contributed to his later criminal behaviour.

Borstal Institutions: A Snapshot

Borstals were a type of youth detention centre prevalent in the United Kingdom during the early 20th century. They were established as an alternative to adult prisons, with a primary focus on rehabilitation and education for young offenders. Manuel's encounters with the Borstal system would have a profound impact on his life.

Daily Routine and Discipline

Life in Borstal was marked by a regimented daily routine that aimed to instil discipline and structure in the lives of young offenders. The typical day would begin early, with inmates rising at a designated time. Meals were provided at specific intervals, and there were scheduled periods for work, education, and recreation.

Educational Opportunities: A Double-Edged Sword

One of the key components of Borstal rehabilitation was education. Young offenders were provided with educational opportunities, including basic literacy and numeracy classes. However, the quality of education varied between institutions, and some Borstals struggled to provide a comprehensive educational program.

For someone like Manuel, who displayed a certain level of intelligence and charm, the limited educational opportunities might have left him feeling unchallenged. This lack of stimulation could have contributed to his growing sense of frustration and restlessness.

Work Assignments: Skill Development and Monotony

In addition to education, Borstals emphasized vocational training. Inmates were assigned various work tasks, such as carpentry, plumbing, or farm labour. The goal was to equip young offenders with practical skills that could be valuable upon release.

However, the nature of the work assignments could vary widely. While some inmates found purpose and skill development in their tasks, others might have experienced monotony and frustration, especially if they felt their talents were underutilized.

Peer Influence: The Borstal Community

Borstals exposed Manuel to a peer group of young offenders, some of whom had committed serious crimes. Peer influence can be a powerful force, and interactions with fellow inmates could have a significant impact on shaping his criminal mindset.

Within the Borstal community, Manuel might have encountered individuals with varying levels of criminal sophistication. These interactions could have provided him with insights into different criminal techniques, as well as a sense of belonging within a group that shared his rebellious tendencies.

Isolation from the Outside World

One of the most challenging aspects of life in Borstal was the limited contact with the outside world. Inmates had restricted access to family and friends. This isolation from loved ones and the broader community could foster a sense of abandonment or resentment.

For a young offender like Manuel, who was known to have a complex relationship with his family, this isolation might have deepened his feelings of detachment from mainstream society. The lack of external support systems could have left him emotionally vulnerable and prone to further criminal influences within the institution.

Psychological Impact: Frustration and Resentment

Extended confinement in Borstals could have had psychological consequences on Manuel. Frustration, anger, and a sense of hopelessness might have welled up within him. These emotions could have played a pivotal role in shaping his criminal mindset.

The strict discipline, limited freedoms, and perceived injustices within the Borstal system might have fuelled a growing resentment toward authority figures and society at large. Such resentment could have contributed to a sense of rebellion and defiance that Manuel would carry with him beyond the confines of the institution.

Conclusion: The Crucible of Borstal

In the crucible of Borstal institutions, Peter Manuel's character and criminal tendencies were forged. The combination of limited educational opportunities, peer influence, isolation, and psychological impact contributed to the development of a troubled young man who would go on to commit a string of heinous crimes.

Understanding Manuel's experiences in Borstals is crucial for gaining insight into the factors that shaped his criminal behaviour. While Borstals were intended for rehabilitation, they were not always effective in reforming young offenders like Manuel, whose encounters with the system would have a lasting impact on Scotland's history and criminal justice system.

Rehabilitation Efforts in Borstal: The Impact on Peter Manuel's Path

The concept of rehabilitation lies at the core of the Borstal system, aiming to reform young offenders and reintegrate them into society as law-abiding citizens. However, the success of rehabilitation programs can vary widely. In the case of Peter Manuel, it's essential to explore whether he participated in any rehabilitation or counselling programs during his time in Borstal and whether these efforts had any discernible impact on his behaviour or mindset.

Rehabilitation Programs in Borstal

Borstal institutions were designed to offer a multifaceted approach to rehabilitation. These programs typically included education, vocational training, physical exercise, and opportunities for counselling and personal development.

1. Educational Programs: Borstal inmates, including Manuel, were provided with educational opportunities. They could attend basic literacy and numeracy classes, which were intended to improve their educational deficits. The idea was to equip them with the skills necessary to secure lawful employment upon release.

2. Vocational Training: Manuel, like other inmates, would have been exposed to vocational training programs. These programs aimed to provide practical skills that could facilitate employment after leaving Borstal. Depending on the specific Borstal, Manuel may have received training in areas like carpentry, metalwork, or farming.

3. Physical Exercise and Sports: Physical activities were encouraged in Borstals to promote discipline and physical fitness. Engaging in sports and exercise routines was believed to foster self-discipline and teamwork.

4. Counselling and Personal Development: Some Borstals offered counselling and personal development programs. These sessions were designed to address emotional and psychological issues that young offenders might face. They could include individual counselling, group therapy, or discussions on anger management and conflict resolution.

Peter Manuel's Participation and Impact

While it is challenging to find specific records detailing Manuel's participation in these rehabilitation efforts, it is likely that he would have been exposed to at least some of these programs during his time in Borstal. However, the impact of such programs on Manuel's behaviour and mindset remains speculative.

Given Manuel's complex personality and propensity for manipulation, it is possible that he may have superficially engaged with these programs without undergoing significant behavioural change. Some individuals with antisocial or psychopathic tendencies can be adept at presenting themselves in ways that align with rehabilitation efforts while concealing their true intentions.

Furthermore, the effectiveness of rehabilitation programs in Borstals during the mid-20th century varied widely. In some cases, limited resources and the sheer volume of inmates could have hindered the ability of these programs to achieve substantial results.

Conclusion: A Complex Portrait

The question of whether rehabilitation efforts in Borstal had a lasting impact on Peter Manuel's behaviour and mindset is difficult to answer definitively. His later criminal activities and escalating violence suggest that any potential positive effects of these programs may have been limited in their influence.

In the case of Peter Manuel, the complex interplay of his personality traits, upbringing, and early encounters with the criminal justice system likely had a more profound impact on his criminal path than any rehabilitation efforts. His eventual transformation into a notorious serial killer remains a haunting chapter in the annals of criminal history, showcasing the intricate and often elusive nature of rehabilitation in the face of severe criminal tendencies.

Release and Return to Criminal Activity: Peter Manuel's Troubled Journey

Peter Manuel's release from Borstal marked a critical juncture in his life. It represented a chance for rehabilitation and reintegration into society, as Borstal institutions were intended to provide young offenders with the tools to lead law-abiding lives. However, the question remains whether his time in Borstal had any observable effects on his criminal behaviour or if it merely served as a temporary respite before he embarked on a more violent and murderous path.

The Borstal Experience: Limited Impact?

Manuel's time in Borstal exposed him to a range of programs and activities aimed at rehabilitation and personal development. These programs were designed to address the root causes of criminal behaviour and equip inmates with the skills and mindset needed for a lawful life after release.

1. Education and Vocational Training: Borstals offered educational opportunities that aimed to improve basic literacy and numeracy skills. Vocational training was also provided to give inmates practical skills for employment. While these programs were available to Manuel, it's unclear to what extent he engaged with them and whether they influenced his future actions.

2. Physical Exercise and Sports: Physical activities and sports were encouraged in Borstals to promote discipline and physical fitness. Participation in these activities was meant to foster a sense of teamwork and self-discipline. Manuel's involvement in such programs is difficult to ascertain but could have contributed to his physical fitness.

3. Counselling and Personal Development: Some Borstals offered counselling and personal development programs to address emotional and psychological issues. These sessions could have helped inmates like Manuel confront underlying problems. However, it's unclear whether Manuel actively participated or benefited from these services.

Release into Society: A Tumultuous Transition

Upon his release from Borstal, Manuel faced a challenging transition back into society. This transition could have been an opportunity for genuine reform, but it also presented risks, particularly if his time in Borstal failed to address the root causes of his criminal behaviour.

1. Employment and Social Reintegration: Borstals aimed to equip inmates with skills for lawful employment. Manuel may have sought employment, but the types of jobs available to him and his ability to secure stable work remain uncertain. His ability to reintegrate into society likely depended on factors such as his educational achievements and social support networks.

2. Influence of Peer Groups: The post-release environment can significantly influence an individual's behaviour. If Manuel returned to a criminal milieu or associated with individuals engaged in unlawful activities, it could have led him down a troubling path once more. His ability to resist criminal temptations may have been tested.

The Escalation of Violence: A Grim Path

Unfortunately, the years following Manuel's release did not see a transformation toward law-abiding behaviour. Instead, his criminal activities escalated, eventually culminating in a reign of terror that would earn him the moniker "The Beast of Birkenshaw." Here's a closer look at Manuel's post-release criminal activities:

1. Petty Crimes: Manuel's early post-release activities reportedly involved relatively minor offenses, such as housebreaking and theft. While these

crimes were concerning, they did not immediately foreshadow the brutality and violence that would later define his criminal career.

2. Escalation to Murder: Over time, Manuel's criminal behaviour escalated dramatically. He evolved from committing property crimes to perpetrating horrific acts of violence, including rape and murder. His willingness to target and harm innocent individuals shocked the nation.

3. Taunting of Police: A chilling aspect of Manuel's post-release behaviour was his propensity to taunt and mock the police. He left cryptic messages and engaged in a cat-and-mouse game with law enforcement, undermining their efforts to apprehend him.

Unanswered Questions and Complex Factors

The question of whether Manuel's time in Borstal had any observable effects on his criminal behaviour is complex and challenging to definitively answer. It is possible that some aspects of rehabilitation and personal development programs had limited short-term impacts. Still, the escalation of his criminal activities, including multiple murders, suggests that any potential influence may have been overshadowed by deeper-seated issues.

Manuel's transformation from a Borstal inmate into a notorious serial killer remains a haunting and perplexing case in the annals of criminal history. It underscores the complexity of addressing the underlying causes of criminal behaviour and the limitations of rehabilitation efforts when dealing with individuals with severe antisocial tendencies.

Chapter 3

The Murder Spree Begins

The First Kill

The year was 1956, and the residents of Scotland's Lanarkshire region were blissfully unaware of the impending nightmare that would soon shatter their peaceful existence. It was on an ordinary summer's day that Peter Manuel, the man who would become a harbinger of terror, committed his first murder—a crime that would set in motion a reign of darkness.

On the 2nd of September, 1956, Peter Manuel claimed his first victim: Anne Kneilands, a young, vibrant woman with her whole life ahead of her. Anne was only 17 years old, a symbol of youthful innocence that would be brutally extinguished by the malevolence of Peter Manuel.

Anne Kneilands: The First Tragedy

Anne, a nurse's assistant, had been enjoying an evening out with friends when she encountered Manuel. He was no stranger to Anne; they lived in the same neighbourhood, and her trusting nature would become her tragic downfall. Peter Manuel, with his charming facade and disarming smile, lured her into his web of deception.

As the night wore on, Anne and Manuel found themselves in a wooded area, far removed from the watchful eyes of the community. It was there, hidden beneath the cover of darkness, that Manuel's true nature emerged. He subjected Anne to a horrifying ordeal, one that would culminate in her life being violently extinguished.

The Impact on the Community

The discovery of Anne Kneilands' lifeless body sent shockwaves through Lanarkshire. The quiet, close-knit community was suddenly thrust into the harsh glare of the public spotlight. The brutal nature of the crime left residents in a state of fear and disbelief. The illusion of safety, once taken for granted, had been shattered.

In the aftermath of Anne's murder, the community rallied together, determined to bring her killer to justice. Fear and anger united neighbours, as they began to look over their shoulders, questioning the faces they thought they knew. But little did they realize that the man they sought was among them, a wolf in sheep's clothing, lurking in plain sight.

The Beginnings of a Pattern: Unravelling a Web of Darkness

The murder of Anne Kneilands was not a solitary, isolated incident, but rather the chilling inception of a deeply disturbing pattern that would leave a trail of horror in its wake. As the investigation into her tragic death began to unfold, law enforcement officials found themselves peeling back layers of darkness that stretched far beyond the confines of one victim. It became glaringly evident that Peter Manuel possessed not only a capacity for violence but also a deep-seated predilection for it, and his insatiable desires were far from being sated.

1: A Gruesome Revelation

The investigation into Anne Kneilands' murder opened a window into a nightmarish world that lay hidden beneath the surface of suburban tranquillity. What initially appeared as an isolated act of brutality soon revealed itself as the harbinger of something far more sinister—a sinister web that ensnared not just one victim but threatened an entire community.

The discovery of Anne's lifeless body was like a thunderclap in the peaceful neighbourhood, shattering the illusion of safety. It was a grotesque tableau, her life extinguished in the most horrifying manner imaginable. But as the investigators descended upon the crime scene, their flashlights cutting through the darkness, they couldn't fathom the depths of darkness they were about to plunge into.

The tiny details spoke of horror—the eerie silence of the night, the chilling stillness of Anne's home, and the remnants of a life now lost forever. But beyond the obvious lay a puzzle, one that seemed to defy comprehension. Anne Kneilands had been living a quiet, ordinary life, and the idea that such brutality could touch her world was inconceivable.

As the hours turned into days, the revelation took a more sinister form. Patterns began to emerge, threads connecting Anne's fate to other unsolved mysteries that had haunted the community for years. Whispers of a serial killer hung in the air, and the unease that had settled over the neighbourhood was palpable.

The gruesome revelation was not confined to the crime scene; it spread like a contagion, affecting every aspect of daily life. Fear and suspicion crept into the hearts of residents who had once trusted their neighbours implicitly. Locks were strengthened, windows barred, and children were cautioned never to wander alone.

The investigation that began with Anne's murder soon became a relentless quest for answers, an urgent mission to unmask the face of evil lurking among them. It was a journey that would lead to more horrors, test the limits of human endurance, and ultimately reveal a truth that would forever change the lives of those who dared to confront the darkness.

In the heart of that sleepy neighbourhood, a storm was brewing, and the gruesome revelation was only the first thunderclap in a tempest that would shake their community to its core.

2. The Disturbing Unravelling

What they discovered was far from ordinary. Anne's life, it appeared, was intertwined with something far more sinister than anyone could have imagined. The disturbing revelations began to paint a chilling portrait of a predator who had operated in the shadows, preying on the vulnerability of innocence.

As the investigation expanded its scope, it unearthed a series of unsolved mysteries, each more haunting than the last. Violent crimes that had once perplexed investigators now seemed to fall into a grim pattern. Homes invaded, lives extinguished, and families torn apart—all at the hands of an unseen, malevolent force.

Peter Manuel's name began to surface with increasing frequency, like a sinister spectre hovering on the periphery of every crime scene. The unsettling connection between Anne's murder and the man who had once resided in their quiet neighbourhood was undeniable.

But understanding the mind of a killer is never a straightforward endeavour. The detectives found themselves grappling with the enigma of Peter Manuel—a man whose actions defied rational explanation. What drove him to commit such heinous acts? Was it a thirst for power, a sadistic pleasure derived from inflicting pain, or a profound darkness that lurked within him?

The disturbing unravelling of Peter Manuel's crimes was a descent into a nightmare that gripped not only the investigators but an entire community. Fear gave way to obsession as they sought to expose the malevolence that had hidden in plain sight for so long.

In the heart of their once-peaceful neighbourhood, a battle of wits had begun—a relentless pursuit of answers that would lead them deeper into the abyss of Peter Manuel's psyche. The disturbing pattern they had uncovered was not just the mark of a cold-blooded murderer; it was a reflection of the profound darkness that resided within the human soul itself.

3. A Predilection for Violence

As the investigation into Peter Manuel's crimes continued to unfold, a disturbing and unsettling truth emerged—an insidious predilection for violence that seemed to define his very existence. It became increasingly evident that Peter Manuel possessed not only the capability but also a sinister appetite for acts of brutality that transcended the boundaries of mere criminality.

The unsettling realization dawned on those involved in the pursuit of justice that Peter Manuel's actions were not confined to a single, isolated incident of violence. No, his deeds were far more insidious and calculated than anyone had initially comprehended. The chilling revelation that he had not been satisfied with one act of violence sent shivers down the spines of all those tasked with bringing him to justice.

What had once appeared as a perplexing, singular murder had morphed into something far more ominous. Peter Manuel's appetite for violence seemed insatiable, as if he derived a perverse pleasure from the pain and suffering he inflicted upon others. His actions were characterized not only by the taking of lives but by a sadistic enjoyment of the torment he wrought.

The crimes he committed painted a harrowing tableau of malevolence. Homes violated, lives cruelly extinguished, and communities left in perpetual fear—all bore the unmistakable signature of a mind that revelled in violence. His victims became more than statistics; they were symbols of his depravity, testaments to the depths of darkness within him.

The investigators found themselves grappling with an unsettling question: What could drive a man to descend to such depths of brutality? Was it a thirst for power, a perverse form of control, or a chilling indifference to the sanctity of human life? The answers remained elusive, buried within the enigmatic recesses of Peter Manuel's psyche.

As the web of violence continued to unravel, those tasked with apprehending him were haunted by the realization that they were not dealing with a conventional criminal. This was a predator of a different breed, one whose motivations defied easy categorization. It was a disturbing reality that fuelled their determination to unravel the mystery and bring him to justice.

The chilling predilection for violence that Peter Manuel exhibited was a stark reminder that evil could take on many forms, often lurking beneath the surface of the seemingly ordinary. It was a stark warning to a community that had been thrust into a nightmare—a nightmare that could only be confronted by those willing to stare unflinchingly into the abyss of human malevolence.

4. The Disturbing Revelation

As detectives diligently pieced together the puzzle of Peter Manuel's reign of terror, a chilling pattern began to emerge. It was a pattern characterized by violence, manipulation, and a complete disregard for the sanctity of human life. The threads of this dark tapestry led investigators deeper into the heart of darkness that was Peter Manuel's psyche.

The unravelling of this sinister pattern raised deeply unsettling questions about the depths of human depravity. It was a revelation that shook the foundations of understanding, pushing the boundaries of what society believed an individual could be capable of. How could one person harbour such a profound and insatiable thirst for violence and cruelty?

What malevolent forces had converged to shape Peter Manuel into the embodiment of evil that he had become?

The crimes committed by Peter Manuel transcended the realm of ordinary criminal behaviour. They were not the impulsive acts of a desperate individual but the calculated, deliberate actions of a predator who seemed to relish in the pain and suffering he inflicted upon others. This was a disturbing revelation that challenged the very core of human morality and compassion.

The investigators found themselves grappling with an unsettling question that lingered like a shadow in their minds: What were the origins of such malevolence? Had Peter Manuel been shaped by traumatic experiences, or was there something inherently dark within him from the beginning? Understanding the genesis of his depravity became a critical aspect of the investigation, as it held the key to unravelling the twisted tapestry of his crimes.

It was as if Peter Manuel had become a manifestation of society's most profound fears—a living embodiment of the darkest recesses of the human soul. His actions defied rational explanation, leaving those tasked with bringing him to justice in a state of perpetual unease. The crimes he committed transcended mere criminality; they were windows into a mind consumed by a sinister darkness.

As the investigation delved deeper into Peter Manuel's psyche, it became increasingly evident that this was not a conventional criminal they were dealing with. His motivations were shrouded in enigma, his psyche a labyrinth of malevolent desires. It was a chilling revelation that compelled those pursuing him to confront the very nature of evil itself.

The disturbing pattern that had emerged was a testament to the complexity of human nature. It served as a stark reminder that the capacity for both good and evil resided within each individual, and that the line between them could be disturbingly thin. Peter Manuel's reign of terror forced society to confront the uncomfortable reality that true malevolence could exist in the most unexpected of places, lurking beneath the façade of normalcy.

As the investigators continued to peel back the layers of darkness that enshrouded Peter Manuel's life, they knew that answers lay buried within the recesses of his past and psyche. The disturbing revelation of his capacity for cruelty was a grim testament to the relentless pursuit of justice in the face of incomprehensible evil.

5. A Community Gripped by Fear

The revelation of the sinister pattern that had emerged from Peter Manuel's crimes sent shockwaves not only through the investigation but also reverberated through the entire community. Fear and unease spread like wildfire as residents grappled with the horrifying reality that a predator, a veritable embodiment of evil, lurked among them, capable of unspeakable acts. The sense of security that had once enveloped their lives was shattered, replaced by an ominous atmosphere that left a community in the relentless grip of terror.

In the peaceful neighbourhoods and quiet streets where families had once felt safe and protected, a dark cloud of fear descended. The idea that the sanctity of their homes and the tranquillity of their lives could be shattered at any moment was a haunting notion that kept them awake at night. The simple act of locking doors and windows became a feeble defence against the unknown menace that haunted their collective nightmares.

For many, the sinister revelation of Peter Manuel's crimes felt like a breach in the fabric of their reality. The trust that had once bound neighbours together began to erode, replaced by suspicion and caution. No longer could they view their fellow community members through the lens of familiarity; instead, each person became a potential harbinger of danger.

Parents clutched their children closer, their protective instincts on high alert. The laughter of playing children grew muted, replaced by the hushed conversations of worried parents who dared not let their offspring out of sight. The simple act of walking alone at night, once a symbol of freedom, had transformed into an act of bravery, undertaken only with trepidation.

Even the routine tasks of daily life took on an air of caution. Residents watched their surroundings with a vigilance born of fear, second-guessing the intentions of strangers and acquaintances alike. A sense of vulnerability permeated every aspect of their existence, as the sinister revelation of Peter Manuel's actions had shattered their collective innocence.

As the investigation pressed on and the community remained in the relentless grip of fear, a heavy sense of unease settled over the region.

The once-close-knit neighbourhoods, where trust and familiarity had reigned supreme, now bore the scars of uncertainty. The terror that had been unleashed upon them was an insidious force that could not be easily vanquished.

In the midst of this pervasive fear, however, there was a glimmer of resilience. The community rallied together, determined to support one another in the face of an unrelenting threat. Neighbours became more vigilant, looking out for one another's safety. A newfound solidarity emerged as they collectively defied the darkness that sought to envelop their lives.

Yet, the fear remained, a constant reminder that evil could manifest itself in the most unexpected of forms. The sinister revelation of Peter Manuel's crimes had left an indelible mark on the community, forever altering the way they perceived the world around them. The community that had once thrived in harmony was now a place where shadows seemed to lurk at every corner, where the sinister revelation had given rise to an enduring sense of vulnerability.

The Unearthing of Evil

The murder of Anne Kneilands marked the beginnings of a pattern that would come to define Peter Manuel's reign of terror. It was a pattern characterized by violence, manipulation, and a chilling predilection for cruelty. As the investigation delved deeper into the heart of darkness, it became evident that the evil within him knew no bounds. The unearthing of this malevolence left a community and a nation grappling with the unsettling question of what drives an individual to commit such heinous acts.

Modus Operandi: Unveiling the Calculated Cruelty

To comprehend the full extent of Peter Manuel's depravity, it is imperative to delve into his modus operandi—the intricate methods and patterns he meticulously crafted to select and victimize individuals. Manuel's chilling ability to evade capture and perpetuate his murderous spree was inextricably intertwined with his cunning and calculated approach.

1. The Selection of Victims

Peter Manuel's reign of terror unfolded with a chilling sense of order, a methodical approach to selecting victims that revealed the depths of his twisted psychology. His crimes were not the result of random chance but rather a manifestation of his calculated and sinister planning. Behind his facade of normalcy, he harboured a dark compulsion to seek out and harm others, leaving investigators to unravel the disturbing pattern that defined his predatory actions.

Manuel's selection of victims was not haphazard; it was a calculated process that showcased his cold and calculating nature. He often chose individuals who shared commonalities, weaving a web of connections that initially eluded investigators. These connections, whether through acquaintanceship or geographical proximity, became the threads of a sinister tapestry that concealed the true extent of his malevolence.

In many instances, his victims were familiar faces in his life, people who had unwittingly crossed paths with a man harbouring a deadly secret. Manuel's ability to blend into his surroundings, to assume the role of an ordinary member of society, made him a phantom in plain sight. This, in turn, allowed him to get close to his victims without raising suspicion.

The process of victim selection was characterized by a chilling blend of opportunism and calculation. Manuel would identify individuals who seemed vulnerable, whether due to their circumstances or their trust in him as an acquaintance. This predatory instinct was underpinned by a deep-seated compulsion, an insatiable urge to exert power and control over others, to inflict fear and suffering upon those who crossed his path.

As investigators delved deeper into the cases associated with Peter Manuel, the threads connecting his victims became increasingly apparent. The shared neighbourhoods, the overlapping social circles, and the seemingly innocuous connections began to form a sinister web. It was a web that would eventually ensnare Manuel himself, but not before he continued his reign of terror, leaving a trail of victims in his wake.

Understanding the meticulous process of victim selection was a chilling revelation for investigators, a glimpse into the mind of a serial predator who methodically sought out those he deemed suitable targets. It was a stark reminder that evil could lurk in the most unexpected of places,

concealed behind a facade of normalcy, waiting to strike with calculated precision.

2. A Mask of Deception

One of the most unsettling facets of Peter Manuel's criminal methodology lay in his uncanny ability to wear a mask of deception. Behind his façade of normalcy, he possessed a chilling talent for presenting himself as a charming and trustworthy individual, a wolf in sheep's clothing. This duplicitous guise served as the key to his sinister success, allowing him to weave a web of deceit around his unsuspecting victims.

Manuel's charm was not a superficial veneer but a calculated and manipulative tool. He had an innate capacity to appear unthreatening, even amiable, to those he targeted. This beguiling charisma was the linchpin of his predatory strategy. It enabled him to gain the trust of his victims swiftly and with disconcerting ease, creating a false sense of security that would ultimately seal their fates.

He could be the friendly neighbour, the affable acquaintance, or the personable stranger—roles he adopted with chilling precision. His capacity to adapt his persona to suit the circumstances allowed him to infiltrate the lives of his victims, often leaving them entirely unaware of the malevolent intentions that lay beneath the surface.

This gift for deception went beyond mere charm. Manuel possessed an acute understanding of human psychology, an insight into the vulnerabilities and desires of his victims. He knew precisely which emotional strings to pull to engender trust and compliance. It was as if he possessed an eerie intuition, an ability to read people's needs and aspirations with an unnerving accuracy.

The consequences of this duplicitous charm were twofold. First, it lulled his victims into a false sense of security. They would willingly let down their guard, believing they were in the company of someone they could trust. This misplaced trust was the cornerstone of his ability to approach and subdue them without raising alarm.

Second, it left a trail of confusion and disbelief in the aftermath of his crimes. Friends, family, and acquaintances of the victims struggled to reconcile the affable façade they had encountered with the heinous acts he had committed. It was a bewildering paradox that compounded the horror of his actions, making it all the more difficult for authorities to connect the dots and apprehend the elusive predator.

For investigators, the realization that behind Manuel's charming exterior lurked a remorseless and calculating killer was a stark reminder of the capacity for evil that could exist within the most unassuming individuals. His mask of deception was not only a tool for manipulation but a testament to the chilling duality of his nature—a nature that revelled in the suffering and terror he inflicted upon those who had mistakenly placed their trust in him.

3. The Element of Surprise

Peter Manuel's sinister predilection for violence was further magnified by his calculated use of surprise as a weapon. This chilling aspect of his modus operandi was a testament to the meticulous planning and sadistic thrill he derived from catching his victims unawares, often in the very sanctuaries where they should have felt safest—their own homes.

The element of surprise was a cornerstone of Manuel's predatory strategy. He didn't merely rely on his duplicitous charm to gain access to his victims' lives; he meticulously orchestrated his attacks to catch them off guard. This methodical approach allowed him to subdue and control his victims swiftly, rendering them vulnerable and defenceless in the face of his malevolent intentions.

Manuel's attacks were brazen, yet cunning. He would stalk his victims, studying their routines and patterns, learning when they were most likely to be alone. He understood the vulnerability that accompanied the comfort of home, a place where one's guard was naturally lowered. It was within the confines of these supposedly secure spaces that he struck with ruthless efficiency.

In many instances, he would gain access to his victims' homes through a combination of ruses and manipulation. He might pose as a friendly neighbour in need, an acquaintance seeking assistance, or even a stranger in distress. His mastery of deception allowed him to exploit the inherent trust that people often extended to those they encountered within their own living spaces.

Once inside, Manuel would pounce with terrifying swiftness. His victims would find themselves suddenly face to face with the embodiment of their worst nightmares—a man who had infiltrated the very heart of their personal space, someone they had unwittingly welcomed in. The shock and fear that accompanied this moment were palpable, leaving them paralyzed and disoriented.

It was at this critical juncture that Manuel's propensity for violence reached its zenith. The element of surprise ensured that his victims had little opportunity to react or defend themselves. He would subdue them before they could comprehend the impending danger, using physical force, threats, or a combination of both. The feeling of helplessness that overcame them was an integral component of the psychological torment he inflicted.

The element of surprise also played a crucial role in his ability to maintain control throughout the course of his crimes. By catching his victims off guard, he could dominate and manipulate them with a sadistic satisfaction that stemmed from the knowledge that they had no recourse. It was a calculated strategy that allowed him to assert power and dominance over those who fell victim to his brutality.

For investigators, the realization that Manuel's attacks were marked by this element of surprise added another layer of horror to an already chilling case. It underscored the depths of his predatory nature and the extent to which he was willing to go in pursuit of his malevolent desires. It was a strategy that instilled terror not only in his victims but also in an entire community left reeling from the realization that their perceived safety could be shattered in an instant by a predator lurking in the shadows.

4. Sexual Sadism

One of the most chilling dimensions of Peter Manuel's sinister modus operandi delved into the darkest realms of human depravity: sexual sadism. While his crimes were already marked by a calculated and brutal violence, it was the sadistic element that sent shockwaves through the investigators and the community alike. Manuel's actions transcended mere violence; they revealed a profound desire for power, control, and cruelty.

Sexual sadism, in the context of Manuel's crimes, introduced an additional layer of horror and violation for his victims. His attacks were not confined to physical brutality but were accompanied by sexual assaults that left a lasting scar on those who survived to recount their ordeals. This aspect of his criminal behaviour showcased a level of malevolence that defied comprehension.

For Manuel, sexual sadism served as a means to exert dominance and control over his victims in the most degrading and violating manner possible. The violation was not solely physical; it extended into the psychological realm, leaving his victims traumatized and shattered. The sadistic nature of his crimes was evident in the callousness with which he treated those who fell prey to his malevolent desires.

The sexual sadism that permeated Manuel's attacks was characterized by the deliberate infliction of pain and suffering for his own perverse gratification. It was a manifestation of his insatiable thirst for power, control, and the degradation of his victims. This form of cruelty went beyond the bounds of any rational explanation; it was a descent into the depths of human malevolence.

Investigators tasked with unravelling the complexities of Manuel's crimes were left grappling with the profound psychological darkness that lurked within him. The sadistic component of his modus operandi served as a haunting reminder of the depths to which he was willing to sink in his pursuit of dominance and cruelty. It was a dimension of his criminal behaviour that challenged the very limits of comprehension.

For the survivors of Manuel's attacks, the scars left by his sexual sadism ran deep, both physically and emotionally. The trauma inflicted upon them was immeasurable, and their stories served as a stark testament to the sadistic nature of the "Beast of Birkenshaw." It was a dimension of his crimes that added an extra layer of horror to an already gruesome narrative.

The sexual sadism that pervaded Manuel's actions went beyond the realm of violence; it was a manifestation of his insidious desire for power and control. It was a reminder that his malevolence knew no bounds, and that the depths of his depravity were as unfathomable as they were terrifying.

5. Precise Timing and Escape

In the malevolent tapestry of Peter Manuel's crimes, a chilling thread emerged—his uncanny ability for precise timing and escape. This aspect of his modus operandi revealed not only his capacity for meticulous planning but also a cunning intellect that left investigators astounded. Manuel's crimes were marked not only by their brutality but by his calculated strategy to strike when he believed law enforcement to be least vigilant.

Timing, in the world of Peter Manuel, was a critical factor that played to his advantage. He didn't strike randomly; instead, he meticulously selected moments when he believed the odds of detection were lowest. This calculated approach allowed him to carry out his heinous acts with a cold, clinical precision that left no room for error. It showcased his deep understanding of the psychological dynamics at play in law enforcement's efforts to apprehend him.

By choosing moments of perceived vulnerability within the law enforcement apparatus, Manuel managed to evade capture time and time again. It was as though he possessed an eerie intuition, an ability to slip through the cracks of the justice system. This escape was not merely a stroke of luck; it was a testament to his calculated cunning and an integral part of his modus operandi.

Manuel's escapes following his crimes were characterized by an ability to blend seamlessly back into the community. He could shift from the role of a ruthless predator to that of an unassuming neighbour, leaving those around him oblivious to the darkness that lurked within. This duality was a hallmark of his criminal career, allowing him to prolong the reign of terror he inflicted upon the community.

For investigators, Manuel's precise timing and ability to escape posed a formidable challenge. It was as if he possessed an innate understanding of the rhythms and routines of law enforcement. His capacity to evade capture frustrated their efforts at every turn, leaving them grappling with the enigma of the "Beast of Birkenshaw."

The calculated strategy of timing and escape served as a haunting reminder that Manuel was not merely an impulsive criminal but a meticulous planner. He exhibited a level of patience and cunning that set him apart from more conventional offenders. It was this aspect of his modus operandi that prolonged the terror he inflicted on the community and added an extra layer of complexity to the investigation.

Ultimately, the art of precise timing and escape showcased Peter Manuel's dark genius—a chilling intellect that allowed him to operate in the shadows, striking fear into the hearts of those who crossed his path. His ability to evade justice for an extended period would leave investigators and the community in a state of unease, wondering when and where he would strike next.

6. The Dark Pattern Unveiled

As the relentless investigators delved deeper into the web of Peter Manuel's crimes, a haunting and sinister pattern slowly emerged from the shadows. It was a pattern that transcended mere criminality, revealing a chilling tapestry of calculated cruelty, cunning deception, and a relentless desire for control. This insight into his modus operandi not only sent shivers down the spines of those tasked with bringing him to justice but also laid bare the extent of his malevolence.

The dark pattern that unfolded before the eyes of investigators was characterized by a calculated approach to violence that defied conventional understanding. Manuel's actions were not those of a mere criminal; they were the manifestations of a mind deeply steeped in malevolence. His cruelty knew no bounds, and his victims would soon come to realize that they were dealing with a force far more sinister than they could have ever imagined.

At the heart of this pattern lay a disturbing desire for control. Manuel's need for power over his victims was relentless, and he went to great lengths to ensure it. His manipulation knew no bounds, and he would often present himself as charming and trustworthy, lulling his victims into a false sense of security. It was a deception that showcased not only his cunning but his deep understanding of the human psyche.

The unveiling of this dark pattern was not a mere academic exercise but a chilling revelation of the depths of depravity to which Manuel was willing to sink. It was a reminder that his actions went beyond the realm of impulsive criminality; they were the calculated manoeuvres of a man whose malevolence knew no boundaries. This revelation sent shockwaves through the investigation, forcing those involved to confront the sheer horror of the "Beast of Birkenshaw."

In the chapters that followed, the dark pattern would be explored in greater detail, revealing the true extent of Manuel's calculated cruelty, cunning deception, and relentless desire for control. It was a pattern that would haunt the collective psyche of the community and investigators alike, as they grappled with the unsettling truth that the terror they faced was unlike anything they had ever encountered before.

Conclusion: A Calculated Reign of Terror

Peter Manuel's modus operandi was a chilling testament to his calculated reign of terror. His ability to meticulously plan and execute his crimes, coupled with his capacity to evade capture, showcased a mind twisted by darkness. Understanding the depths of his depravity through his modus operandi is essential in unravelling the complexities of his criminality and the profound impact it had on his victims and the community at large.

The Charm Offensive: Disarming Deception

One of the most disconcerting facets of Peter Manuel's method was his uncanny ability to wield charm as a potent weapon. He possessed an innate charisma that could disarm even the most cautious individuals, luring them into his web of deception and darkness. This charm offensive allowed him to gain the trust of his victims and lower their guard, often leading them willingly to secluded and perilous locations.

1. The Charismatic Facade

Peter Manuel's charm was not a mere surface-level quality but a carefully cultivated and deeply ingrained aspect of his persona. It was a charisma that left an indelible impression on those who had the misfortune of crossing his path. To friends and acquaintances alike, Manuel exuded an air of affability and magnetism that was, at first glance, nearly impossible to resist. It was this very charm that allowed him to navigate the social world with ease, all while concealing the malevolence that lay hidden beneath the surface.

At its core, Manuel's charismatic facade was a masterful act of deception. He knew precisely how to present himself to others, crafting an image of trustworthiness, approachability, and harmlessness. His ability to wear this mask of charisma was not a random quirk of personality but a calculated tool he employed to manipulate those around him.

One of the most disarming aspects of Manuel's charm was its authenticity. It did not come across as contrived or forced, making it all the more convincing. People genuinely believed that he was a friendly and engaging individual, unaware of the dark secrets he harboured.

This charisma was particularly effective in disarming potential victims. They would lower their guard in his presence, lulled into a false sense of security by his captivating charm. Little did they know that beneath the charm lay a predator who revelled in the control and power he could exert over others.

The facade was not a one-dimensional act but a multi-faceted performance that allowed Manuel to navigate various social circles. He could effortlessly blend into different environments, whether mingling with acquaintances, engaging in casual conversation, or infiltrating the lives of his unsuspecting victims.

As the investigation into his crimes progressed, the revelation of this charismatic facade added another layer of complexity to the enigma that was Peter Manuel. It forced those tasked with apprehending him to grapple with the unsettling truth that the malevolence they sought to expose was concealed beneath the veneer of charm—a deception that had allowed Manuel to operate in plain sight, masking his true nature with a charisma that was, in its own way, as chilling as the crimes he committed.

2. Gaining Trust

Among the many tools in Peter Manuel's sinister arsenal, one stood out as particularly potent—his uncanny ability to gain the trust of his victims. It was a skill that showcased his manipulative prowess and played a pivotal role in his crimes. Manuel didn't strike as a stranger in the night; he was a wolf in sheep's clothing, gradually weaving a web of trust around his unsuspecting prey.

What set Manuel apart was his patient and calculated approach. He didn't rush his victims; instead, he bided his time, often befriending individuals over an extended period. His modus operandi involved gradually insinuating himself into their lives, meticulously building rapport, and winning their trust step by insidious step.

The process of gaining trust was a slow and deliberate one. Manuel would present himself as a reliable, caring, and empathetic individual. He became a confidant, someone his victims could turn to in times of need. This facade of a trustworthy friend created an emotional bond that made his victims more susceptible to his manipulations.

Manuel's victims, unknowingly drawn into his web of deceit, found solace in his apparent friendship. They lowered their guard, believing they were in the company of a person who had their best interests at heart. This misplaced trust allowed Manuel to get closer, both physically and emotionally, to those he intended to harm.

The gradual nature of Manuel's approach had a paralyzing effect on his victims' instincts. By the time they began to sense that something was amiss, they were already ensnared in his trap. Doubts were dismissed, and suspicions were suppressed as they clung to the belief that this charming confidant was incapable of harm.

This artful manipulation of trust not only made his victims more vulnerable but also allowed Manuel to control the narrative. He could dictate the course of their interactions, lulling them into a sense of complacency until the moment he chose to strike.

As investigators unravelled the details of Manuel's crimes, the chilling revelation of how he gained the trust of his victims added a layer of horror to his already disturbing profile. It underscored the depths of his malevolence and his capacity to exploit the very qualities that make us human—our ability to trust and connect with others. In the mind of Peter Manuel, trust was not a virtue to be celebrated but a weapon to be wielded with deadly precision.

3. Lowering Their Guard

Peter Manuel's ability to lower the guard of his victims was a pivotal aspect of his predatory strategy. It was the next step in the dark dance of manipulation that he orchestrated with chilling precision. As victims succumbed to his charm offensive, their initial reservations and instincts would inevitably give way to a sense of false security, setting the stage for his malevolent intentions.

The first encounter with Manuel often left his victims with a sense of unease—a nagging feeling that something about this charming stranger was amiss. It was a natural response, a primal instinct that whispered warnings of potential danger. However, Manuel was a master of eroding these early doubts.

His charisma was a weapon honed to perfection. Manuel exuded an air of affability and magnetism that was difficult to resist. His infectious laughter, engaging conversation, and apparent concern for his victims created a facade that appeared genuine and trustworthy. This veneer of warmth and sincerity lulled his victims into a state of complacency.

As time passed, doubts and reservations began to dissipate. Victims would dismiss their initial unease as unwarranted, attributing it to mere paranoia or a misunderstanding. They couldn't fathom that the charming individual who had entered their lives could pose any harm. Manuel's calculated approach ensured that their perception of him shifted from a potential threat to a benevolent presence.

This lowering of defences was crucial to Manuel's modus operandi. As victims embraced a false sense of security, they became more pliable, more easily manipulated. They no longer questioned his intentions or the increasingly inappropriate nature of his interactions. Instead, they leaned into the growing connection, convinced that this newfound friendship was genuine.

The process of lowering their guard also played into Manuel's strategy of isolating his victims. With their reservations quelled, they were less likely to seek advice or share concerns about their interactions with others. Instead, they would withdraw from their social circles, investing more time and emotional energy into their relationship with Manuel.

The chilling realization was that, by the time victims began to sense that something was amiss, it was often too late. Their lowered guard had placed them firmly within Manuel's grasp, and escape from his web of manipulation became increasingly challenging.

The psychological impact of realizing they had been deceived by someone they had grown to trust was profound. It left victims not only physically vulnerable but also emotionally scarred. As investigators delved into Manuel's crimes, this aspect of his predatory behaviour added another layer of horror to an already disturbing profile. It underscored his cold, calculated approach to exploiting human nature's vulnerabilities, turning trust into a weapon that would ultimately be used against his victims.

4. The Willing Companions

The depths of Peter Manuel's sinister charm offensive reached its most chilling crescendo when victims found themselves willingly accompanying him to secluded or vulnerable locations. It was a testament to his manipulative prowess that he could not only lower their guard but also entice them to participate in their own vulnerability.

For his victims, it often began with an innocent proposition or an invitation framed as a simple outing. Manuel's initial interactions were marked by an air of affability and charm that was disarming. He would suggest activities or places to visit, and his victims, lulled into a false sense of security by his charismatic facade, would agree without hesitation.

This willingness to accompany him was a key component of Manuel's predatory strategy. Victims saw no reason to fear the company of someone they believed to be friendly and trustworthy. They had been drawn into his orbit, and his apparent concern for their well-being further cemented their trust in him.

In some instances, the outings appeared completely benign, such as a leisurely walk in the park or a visit to a local cafe. To the victims, it was an opportunity to spend time with a new friend who had entered their lives seemingly by chance. They felt a connection, a sense of camaraderie, and perhaps a hint of excitement at the prospect of this newfound friendship.

However, in other cases, the outings had darker undertones. Manuel's charm offensive had progressed to a point where victims might agree to join him for a more secluded rendezvous, away from the prying eyes of the public. These situations, while appearing innocent on the surface, placed his victims in increasingly vulnerable positions.

The sinister aspect of these outings lay in their ultimate destination. Victims would willingly accompany Manuel to isolated locations, often remote spots where they could spend time together without interruption. In some instances, it was a quiet woodland area, a desolate stretch of road, or an abandoned building—locations that, to the victims, held no inherent threat.

It was this willingness that made them easy prey for his nefarious intentions. As victims found themselves alone with Manuel in these secluded settings, his predatory nature would emerge. The facade of charm and friendliness would crumble, revealing the malevolent intentions he had concealed.

For those investigating Manuel's crimes, the realization that victims had willingly placed themselves in such precarious situations underscored the insidious nature of his manipulation. It was a testament to his ability to exploit trust, to present himself as an affable companion while concealing the darkness that lurked beneath. This aspect of his modus operandi added yet another layer of horror to the chilling narrative of his crimes, highlighting the depth of his depravity and the devastating consequences for those who had unknowingly walked into his trap.

5. The Charmer's Advantage

Peter Manuel's charm was not merely a superficial trait; it was a potent weapon that he wielded with malevolent expertise. This charm provided him with a significant advantage, enabling him to operate within the community without raising suspicion. His victims, friends, and acquaintances often saw no reason to fear him until it was tragically too late.

At first glance, Manuel appeared as an ordinary member of society. He could engage in casual conversations, crack jokes, and present himself as an affable individual. This facade of normalcy allowed him to seamlessly blend into his surroundings, making him virtually invisible among his unsuspecting neighbours and peers.

His charm was a chameleon-like quality that adapted to various social situations. To his victims, he was a friendly companion, someone who could be trusted with their time and company. They saw no cause for alarm in his presence, given the genuine-seeming warmth he projected.

This ability to ingratiate himself into the lives of others was crucial to Manuel's predatory strategy. He would often befriend individuals, whether they were neighbours, acquaintances, or casual friends, gradually insinuating himself into their social circles. His actions gave no hint of the darkness that lurked beneath the surface.

What made Manuel's charm particularly insidious was the element of surprise. His victims and those around him were taken off guard by the brutality he was capable of. They might have dismissed their initial reservations and instincts as unwarranted, lulled into a sense of false security by his charismatic demeanour. This lowering of defences was a calculated tactic, enabling him to strike when least expected.

As a result, many who knew him remained blissfully ignorant of the sinister reality. Manuel's charm served as a shield, obscuring the malevolence that dwelled within. Friends and acquaintances were left in the dark, unable to discern the true nature of the person they believed they knew.

The advantage of this charm lay in its ability to facilitate his predatory actions while eluding suspicion. His victims willingly placed themselves in vulnerable positions, assuming they were in the company of a trustworthy friend. By the time the mask of deception fell away, it was often too late for them to escape the horrors that awaited.

This ability to blend into society while concealing his dark intentions added an additional layer of menace to his reign of terror. Manuel's charm was a weapon that allowed him to move undetected through the community, preying upon those who had no reason to suspect the true nature of the man who had insinuated himself into their lives. It was a stark reminder that evil could wear a friendly face, and that the most dangerous predators could lurk within the most ordinary of settings.

The Charmer's Dark Secret

The charm offensive wielded by Peter Manuel was a sinister and calculated deception. His charisma allowed him to navigate society with ease, gaining the trust of those around him while concealing his malevolent desires. Understanding the chilling effectiveness of his charm is essential in comprehending the depths of his manipulation and the profound impact it had on his victims, who often had no reason to suspect the true nature of the man behind the facade.

Target Selection: The Unpredictable Predation

Peter Manuel's victims were a chilling testament to the unpredictable nature of his predation. They spanned the spectrum of age, gender, and background, creating a perplexing puzzle for law enforcement. Manuel's ability to prey upon both men and women, young and old, left investigators grappling with motives that often appeared muddled and elusive. It was this very unpredictability that added an extra layer of terror to his crimes, as no one knew who might be next in his twisted game of malevolence.

1. A Diverse Array of Victims

Peter Manuel's insidious reign of terror was marked by a victim selection process that defied easy categorization. Unlike many serial killers who exhibit a specific victim profile, Manuel's approach was disturbingly diverse. He did not discriminate based on age, gender, or social status. His victims encompassed both men and women, the young and the old, creating a baffling and perplexing mosaic of targets.

This bewildering diversity in victimology was one of the factors that confounded law enforcement efforts to establish a clear profile of the killer. Serial killers often adhere to a pattern, targeting victims who share common characteristics or vulnerabilities. Manuel, however, shattered this conventional understanding by choosing victims from a broad spectrum of society.

His indiscriminate selection revealed a deeply unpredictable and malevolent nature. He did not conform to the expectations of law enforcement or the public, making it exceedingly difficult to anticipate his next move. This unpredictability became one of his most unsettling trademarks, leaving communities in a constant state of unease.

For those tasked with solving the case, the absence of a clear victim profile presented a formidable challenge. Serial killer investigations often rely on patterns and similarities among victims to build a coherent picture of the offender. In Manuel's case, the absence of such patterns left investigators grasping at straws.

Manuel's ability to transcend societal boundaries when selecting victims highlighted the extent of his depravity. His crimes did not discriminate based on age, gender, or social standing. This diversity served as a chilling reminder that evil could strike anyone, regardless of their circumstances.

The diversity of his victims also underscores the notion that Manuel's motivations transcended conventional understanding. While some serial killers fixate on specific traits or characteristics in their victims, Manuel's motivations appeared to be rooted in a more profound and disturbing realm—one that defied easy explanation.

Ultimately, the mosaic of victims left in Manuel's wake serves as a haunting testament to the depths of his malevolence. He was a predator who could strike at any time, targeting individuals from all walks of life. This unsettling unpredictability made him a uniquely dangerous and enigmatic figure in the annals of criminal history.

2. The Perplexing Motives

In the chilling chronicles of Peter Manuel's crimes, one of the most enigmatic and unsettling aspects was the seeming absence of a clear motive. Unlike many criminals whose actions can be linked to financial gain, personal vendettas, or specific psychological triggers, Manuel's crimes often defied conventional understanding. His malevolent acts lacked a discernible pattern or rationale, leaving investigators and the public grappling with the unsettling question: why did he target specific individuals?

This ambiguity surrounding Manuel's motives further fuelled the sense of terror that permeated the communities he terrorized. Residents could not grasp the logic behind his predation. In the absence of a clear motive, the spectre of the "Beast of Birkenshaw" loomed larger, casting a long and dark shadow over everyday life.

Serial killers typically operate within a framework of motivation. Some are driven by a desire for power and control, others by sexual gratification, and still, others by deeply rooted psychological issues. In Manuel's case, identifying a singular motive proved to be a complex and elusive task.

Some experts have posited that Manuel's motivation was rooted in a twisted thirst for power and domination. His crimes often involved sexual assaults and brutal acts of violence, suggesting a sadistic desire to exert control over his victims. This notion aligns with his reputation as a psychopath, devoid of empathy or remorse.

Others have theorized that Manuel's crimes were driven by a profound need for attention and recognition. He revelled in the notoriety and media attention that his actions garnered, a trait that set him apart from many other serial killers who prefer to remain hidden in the shadows.

The absence of a clear motive did not mean that Manuel's actions were arbitrary or random. Rather, they were calculated and deliberate, reflecting a mind that was not bound by conventional moral or ethical constraints. His actions were a manifestation of his inner malevolence, a darkness that defied easy comprehension.

For those tasked with solving the case, this ambiguity regarding Manuel's motives presented a formidable challenge. Criminal profiling often relies on understanding why an offender commits specific acts. In Manuel's case, the absence of a clear motive left investigators with a complex puzzle, one that would take years to unravel.

The enigma of Peter Manuel's motives remains an enduring aspect of his criminal legacy. It serves as a stark reminder that some individuals defy conventional psychological explanations. Manuel was not driven by the usual motivations that guide criminal behaviour. Instead, he inhabited a realm of darkness where the boundaries of reason and morality dissolved, leaving only chaos and malevolence in their wake.

3. The Unsettling Unpredictability

In the dark annals of Peter Manuel's reign of terror, one unnerving aspect that sent shockwaves of fear throughout the community was the unsettling unpredictability of his victim selection. Unlike some serial killers who adhere to a specific victim profile or exhibit a consistent pattern in their crimes, Manuel seemed to operate with a chilling randomness that defied easy categorization. This unpredictability, or rather the perception of it, had profound and far-reaching effects on the psyche of the community.

Imagine living in a neighbourhood where the night held not just the mystery of darkness but also the lurking terror of the unknown. For the residents of Glasgow and its surrounding areas during Manuel's reign, this was a haunting reality. The absence of a discernible pattern meant that anyone, regardless of age, gender, or social status, could potentially become a victim. It was as if a shadowy hand could reach out at any moment, plunging an individual into a nightmare from which there might be no awakening.

This atmosphere of uncertainty was akin to living in a perpetual state of vulnerability and paranoia. People looked over their shoulders, questioned the intentions of acquaintances, and second-guessed even the most routine activities. The sense of safety that one typically associates with home and community was eroded by the knowledge that the "Beast of Birkenshaw" could strike at any time, in any place.

The unsettling unpredictability of Manuel's victim selection left no one untouched. It was not just the victims themselves who lived in fear; it was an entire community held captive by the spectre of an invisible and malevolent presence. Friends and neighbours became potential suspects in the minds of others. Innocent encounters took on sinister undertones. The bonds of trust that typically bind a community were strained to the breaking point.

For law enforcement tasked with solving the case, the unpredictability of Manuel's actions presented an unprecedented challenge. Serial killers are often profiled based on their choice of victims, the locations of their crimes, and the methods they employ. Manuel, however, seemed to defy such categorization. He moved with a capriciousness that was as maddening as it was terrifying.

In many ways, the unpredictable nature of Manuel's crimes served as a psychological weapon, amplifying the fear he instilled. It was as if he revelled in the knowledge that no one could predict his next move, that he held the community in a state of perpetual anxiety.

This chapter in the dark saga of Peter Manuel underscores the psychological torment he inflicted on an entire community. The fear of the unknown, the terror of unpredictability, and the erosion of trust were all tools in his arsenal, wielded with a malevolence that defied easy explanation. In the face of such a relentless and enigmatic adversary, the community of Glasgow was left to grapple with the unsettling question: who could be the next victim of the "Beast of Birkenshaw"?

4. Law Enforcement's Perplexity

As the chilling reign of Peter Manuel cast a long and ominous shadow over Glasgow and its surrounding areas, law enforcement faced a vexing and seemingly insurmountable challenge. The diverse array of victims, coupled with the glaring absence of clear motives, created a perplexing puzzle that confounded detectives, investigators, and profilers alike. The enigma of Manuel's crimes extended far beyond the acts themselves; it lay in the very heart of his unpredictable and chaotic modus operandi.

In the realm of criminal investigation, patterns are often sought as guiding lights, providing insights into the mind of the offender. Serial killers typically adhere to a certain victim profile, exhibit consistent methods, or follow a particular geographical pattern in their crimes. However, Peter Manuel defied such conventions with a diabolical glee. He seemed to revel in the chaos and uncertainty he sowed, taunting those who sought to stop him.

Law enforcement, trained to uncover patterns and motives, found themselves navigating uncharted waters. They could not rely on the comfort of established norms in criminal behaviour. Manuel's victims spanned a wide spectrum, ranging in age, gender, and social background. This diversity left investigators without the customary anchor points they depended upon to build a profile of the killer.

The lack of clear motives further compounded the perplexity. In many serial killer cases, investigators can discern a motive rooted in psychological pathology, a desire for power, or some form of personal gratification. In Manuel's case, the motives often seemed arbitrary or absent altogether. Why did he choose certain victims over others? What drove him to commit these heinous acts?

The chaos and unpredictability of Manuel's crimes were not accidental but rather calculated. He understood that by eschewing a discernible pattern, he could confound those who pursued him. Detectives scrambled to anticipate his next move, a task made infinitely more difficult by the absence of any clear method to his madness.

As the investigation progressed, detectives grappled with an adversary who seemed to mock their efforts at every turn. Manuel's brazenness, cunning, and capacity to vanish into the shadows only added to the frustration. It was as if he thrived on the psychological torment he inflicted, a sadistic puppeteer pulling the strings of those trying to catch him.

This chapter in the harrowing chronicle of Peter Manuel's crimes shines a spotlight on the formidable challenge faced by law enforcement. The absence of patterns, motives shrouded in ambiguity, and the relentless unpredictability of the "Beast of Birkenshaw" created an investigative labyrinth that seemed impossible to navigate. In their pursuit of this elusive killer, detectives would be forced to confront not only the darkness lurking within Peter Manuel but also the limits of their own understanding of criminal behaviour.

5. The Shadow of Fear

In the wake of Peter Manuel's reign of terror, a palpable and pervasive shadow of fear blanketed Glasgow and its surrounding areas. The unsettling unpredictability of Manuel's victim selection had far-reaching consequences, plunging the community into a state of perpetual unease. Residents, once secure in their neighbourhoods, now found themselves haunted by the chilling uncertainty of who might become the next target of this malevolent predator.

Fear has a profound and insidious way of infiltrating the human psyche. It creeps into the most mundane aspects of daily life, casting doubt and suspicion upon even the most ordinary interactions. In the case of Peter Manuel, this fear took root in the hearts and minds of the populace, slowly but inexorably altering the way they went about their lives.

The absence of a clear pattern in Manuel's choice of victims was perhaps the most unsettling aspect of his reign. In many instances of serial predation, communities can find some semblance of solace in the belief that certain demographics or behaviours make them less likely targets. Yet, in the case of the "Beast of Birkenshaw," no such comfort could be found. He did not discriminate based on age, gender, or social status, leaving the entire community on edge.

Families locked their doors and windows with newfound vigilance. Parents clutched their children a little tighter as they walked to school. Neighbours eyed each other with a mix of suspicion and fear, wondering if the friendly facade of a fellow resident concealed something more sinister. The streets, once vibrant with life, now seemed to pulse with an undercurrent of trepidation.

The shadow of fear had a tangible impact on daily routines. People hesitated to venture out alone, especially after dark. Women, in particular, were cautious, often accompanied by friends or family members when going about their business. The once-familiar paths and parks became haunting grounds of uncertainty.

In the absence of a clear pattern, the terror deepened. There was no rhyme or reason to Manuel's selection of victims. This unpredictability played directly into his sadistic strategy, as it left everyone vulnerable, perpetuating a constant state of fear. The community, typically a source of safety and support, had become a breeding ground for paranoia.

This chapter delves into the profound psychological and emotional impact of living under the shadow of fear. It explores how a once-thriving community was transformed into a place of unease, as residents grappled with the unsettling uncertainty of who might be the next victim of the "Beast of Birkenshaw." Fear had become an inescapable presence, a haunting reminder that the malevolent predator was still at large, lurking in the shadows, and that no one was truly safe.

The Enigma of Target Selection

Peter Manuel's choice of victims remained an enigma, defying easy analysis or understanding. His ability to prey upon a diverse array of individuals, regardless of age, gender, or background, created a chilling atmosphere of unpredictability. The absence of clear motives left a community in the grip of fear, haunted by the knowledge that the next victim could be anyone—a sinister testament to the depths of Manuel's malevolence.

The Use of Firearms: Instruments of Terror

A distinguishing and deeply unsettling feature of Peter Manuel's murderous spree was his frequent reliance on firearms. He wielded these deadly weapons not only to assert dominance but also to instil paralyzing fear in his victims. In his hands, the cold, metallic barrel of a gun became an instrument of terror, leaving those in his grasp vulnerable and compliant to his malevolent desires.

1. The Power of the Firearm

Firearms, with their innate ability to inflict harm from a distance, hold a unique power over the human psyche. Manuel understood this power all too well and harnessed it to assert control over his victims. The mere presence of a gun in his hands transformed the dynamics of any encounter, plunging his victims into a nightmarish reality where their lives hung in the balance.

2. The Forced Submission

Manuel's use of firearms was not limited to intimidation; he often compelled his victims to submit to his will at gunpoint. The looming threat of deadly force rendered his targets powerless, forcing them to comply with his every demand. It was a harrowing display of the extent to which he was willing to exert control.

3. The Psychological Impact

The psychological impact of facing a firearm-wielding assailant cannot be overstated. The fear instilled by the sight of a gun is paralyzing, eroding rational thought and replacing it with a primal instinct for self-preservation. Manuel's victims, confronted with this chilling reality, were left with little choice but to obey his commands.

4. The Instrument of Terror

In the hands of Peter Manuel, firearms transcended their utilitarian function and became instruments of terror. He exploited the innate fear they provoked, using it to manipulate and subdue those who fell under his malevolent gaze. The cold, metallic presence of the gun symbolized the ultimate authority he held over life and death.

5. A Perpetual Threat

For Manuel's victims, the knowledge that he possessed firearms transformed their lives into a perpetual state of uncertainty and dread. They lived with the constant awareness that at any moment, the deadly weapon could be turned against them, snuffing out their existence at his whim.

The Reign of Terror

Peter Manuel's use of firearms was a chilling manifestation of his desire for power and control. These deadly instruments amplified the fear he instilled in his victims, leaving them utterly vulnerable and compliant. The psychological trauma inflicted by the presence of a gun served as a stark reminder of the depths of his malevolence and the reign of terror he imposed upon those unfortunate enough to cross his path.

Sexual Assault and Sadism: The Twisted Intersection

In the grim tapestry of Peter Manuel's crimes, sexual assault and sadistic tendencies emerged as deeply disturbing and prevalent elements. Manuel derived perverse pleasure from inflicting pain, humiliation, and degradation upon his victims, and the introduction of a sexual component to his crimes added an especially disturbing dimension to his malevolence. This twisted interplay of violence and sexual gratification marked him as a true psychopath, plumbing the darkest depths of human depravity.

1. The Sadistic Thrill

Peter Manuel's descent into sadism marked a chilling and grotesque chapter in the annals of criminal history. While many criminals may commit acts of violence out of necessity or desperation, for Manuel, sadism was not merely a means to an end. It was an insatiable source of gratification, a perverse thrill that he actively sought out.

At the heart of Manuel's sadism lay a desire for power and control, a need to dominate and manipulate his victims in the most heinous ways imaginable. His crimes were not driven by financial gain or self-preservation but by an insidious pleasure derived from the suffering he inflicted.

The sadistic elements of Manuel's crimes often went beyond the mere act of violence. He subjected his victims to sexual assaults that added an additional layer of horror to his already gruesome acts. It was not enough for him to physically harm them; he sought to debase and humiliate them, savouring their anguish and helplessness.

This sadistic satisfaction was evident in the sheer brutality of his crimes. Manuel did not merely kill; he tortured, terrorized, and tormented his victims. Their suffering seemed to fuel his malevolence, driving him to increasingly depraved acts. He revelled in their pain, taking perverse pleasure in their anguish.

For Manuel, the crimes themselves became a grotesque theatre of cruelty. He meticulously planned and executed each act, relishing the power he held over his victims. His sadism was not a momentary lapse of morality but a deeply ingrained aspect of his personality, a wellspring of darkness that seemed bottomless.

This section delves into the disturbing psychology of Peter Manuel, exploring the sadistic thrill he derived from his crimes. It examines the depths of his depravity and the ways in which he actively sought out opportunities to inflict suffering upon his victims. Manuel's sadism was not a side note to his criminal activities; it was at the core of his malevolent essence, driving him to commit acts of unimaginable horror.

2. The Sexual Component

Peter Manuel's crimes were not solely about violence; they were marked by a disturbing fusion of brutality and sexuality that intensified the horror of his acts. The inclusion of a sexual component in his crimes was a chilling manifestation of his psychopathic proclivities, revealing an even darker facet of his malevolent nature.

For Manuel, sexual assault was not a mere byproduct of his violence; it was a deliberate and calculated tool to exert dominance and control over his victims. He used the fusion of violence and sexuality to amplify their terror, leaving them not only physically violated but psychologically scarred.

The sexual component of Manuel's crimes was not about gratification in the conventional sense but about power and degradation. It was a means of reducing his victims to objects of his sadistic desires, stripping away their humanity, and leaving them utterly vulnerable and humiliated.

This passage delves into the disturbing intersection of violence and sexuality in Manuel's crimes, exploring the psychological motivations behind this chilling fusion. It examines how he meticulously planned and executed acts of sexual assault, using them as tools of terror and control. The inclusion of a sexual component painted a harrowing portrait of his psychopathic nature and added an even more horrifying layer to the already gruesome tableau of his crimes.

3. The Power Dynamics

Within the nightmarish realm of Peter Manuel's crimes, the power dynamics he imposed were nothing short of horrifying. His sadistic tendencies found expression in the absolute control he wielded over his victims, and sexual assault was a potent tool in this twisted arsenal.

Manuel revelled in the sense of dominion he held over those he targeted. The violation of his victims' bodies and the degradation of their dignity were not incidental but rather integral to his pursuit of power. The act of sexual assault became a grotesque symbol of his insatiable appetite for control.

This passage delves into the chilling power dynamics at play in Manuel's crimes. It examines how he meticulously orchestrated scenarios that left his victims utterly powerless and vulnerable. His manipulation and cruelty were aimed at not just physical domination but the crushing of their spirits. It was a dark manifestation of his psychopathy, where the thirst for power and the infliction of suffering became inseparable elements of his crimes.

4. A True Psychopath

Peter Manuel's descent into the realm of sexual sadism marked him as a true psychopath, a character study in malevolence that transcended conventional criminality. His actions were not merely criminal acts; they were a manifestation of the darkest corners of the human psyche.

This section explores the disturbing facets of Manuel's personality that led him to derive pleasure from the suffering he inflicted on his victims. It delves into the psychological underpinnings of his sadistic tendencies, examining the complex interplay between power, control, and cruelty. Manuel's crimes were a testament to the chilling depths of his depravity, an exploration of the psyche of a man who found gratification in the torment of others.

As we delve into the mind of a true psychopath, we confront uncomfortable questions about the nature of evil, the limits of human empathy, and the disturbing allure of sadism. Peter Manuel's journey into the heart of darkness serves as a chilling reminder of the capacity for malevolence that can reside within the human soul.

5. The Profound Impact

The aftermath of Peter Manuel's sadistic and sexually motivated crimes left a trail of profound impact that stretched far beyond the immediate physical harm inflicted upon his victims. This chapter delves into the lasting consequences of his actions, highlighting the enduring scars of both physical agony and psychological trauma.

As we explore the lives of those who survived Manuel's brutality, we bear witness to the profound ways in which their existence was irrevocably altered. The violation of their bodies and their sense of self created a complex tapestry of emotional and psychological turmoil. The victims grappled with the haunting memories of their ordeals, often enduring a lifelong struggle to regain a sense of normalcy and security.

This passage shines a light on the indomitable spirit of survivors, their resilience in the face of unimaginable horror, and the enduring impact of a predator who revelled in their suffering. It is a testament to the strength of the human spirit and the ongoing journey towards healing and recovery in the wake of unspeakable cruelty.

Conclusion: A Portrait of Darkness

The presence of sexual assault and sadistic tendencies in Peter Manuel's crimes painted a chilling portrait of a true psychopath. His malevolent actions went beyond conventional criminality, plunging into the darkest depths of human depravity. Understanding this disturbing dimension of his crimes is essential in unravelling the complexities of his psyche and the profound trauma inflicted upon his victims

The Evasion of Capture: The Cat-and-Mouse Game

One of the most perplexing and infuriating aspects of Peter Manuel's murder spree was his uncanny ability to evade capture. As the body count rose, despite mounting evidence and growing public hysteria, he managed to stay one step ahead of law enforcement, taunting them with his audacity and elusiveness. His evasion tactics transformed his reign of terror into a chilling cat-and-mouse game that left both investigators and the public on edge.

1. The Slippery Perpetrator

In this section, we delve into the astonishing ability of Peter Manuel to elude the grasp of law enforcement time and again. His capacity to slip through the fingers of detectives, often in the most audacious of circumstances, left both investigators and the public in a state of disbelief.

As we explore the various instances when Manuel managed to evade capture, a pattern of cunning and meticulous planning begins to emerge. He seemed to possess an innate understanding of police procedures and a remarkable talent for exploiting weaknesses in the system. Whether it was his ability to disappear into the shadows, change his appearance, or manipulate those around him, Manuel's elusive nature became a hallmark of his criminal career.

This passage sheds light on the relentless pursuit of justice by detectives who were determined to bring Manuel to account for his heinous crimes. It is a testament to the enduring dedication of those who tirelessly worked to unravel the mysteries surrounding this slippery perpetrator and ultimately bring him to justice.

2. An Elusive Trail

This section delves into the perplexing nature of Peter Manuel's ability to remain an enigmatic and elusive figure in the eyes of law enforcement.

Despite the trail of evidence left behind at his crime scenes, Manuel consistently managed to outmanoeuvre the authorities, leaving detectives grappling with the challenge of capturing this slippery criminal.

As we explore the various instances when Manuel skilfully evaded capture, a picture of his cunning and adaptability comes into focus. He seemed to possess an intuitive understanding of criminal investigations, allowing him to exploit weaknesses and blind spots in the police's efforts to apprehend him. His capacity to disappear into the shadows, change his identity, and stay one step ahead only added to the mystique surrounding his criminal career.

This passage also examines the tireless efforts of the detectives who were determined to close in on Manuel, revealing the cat-and-mouse game that unfolded between law enforcement and their elusive quarry. Manuel's ability to confound his pursuers serves as a testament to the complexities and challenges faced by those tasked with bringing him to justice.

3. Taunting the Authorities

Beyond the practical aspects of eluding capture, Peter Manuel took perverse pleasure in taunting and mocking the very authorities charged with apprehending him. His evasion tactics were not merely a means to an end but a source of sadistic delight.

Manuel's crimes were not committed in the shadows; rather, they were staged for an audience. He understood the profound fear and frustration he instilled in both law enforcement and the public, and he thrived on this sense of power. The headlines, the investigations, and the manhunt all provided him with the notoriety he craved.

This section delves into Manuel's sinister glee as he defied authority figures. It explores the mind of a criminal who saw his actions not only as a means of satisfying his own dark desires but as a way to exert dominance over those who sought to bring him to justice. Manuel's ability to manipulate the narrative surrounding his crimes and cast himself as a criminal mastermind added an unsettling layer to his already chilling persona.

4. A Community Gripped by Fear

The reign of terror orchestrated by Peter Manuel didn't just affect individual victims; it sent shockwaves through the entire community, leaving it in a perpetual state of fear and uncertainty. Manuel's ability to remain elusive, slipping through the fingers of law enforcement, created a climate of paranoia and mistrust.

Residents lived in dread, their daily lives overshadowed by the fear that they could be the next target of this cold-blooded killer. It was a time when locking doors and windows became an act of self-preservation, when evening strolls turned into nerve-wracking experiences, and when trusting even familiar faces became a dilemma.

5. The Elusiveness Continues

As the body count rose, the elusiveness of Peter Manuel continued to confound those tasked with bringing him to justice. Despite intense scrutiny and a heightened police presence, he managed to evade capture, prolonging the nightmare for both his victims and the community.

A Chilling Game of Cat and Mouse

Peter Manuel's evasion of capture turned his murder spree into a chilling and protracted game of cat and mouse. His ability to outmanoeuvre law enforcement, taunt the authorities, and elude justice for an extended period only deepened the sense of terror that gripped the community. His story serves as a haunting reminder of the complexities and challenges inherent in tracking down a ruthless and cunning predator who seemed always to be one step ahead.

Conclusion: A Dark Prelude

The murder of Anne Kneilands marked the beginning of a reign of terror that would grip Scotland in a vice of fear and uncertainty. Peter Manuel's first kill was a harbinger of the horrors to come, and the impact on the community was profound.

As we delve deeper into the chilling world of Peter Manuel, we will explore the full extent of his murderous rampage, the investigations that sought to unmask him, and the courtroom dramas that would determine his fate. But always, in the background, the shadow of his initial kill will linger—a reminder of the darkness that lurked within, waiting to consume all in its path.

In the following chapters, we will confront the harrowing stories of Manuel's victims, the tireless efforts of law enforcement to bring him to justice, and the moral and ethical questions raised by his heinous acts. Together, we will seek to unravel the enigma of Peter Manuel, a man whose name would become synonymous with terror and whose crimes would etch a bloody stain on the annals of true crime history.

Chapter 4

The Investigation

Law Enforcement Response

As the chilling details of Peter Manuel's first murder emerged, a sense of urgency gripped the Lanarkshire region. The hunt for this emerging serial killer became the top priority for law enforcement agencies, and detectives embarked on a relentless pursuit that would ultimately span years. In this chapter, we delve into the painstaking efforts of the police and detectives in their quest to bring the elusive killer to justice.

The Gruelling Task Ahead: Unravelling Manuel's Web of Terror

The investigation into Peter Manuel's heinous crimes presented a daunting and unprecedented challenge for law enforcement from the very outset. Scotland had not witnessed a serial killer of this magnitude in recent memory, and the police were ill-prepared for the complexities and horrors that lay ahead. Manuel's uncanny ability to seamlessly blend into the community, his cunning manipulation of his victims, and his ever-changing patterns of behaviour all combined to create a gruelling and formidable task for investigators.

1. A Lack of Precedent

The absence of recent precedent for such a prolific serial killer in Scotland left law enforcement grappling with unfamiliar territory. The sheer scale and audacity of Manuel's crimes defied conventional investigative methods, necessitating a new approach to tracking down this elusive predator.

2. The Chameleon in Their Midst

Manuel's ability to blend into the community was a significant obstacle. He was not an outsider; he was a resident who lived among his potential victims, making him all the more difficult to identify and apprehend. This inherent advantage placed the investigators at a disadvantage as they struggled to unmask the killer in their midst.

3. Cunning Manipulation

Another formidable challenge lay in Manuel's capacity for cunning manipulation. He exploited the trust and vulnerability of his victims, leaving behind a trail of confusion and psychological trauma. Untangling the web of deceit he wove around his victims was a complex and emotionally gruelling task for detectives.

4. Shifting Patterns of Behaviour

Manuel's unpredictable and shifting patterns of behaviour further complicated the investigation. His crimes did not conform to a consistent modus operandi, making it challenging for investigators to anticipate his next move or establish a clear profile. This volatility left detectives on edge, constantly adapting to a foe who refused to conform to their expectations.

5. The Weight of Public Hysteria

As the body count rose and the public hysteria intensified, investigators faced not only the pressure of solving the case but also the weight of public expectation. Communities lived in fear, demanding answers and action. This added an additional layer of stress and urgency to an already gruelling investigation.

A Herculean Effort

The investigation into Peter Manuel's crimes demanded a Herculean effort from law enforcement. It was a relentless pursuit marked by unprecedented challenges, the likes of which Scotland had not seen before. The detectives tasked with tracking down this elusive and sadistic killer faced a relentless adversary who seemed to always be one step ahead. Manuel's reign of terror would ultimately test their resolve, resourcefulness, and resilience in the face of unimaginable horror.

The Role of Local Law Enforcement: A Desperate Struggle for Answers

In the wake of Anne Kneilands' murder, local police departments across Lanarkshire found themselves thrust into a gruelling and emotionally charged investigation. Detectives embarked on an arduous journey, combing through leads, interviewing witnesses, and painstakingly reconstructing the events leading up to the heinous crime. But as the body count rose and it became increasingly apparent that a serial killer was on the loose, it also became evident that a more coordinated and specialized approach was desperately needed.

1. The Initial Response

Rapid Mobilization: The Community's Cry for Justice

When news of Anne Kneilands' murder broke, it sent shockwaves through the community. The brutality of the crime and the senselessness of her death struck fear into the hearts of residents. However, it also galvanized local law enforcement into action. The initial response from the police was characterized by a resolute determination to solve the case and bring the perpetrator to justice.

Detectives and officers worked around the clock, combing through the crime scene for any trace of evidence. They interviewed witnesses, collected statements, and pursued leads with unwavering diligence. The urgency of the situation was palpable; the entire community clamoured for answers, and the pressure on law enforcement to deliver them was immense.

This section delves into the immediate aftermath of Anne Kneilands' murder, portraying the fervour and dedication with which law enforcement responded. It highlights the shock and horror that gripped the community and how this collective cry for justice propelled investigators forward in their quest to apprehend the perpetrator.

2. A Growing Sense of Dread

Unveiling a Disturbing Pattern: The Emergence of a Serial Killer

With each passing day of the investigation into Anne Kneilands' murder, Lanarkshire descended further into a gripping sense of dread. What initially appeared to be an isolated act of brutality had now unveiled a dark pattern of violence. The community's worst fears were taking shape, and the realization that they were dealing with a serial killer began to set in.

Local police departments found themselves faced with a daunting and unsettling scenario. In the relatively peaceful region of Lanarkshire, the concept of a serial killer was something they had not encountered in their recent history. The emergence of this pattern added a chilling layer of complexity to the case.

This section explores the growing sense of unease and fear that pervaded Lanarkshire as the investigation progressed. It delves into the shockwaves sent through the community as the realization of a serial killer in their midst sunk in. The police's shifting focus from a single isolated incident to a broader pattern of violence is examined, highlighting the challenges they faced in dealing with this unprecedented threat.

3. The Need for Specialization

Adapting to the Unprecedented: The Demand for Specialized Expertise

As the investigation into the gruesome murder of Anne Kneilands unfolded and the realization of a serial killer stalking Lanarkshire took hold, local law enforcement faced an unprecedented challenge. The complexities of the case and the evolving patterns of the killer's behaviour demanded a shift in their investigative approach.

Recognizing the limitations of traditional investigative methods, authorities understood the need for a more coordinated and specialized effort. The case had transcended the realm of routine criminal investigations; they were now dealing with a predator who demonstrated a disturbing level of cunning and elusiveness.

This necessitated a call for specialized expertise. Detectives and law enforcement agencies began to explore new avenues and strategies, including seeking assistance from experts in profiling and serial crime analysis. The community's safety depended on their ability to adapt to this unsettling new reality and collaborate effectively to bring this serial killer to justice.

This section delves into the challenges faced by local law enforcement and their realization that traditional approaches would not suffice. It underscores the need for specialization and the evolving strategies employed to confront the enigmatic killer, Peter Manuel.

4. The Emergence of Task Forces

Uniting Forces: The Birth of Specialized Task Forces

As the fear and tension in Lanarkshire escalated, law enforcement recognized the need for a coordinated and concerted effort to apprehend Peter Manuel. The emergence of a serial killer was an extraordinary challenge, requiring an equally extraordinary response.

In response to this crisis, task forces and joint operations were formed, uniting detectives from various jurisdictions. These specialized units served as the vanguard in the relentless pursuit of Manuel, pooling their resources, expertise, and collective knowledge. The objective was clear: to untangle the intricate web of terror that Manuel had woven across Lanarkshire.

These task forces operated with a singular focus on solving the heinous crimes committed by Manuel. They conducted exhaustive investigations, analysed patterns, and pursued every lead with unwavering determination. This collaborative approach was essential in tackling a criminal who had already demonstrated an unnerving ability to outwit and evade local law enforcement.

This section sheds light on the formation and operations of these specialized task forces, highlighting the dedication and unity of purpose that drove detectives from different jurisdictions to work together in the pursuit of justice.

5. A Desperate Struggle

The Desperate Struggle: Law Enforcement's Battle Against Darkness

Local law enforcement found themselves embroiled in a desperate struggle when faced with the enigmatic and sadistic Peter Manuel. This battle was not just a professional endeavour but a deeply personal one, as detectives grappled with the profound toll of pursuing a serial killer of unparalleled malevolence.

Manuel's crimes were marked by a level of cunning and sadism that left even seasoned investigators shocked and horrified. Each crime scene presented a new layer of darkness, forcing detectives to confront the depths of human depravity. The emotional toll was immense, as they bore witness to the suffering he inflicted upon innocent victims.

While dedicated to their duty, these detectives were not immune to the psychological impact of their work. The relentless pursuit of Manuel took a toll on their emotional well-being, leading to sleepless nights and haunting nightmares. The investigation demanded more than just professional dedication; it required an unwavering resilience in the face of overwhelming horror.

This section delves into the personal struggles of the detectives, highlighting their determination to bring Manuel to justice despite the harrowing challenges they encountered. It provides a glimpse into the emotional turmoil and resilience that defined their quest for answers in the darkest of times.

Conclusion: A Community's Resilience

The early stages of the investigation into Peter Manuel's crimes saw local law enforcement grappling with an unprecedented challenge. Their efforts, driven by a commitment to justice and a desire to protect their community, would ultimately play a crucial role in the broader pursuit of the elusive and sadistic serial killer.

Formation of the Manuel Squad: The Elite Pursuers

As the wave of terror unleashed by Peter Manuel swept through Lanarkshire, local law enforcement realized that a new level of coordination and specialization was imperative. In response to the mounting crisis, a formidable and highly specialized task force emerged, known as the "Manuel Squad." Comprised of seasoned detectives and investigators, this elite team was entrusted with the harrowing mission of unravelling the web of darkness that Manuel had cast over the region, with an unwavering commitment to apprehending him at any cost.

1. The Birth of the Manuel Squad

The formation of the Manuel Squad marked a pivotal moment in the pursuit of justice. Recognizing the unprecedented challenges posed by a serial killer of Manuel's calibre, law enforcement agencies across Lanarkshire pooled their resources, expertise, and manpower. The squad was carefully assembled, bringing together some of the most experienced and determined individuals from various departments.

2. Seasoned Detectives and Investigators

The members of the Manuel Squad were not novices; they were seasoned detectives and investigators with a wealth of experience. Their backgrounds spanned a diverse range of specialties, from homicide investigations to behavioural profiling. This diversity ensured that no stone would be left unturned in the relentless pursuit of the elusive killer.

3. A Singular Focus

The squad's mission was singular and clear: to bring Peter Manuel to justice, no matter the obstacles or the length of the pursuit. Their unwavering commitment was a testament to their dedication to safeguarding their community and ending the reign of terror that had enveloped Lanarkshire.

4. The Challenges Ahead

The formation of the Manuel Squad was not without its challenges. The investigators were acutely aware of the gravity of their task, and they bore the emotional weight of each victim's story. The toll of pursuing a sadistic and cunning serial killer would test their mettle and resilience.

5. A Symbol of Hope

For the community, the Manuel Squad became a symbol of hope in the darkest of times. The presence of this elite task force offered reassurance that every effort was being made to apprehend the killer and bring an end to the nightmare that had gripped Lanarkshire.

The Relentless Pursuit

The formation of the Manuel Squad signalled a turning point in the pursuit of Peter Manuel. It was a determined and relentless force, fuelled by a collective desire to protect the innocent and ensure that justice would ultimately prevail. The squad's unwavering commitment to their mission would set them on a collision course with the malevolent force that had terrorized their community, leading to a confrontation that would test their resolve and skill to the utmost.

The Pursuit Begins: Relentless Hunt for a Sadistic Killer

With the formation of the Manuel Squad, the relentless pursuit of the elusive killer, Peter Manuel, commenced in earnest. This elite team of seasoned detectives and investigators embarked on a mission that would demand their unwavering dedication, resilience, and a relentless pursuit of justice. Their efforts were marked by extensive interviews with surviving victims, meticulous collection of forensic evidence, and a careful review of witness statements—all in a determined bid to create a comprehensive profile of the suspect. Yet, with each new murder, the urgency of their quest intensified, and the weight of solving the case bore heavily on their shoulders.

1. Extensive Victim Interviews

One of the initial steps taken by the Manuel Squad was to conduct extensive interviews with surviving victims. These interviews were not merely fact-finding missions; they were a critical means of gaining insight into the mind of the killer. The victims' harrowing experiences provided valuable clues that could help the squad understand the perpetrator's motivations and modus operandi.

2. Meticulous Forensic Work

Forensic evidence played a pivotal role in the pursuit of justice. The squad spared no effort in meticulously collecting and analysing every piece of evidence left behind at the crime scenes. From fingerprints to ballistics, DNA to trace evidence, no stone was left unturned in the quest to identify the killer and link him to his crimes.

3. Reviewing Witness Statements

The Manuel Squad painstakingly reviewed witness statements, hoping to extract any overlooked details or potential leads. Witnesses, often traumatized by their encounters with the killer, provided critical information that could help build a more comprehensive profile of the suspect. The squad understood the value of these statements in piecing together the puzzle.

4. Escalating Urgency

With each new murder, the urgency of the squad's quest escalated. The mounting body count was a grim reminder that every day Manuel remained at large; more lives hung in the balance. The pressure to solve the case weighed heavily on the shoulders of these dedicated investigators.

5. A Relentless Pursuit

The pursuit of Peter Manuel was marked by relentlessness. The members of the Manuel Squad were acutely aware of the stakes, and they were determined to bring the killer to justice. Their unwavering commitment to the mission was a testament to their resolve in the face of unimaginable horror.

The Beginnings of a Profile

The Manuel Squad's relentless pursuit marked the beginnings of a comprehensive profile of the sadistic killer. With each interview, each piece of evidence, and each witness statement, they moved closer to unravelling the web of darkness that had gripped Lanarkshire. Their quest for justice was unwavering, and their resolve would ultimately set the stage for the dramatic and chilling confrontation that lay ahead.

Forensic Advancements and Limitations: The Challenges of the 1950s

The 1950s marked an era when forensic science was still in its infancy. Detectives, including the members of the Manuel Squad, relied predominantly on traditional investigative techniques to solve crimes, such as fingerprint analysis and witness testimonies. The absence of modern forensic tools, such as DNA analysis, posed significant limitations and challenges in definitively linking Peter Manuel to the crimes he had committed. Nevertheless, the investigators pressed on, driven by their unwavering determination to close in on their elusive prey.

1. Traditional Investigative Techniques

During the 1950s, forensic science had not yet reached the advanced stage it occupies today. Detectives primarily relied on traditional investigative techniques and methodologies that were available at the time. This included fingerprint analysis, which could link a suspect to a crime scene, and witness testimonies, which were crucial in piecing together the events leading up to the crimes.

2. The Absence of DNA Analysis

One of the most significant limitations of forensic science in the 1950s was the absence of DNA analysis. Today, DNA evidence plays a pivotal role in identifying and convicting suspects. However, during Manuel's reign of terror, this powerful tool was not available. This absence made it exceedingly challenging to definitively link him to the crimes through biological evidence.

3. Reliance on Witness Statements

In the absence of modern forensic tools, witness statements took on even greater importance. Witnesses who had encountered Manuel during or around the time of the crimes provided critical information that helped build a case against him. These statements were meticulously reviewed and cross-referenced in the pursuit of leads.

4. The Persistence of Investigators

Despite the limitations of the era's forensic science, the investigators, particularly the Manuel Squad, demonstrated remarkable persistence. They understood the challenges they faced but remained resolute in their determination to bring the killer to justice. Their work showcased the power of dedication and traditional investigative skills in the face of an elusive and cunning adversary.

5. A Challenging Environment

The 1950s presented a challenging environment for law enforcement. The absence of modern forensic advancements and the limited technological resources of the time meant that detectives had to rely on their expertise, intuition, and dogged determination. It was a time when solving complex cases demanded unwavering commitment and resourcefulness.

A Determined Pursuit

The Manuel Squad's pursuit of Peter Manuel unfolded in a challenging forensic landscape. Despite the limitations of the era, they persevered, using the tools and knowledge available to them to build a case against

the elusive killer. Their unwavering determination and relentless pursuit would ultimately prove pivotal in the quest for justice in Lanarkshire.

The Fear Grips Glasgow: A City Paralyzed by Dread

As the investigation into the sadistic serial killer, Peter Manuel, intensified, an ominous and suffocating atmosphere of terror and panic descended upon the city of Glasgow and its surrounding areas. What were once tranquil communities transformed into landscapes of dread and apprehension. Residents now lived in a state of perpetual fear, with every creaking floorboard and unfamiliar face evoking anxiety. Locking doors, avoiding strangers, and keeping a vigilant watch over loved ones became daily rituals. The fear that gripped the city was not merely a passing unease; it was palpable, and the very sense of security that residents had taken for granted had been irrevocably shattered.

1. A Once-Vibrant City

Glasgow, a once-vibrant and bustling city, became a shadow of its former self. The laughter that once echoed through the streets was replaced by whispered concerns and anxious glances. The fear of encountering the faceless menace known as the "Beast of Birkenshaw" was inescapable.

2. A Sense of Vulnerability

The realization that a sadistic killer was on the loose struck at the heart of the community's sense of security. The ordinary routines of life became fraught with danger. Parents worried about their children

playing outside, couples hesitated to walk alone at night, and the safety of one's own home no longer felt assured.

3. Communities in Isolation

The fear not only isolated individuals but also entire communities. Neighbours who once shared a sense of camaraderie were now cautious and suspicious of one another. The prevailing sense of unease meant that people withdrew into their homes, afraid to venture out unless absolutely necessary.

4. The Psychological Toll

The fear that gripped Glasgow exacted a profound psychological toll on its residents. Anxiety, insomnia, and nightmares became commonplace. The trauma of living under the constant threat of violence left scars that would endure long after the killer was apprehended.

5. A Determined Resolve

Despite the pervasive fear, there was also a determined resolve among the people of Glasgow. Communities banded together, and vigilance became a shared responsibility. Residents supported the efforts of law enforcement and awaited the day when the nightmare would come to an end.

A City Forever Altered

The fear that swept through Glasgow during the reign of Peter Manuel was a dark chapter in the city's history. It left an indelible mark on the collective psyche of its residents, forever altering the way they viewed their world. The pursuit of the sadistic killer became not only a quest for justice but also a means of reclaiming the city's sense of security and restoring a semblance of normalcy to its streets.

The Media's Role: A Double-Edged Sword in the Pursuit of Peter Manuel

During the pursuit of Peter Manuel, the media assumed a pivotal and complex role in shaping public perception and exacerbating the atmosphere of fear. Newspapers, in particular, played a significant part in the unfolding drama, their coverage oscillating between spreading awareness and sensationalizing the murders. Each new headline, laden with gruesome details and speculation about the killer's identity, had the power to both fuel public anxiety and aid in the investigation. The media's role became a double-edged sword, with far-reaching consequences.

1. Sensationalism and Speculation

The media's coverage of the Manuel case often leaned toward sensationalism. Headlines featured dramatic descriptions of the crimes, with lurid details that captured the public's morbid curiosity. Speculation about the killer's identity ran rampant, with newspapers offering their own theories and hypotheses, sometimes without substantial evidence.

2. Heightened Public Anxiety

As the media sensationalized the murders, public anxiety reached fever pitch. The gruesome depictions and sensational headlines left residents living in a constant state of fear. Speculation about the identity and motivations of the killer only added to the collective sense of dread.

3. The Spread of Awareness

While sensationalism had its drawbacks, the media also played a crucial role in spreading awareness about the case. News reports informed the public about the ongoing investigation, shared descriptions of the suspect, and encouraged vigilance. This heightened awareness led to increased cooperation with law enforcement and more tips from the community.

4. The Impact on the Investigation

The media's extensive coverage had both positive and negative effects on the investigation. On one hand, it ensured that the case remained in the public eye and kept the pressure on law enforcement to solve it. On the other hand, sensationalism and speculative reporting occasionally led to misinformation, false leads, and distractions for investigators.

5. A Complex Relationship

The relationship between the media and the investigation into Peter Manuel was complex. The media, driven by the public's insatiable appetite for sensational stories, had the power to shape public perception and influence the course of the case. This dynamic highlighted the delicate balance between responsible journalism and the potential negative consequences of sensational reporting.

A Pivotal Role

The media's role in the Peter Manuel case was pivotal, leaving an indelible mark on both the investigation and the psyche of the public. It served as a double-edged sword, simultaneously raising awareness and exacerbating fear. Ultimately, it underscored the significant influence that media coverage can have in high-profile criminal cases, for better or worse.

Community Vigilance: Uniting Against the Darkness

Amidst the uncertainty and fear that pervaded Lanarkshire during the reign of Peter Manuel, communities displayed a remarkable resilience by banding together in a remarkable show of unity and vigilance. Neighbourhood watch programs sprang up, and residents, bound by a shared sense of responsibility, began reporting any suspicious activity to the police. This profound sense of collective responsibility was both heartening and a poignant reflection of the profound fear that gripped the region.

1. The Emergence of Neighbourhood Watch Programs

As fear swept through Lanarkshire, many communities responded by forming neighbourhood watch programs. These grassroots initiatives were a direct response to the mounting anxiety and a way for residents to actively participate in safeguarding their neighbourhoods. Neighbours became each other's eyes and ears, working in concert to protect their community from the looming threat.

2. Reporting Suspicious Activity

Residents, no longer content to live in fear, took it upon themselves to report any suspicious activity to the police. This influx of information provided law enforcement with critical leads and tips that would prove invaluable in their pursuit of Peter Manuel. The vigilance of the community became a potent weapon against the darkness that had descended upon them.

3. A Shared Sense of Responsibility

The sense of collective responsibility that emerged was deeply moving. Neighbours looked out for one another, and the bonds of community grew stronger in the face of adversity. The fear that had initially isolated individuals was transformed into a unifying force that transcended divisions.

4. Strength in Unity

The unity displayed by the communities of Lanarkshire was a testament to the human spirit's resilience in the face of terror. While the fear was real and ever-present, it was met with a determination to reclaim a sense of security and normalcy. The unity and vigilance of these communities sent a clear message that they would not be cowed by a malevolent force.

A Beacon of Hope

In the darkest of times, the communities of Lanarkshire became beacons of hope. Their collective vigilance and unwavering determination to protect their neighbourhoods exemplified the strength that can emerge in the face of adversity. While the fear persisted, so did the resolve to confront it, demonstrating that even in the most harrowing circumstances, unity and vigilance can prevail.

The Unyielding Pursuit

The investigation into Peter Manuel's crimes was a herculean effort marked by determination, resourcefulness, and an unwavering commitment to justice. The formation of the Manuel Squad and the tireless work of detectives signalled a resolute response to the terror that had enveloped Lanarkshire.

However, the shadow of fear continued to loom over Glasgow, and the pressure to apprehend Manuel only intensified as the body count rose. In the following chapters, we will explore the chilling stories of Manuel's victims, the psychological toll on the community, and the profound impact of his reign of terror. As we delve deeper into this harrowing narrative, we will witness the unyielding pursuit of justice in the face of unimaginable horror.

Chapter 5

The Courtroom Drama

Arrest and Trial

The culmination of the manhunt for Peter Manuel brought with it a harrowing courtroom drama that would captivate Scotland and the world. In this chapter, we delve into Manuel's arrest, the legal proceedings that followed, and the unfolding drama of his trial.

The Arrest of Peter Manuel: A Momentous Turning Point

The relentless efforts of the police, coupled with tips from vigilant citizens, finally led to a breakthrough in the case that had gripped Lanarkshire in terror. On the fateful day of January 2, 1958, the long and harrowing manhunt for the sadistic serial killer, Peter Manuel, reached its climax when he was apprehended by the police. His arrest was a momentous event, one that sent shockwaves through the region. It offered a glimmer of hope to a terrorized community, but it also marked the beginning of a legal battle that would test the limits of the justice system.

1. The Tensions Mount

As the investigation into Peter Manuel's gruesome murders continued, tensions in Lanarkshire reached a fever pitch. The relentless pursuit of the sadistic killer had taken a toll on the community, and the fear that had gripped the region was palpable. The need for closure and justice was more pressing than ever.

2. A Community on Edge

Lanarkshire had been living in fear for months, with residents locking their doors, avoiding strangers, and living in a state of constant vigilance. The atmosphere was one of unease, with each new headline about Manuel's crimes adding to the collective anxiety.

3. Tips from Vigilant Citizens

Amid this atmosphere of fear and uncertainty, vigilant citizens played a crucial role. Neighbourhood watch programs had sprung up, and residents were actively reporting any suspicious activity to the police. This influx of information provided investigators with valuable leads and tips that gradually closed the net around the elusive killer.

4. The Suspicious Encounter

On that fateful day in early January, a vigilant citizen spotted Peter Manuel acting suspiciously in a neighbourhood in Glasgow. This citizen, emboldened by the prevailing sense of collective responsibility, wasted no time in alerting the police. The sighting would prove to be the critical breakthrough in the case.

5. The Arrest

Responding to the tip, police officers approached Peter Manuel. It was a moment fraught with tension, as they had come face to face with a man suspected of carrying out a horrifying killing spree. Manuel's behaviour, combined with the tip and their own suspicions, gave the officers the grounds they needed to detain him.

6. The Critical Discovery

As they took Peter Manuel into custody, the police made a discovery that would prove to be critical in building their case against him. During the arrest, they found a firearm in Manuel's possession. The significance of this discovery would become evident in the subsequent legal proceedings.

7. Shockwaves Through the Region

News of Peter Manuel's arrest sent shockwaves through Lanarkshire and beyond. The community, which had lived in the shadow of fear for so long, was suddenly confronted with the possibility that the reign of terror might be coming to an end. The relief was palpable, but it was tempered by the knowledge that the legal battle ahead would be arduous and complex.

8. The Legal Battle Begins

The arrest of Peter Manuel marked the beginning of a legal battle that would test the limits of the justice system. The evidence gathered by the police, including the firearm discovered during the arrest, would play a pivotal role in the upcoming trial. The region watched with bated breath as the wheels of justice slowly began to turn.

A Glimmer of Hope

The arrest of Peter Manuel was a momentous turning point in the Lanarkshire killings. It offered a glimmer of hope to a community that had endured months of terror. Yet, it also marked the beginning of a legal saga that would hold the region in its grip, as the pursuit of justice for the victims entered a new and complex phase. The arrest was a testament to the determination of law enforcement and the vigilance of citizens who refused to succumb to fear.

The Legal Proceedings: The Trial of Peter Manuel

The trial of Peter Manuel was not a mere courtroom spectacle; it was a seismic event that would come to define an era. As the accused serial killer stood before the bar of justice, the eyes of the nation turned toward the proceedings, hungry for answers and closure.

1. A Nation's Attention

The trial of Peter Manuel captivated not only the local community but the entire nation. The Lanarkshire killings had struck a chord of fear and intrigue, and people from all walks of life were eager to see justice served. Media coverage of the trial was extensive, with newspapers and radio broadcasts providing daily updates on the proceedings.

2. The Weight of the Charges

Peter Manuel faced an array of charges, including multiple counts of murder, sexual assault, and robbery. The sheer gravity of the accusations cast a long shadow over the courtroom. Each charge represented a heinous act that had terrorized the community, and the victims' families and friends were in attendance, seeking closure for their loved ones.

3. Legal Teams and Strategies

The trial featured skilled legal teams on both sides. Manuel was represented by defence attorneys who sought to challenge the evidence and cast doubt on his guilt. The prosecution, on the other hand, was tasked with presenting a compelling case that would prove beyond a reasonable doubt that Manuel was the sadistic killer responsible for the crimes.

4. Testimonies and Evidence

The courtroom was filled with testimonies from survivors, witnesses, and law enforcement officers who had played a pivotal role in the investigation. The evidence presented included the critical discovery of the firearm during Manuel's arrest, forensic analysis, and the meticulous reconstruction of the events leading up to the murders.

5. The Accused's Demeanour

Throughout the trial, Peter Manuel's demeanour was closely scrutinized. His behaviour in the courtroom, whether it was stoic composure or occasional outbursts, was subject to analysis by both the legal teams and the public. Manuel's demeanour would become a focal point in the narrative surrounding the trial.

6. The Verdict and Sentencing

After weeks of testimonies, arguments, and deliberations, the trial reached its climax with the pronouncement of the verdict. The nation held its collective breath as the jury delivered their decision. The outcome would not only determine the fate of Peter Manuel but also provide closure to the victims' families and a sense of justice to the community.

7. A Seismic Event

The trial of Peter Manuel was more than a legal proceeding; it was a seismic event that had far-reaching implications. It served as a moment of reckoning for a community that had lived in fear and uncertainty. The verdict would not only shape the future of one man but also provide a sense of closure to a region that had endured months of terror.

A Defining Moment

The trial of Peter Manuel was a defining moment in the Lanarkshire killings saga. It was a testament to the pursuit of justice, the resilience of the community, and the weight of the crimes committed. As the courtroom drama unfolded, it held the nation's attention, reminding everyone that the quest for truth and justice was paramount, no matter how dark the circumstances.

The Charges: The Staggering Litany of Crimes Against Peter Manuel

Peter Manuel's day in court was a reckoning, and the charges laid against him were a formidable testament to the reign of terror he had inflicted upon Lanarkshire. The litany of crimes attributed to him was staggering, and the prosecution's case was built on a mountain of evidence, including eyewitness testimonies, forensic analysis, and the recovered murder weapon.

1. Multiple Counts of Murder

At the heart of the charges against Peter Manuel were multiple counts of murder. Each count represented a life cruelly extinguished by the sadistic serial killer. The victims, from Anne Kneilands to Marion Watt and many others in between, had all met their gruesome fates at the hands of Manuel. The weight of these charges hung heavily in the courtroom, a stark reminder of the brutality that had gripped the region.

2. Sexual Assault

In addition to the murders, Peter Manuel faced charges of sexual assault. His crimes often included a chilling blend of violence and sexual gratification, leaving a trail of victims scarred by physical and emotional trauma. The prosecution presented evidence of these disturbing acts, further solidifying the case against him.

3. Robbery

The charges extended beyond violence and sexual assault to include robbery. Manuel's crimes were not only acts of brutality but also driven by a desire for material gain. The victims' belongings and valuables were often taken, adding another layer of criminality to his actions.

4. A Mountain of Evidence

The prosecution's case was fortified by an abundance of evidence. Eyewitness testimonies painted a chilling picture of the crimes, providing harrowing accounts of encounters with Manuel. Forensic analysis, though limited by the standards of the time, still played a crucial role in linking Manuel to the scenes of the crimes. Perhaps most damning of all was the recovery of the murder weapon during Manuel's arrest, a piece of evidence that would loom large in the courtroom.

5. The Weight of the Charges

The charges against Peter Manuel carried a weight that was felt not only in the courtroom but throughout Lanarkshire. The victims' families, who had endured unimaginable grief, sought justice for their loved ones. The community, which had lived in fear for months, looked to the legal proceedings as a means of closure and as a testament to the enduring pursuit of truth and accountability.

A Formidable Case

The litany of charges against Peter Manuel painted a chilling portrait of a man who had terrorized Lanarkshire. The prosecution's case, bolstered by a wealth of evidence, left no room for doubt about the gravity of his crimes. As the trial unfolded, the nation watched with bated breath, eager to see justice served for the victims and a community yearning for closure.

The Defence Strategy

As Peter Manuel's trial got underway, all eyes were on his defence team. Led by experienced barristers, they embarked on a strategy aimed at securing their client's acquittal or, at the very least, avoiding the death penalty.

Analysing the Defence Team: The Battle for Peter Manuel's Freedom

Peter Manuel's defence team was an assembly of accomplished legal professionals, each well-versed in the art of courtroom advocacy. The lead counsel, tasked with navigating the treacherous waters of the trial, was renowned for his legal acumen and persuasive skills. His colleagues brought their own expertise to bear, with some specializing in forensic evidence and others in witness cross-examination.

1. The Lead Counsel

The defence team's most prominent figure was the lead counsel, a legal luminary known for his ability to craft compelling arguments and sway juries. His reputation for defending clients in high-profile cases had earned him the respect of the legal community. He would be the guiding force in the courtroom, seeking to create reasonable doubt in the minds of the jury.

2. Specialized Expertise

The defence team was not a one-dimensional entity. Instead, it was a well-rounded ensemble of legal experts, each contributing a unique set of skills. Some members specialized in forensic evidence, aiming to challenge the reliability of the prosecution's scientific findings. Others were adept at witness cross-examination, with a keen eye for spotting inconsistencies and weaknesses in the testimonies presented.

3. The Formidable Challenge

Defending Peter Manuel was no ordinary task; it was a formidable challenge. The accusations against him were chilling, and the weight of the charges was immense. The defence team was acutely aware of the public sentiment surrounding the case, and they recognized that they had to overcome a considerable burden to secure a fair trial for their client.

4. A Multifaceted Strategy

To mount a robust defence, the team adopted a multifaceted strategy. This strategy drew on a combination of legal tactics, psychological insights, and appeals to the court's sense of justice. They sought to challenge the prosecution's evidence, question the reliability of witnesses, and introduce alternative explanations for the crimes. Additionally, they aimed to portray Peter Manuel as a complex individual whose actions could be attributed to factors beyond pure malevolence.

5. The Pursuit of Reasonable Doubt

Central to the defence's strategy was the pursuit of reasonable doubt. They understood that a successful defence did not necessarily require proving innocence but rather planting seeds of doubt in the minds of the jurors. This approach aimed to create uncertainty about Manuel's guilt, thereby preventing a unanimous verdict of guilty.

Conclusion: A Battle of Legal Titans

The trial of Peter Manuel was not just a battle between the prosecution and the defence; it was a clash of legal titans. Manuel's defence team, armed with legal expertise and a multifaceted strategy, faced the daunting challenge of defending a man accused of heinous crimes that had terrorized the nation. As the trial unfolded, their efforts would be scrutinized by the court, the public, and history itself.

The Insanity Defence: Challenging the Nature of Guilt and Justice

One of the central pillars of Peter Manuel's defence was the assertion of his insanity. The defence argued that Manuel was not in control of his actions at the time of the crimes due to a severe mental illness. To support this claim, they presented expert witnesses, including psychiatrists and psychologists, who testified to Manuel's alleged mental instability.

1. The Assertion of Insanity

The insanity defence was a bold and contentious strategy employed by Manuel's legal team. It hinged on the argument that Peter Manuel's mental state at the time of the crimes rendered him incapable of comprehending the wrongfulness of his actions. This assertion raised profound questions about the nature of guilt, culpability, and the purpose of the justice system.

2. Expert Witnesses

To bolster the insanity claim, the defence called upon a cadre of expert witnesses. Psychiatrists and psychologists were among those who testified, offering their professional opinions on Manuel's mental state. Their testimony delved into the intricacies of his psychological profile, exploring the presence of any severe mental disorders that might have impaired his judgment and self-control.

3. The Prosecution's Response

The prosecution vigorously contested the insanity defence. They presented their own experts, including forensic psychiatrists, who questioned the validity of the insanity claim. These experts scrutinized

Manuel's behaviour, looking for evidence that contradicted the assertion of mental illness. Their aim was to demonstrate that Manuel was fully aware of the consequences of his actions and that his crimes were driven by malevolence rather than mental instability.

4. The Ethical Dilemma

The insanity defence posed a profound ethical dilemma for the court and society at large. If Manuel was indeed found to be legally insane, it would challenge conventional notions of guilt and accountability. Such a verdict would likely result in his confinement to a psychiatric institution rather than a prison, raising questions about the balance between punishment and rehabilitation in the criminal justice system.

5. The Impact on the Verdict

The insanity defence cast a long shadow over the trial, as it forced the jury to grapple with the complex issue of mental illness and culpability. Ultimately, the verdict would hinge on whether the jury accepted the assertion that Manuel's mental state absolved him of responsibility for his actions or whether they believed he was a calculating and sadistic killer.

A Trial Within a Trial

The assertion of insanity in Peter Manuel's defence transformed the trial into a trial within a trial—a battle not only over his guilt but also over the fundamental question of what constitutes justice. As the legal teams clashed over the nature of Manuel's mental state, the court faced a momentous decision that would not only determine his fate but also shape the discourse surrounding mental illness and criminal responsibility.

Challenging the Evidence: The Battle for Reasonable Doubt

Another key element of Peter Manuel's defence strategy involved a meticulous challenge to the prosecution's evidence. His legal team left no stone unturned as they scrutinized the reliability of eyewitness testimonies, raised doubts about the chain of custody of physical evidence, and questioned the admissibility of certain forensic findings. Their aim was crystal clear: to create reasonable doubt in the minds of the jurors, casting uncertainty on the veracity of the charges against Manuel.

1. Eyewitness Testimonies

Eyewitness testimonies, while compelling, are not infallible. Manuel's defence team embarked on a rigorous examination of these accounts, highlighting potential inconsistencies, lapses in memory, and the influence of fear and trauma on the witnesses' recollections. By undermining the credibility of these testimonies, they sought to sow seeds of doubt about Manuel's involvement in the crimes.

2. Chain of Custody

The defence team also scrutinized the chain of custody of physical evidence. They raised questions about whether the evidence had been properly handled and preserved, thereby casting doubt on its reliability. The admissibility of crucial items, such as the murder weapon, became a focal point of contention in the courtroom.

3. Forensic Findings

Forensic evidence, though powerful, is not immune to challenges. Manuel's legal team enlisted their own experts to question the validity of the forensic findings presented by the prosecution. They sought to reveal potential flaws in the collection, analysis, or interpretation of forensic data, further eroding the prosecution's case.

4. Reasonable Doubt

Central to the defence's strategy was the concept of reasonable doubt. They aimed to demonstrate to the jurors that the evidence presented by the prosecution was not ironclad and that there were legitimate reasons to question Manuel's guilt. By raising doubts about the strength and reliability of the evidence, they hoped to prevent a unanimous verdict of guilty.

5. The Jury's Dilemma

The defence's relentless challenge to the evidence placed the jury in a difficult position. They were tasked with evaluating the competing narratives presented by the prosecution and the defence. As the trial unfolded, the jurors had to grapple with the weight of their decision, knowing that the outcome would have profound implications for both Peter Manuel and the community.

The Pursuit of Justice

Challenging the prosecution's evidence was a critical component of Peter Manuel's defence strategy. It was a relentless pursuit of justice—one that demanded a rigorous examination of the facts and a steadfast commitment to the principle that every accused individual is entitled to a fair trial. As the trial reached its climax, the jury faced the daunting task of navigating the complex web of evidence and determining the truth amidst the shadows of doubt.

Appealing to Sympathy: Humanizing Peter Manuel

In a calculated effort to humanize their client, Peter Manuel's defence attorneys embarked on a strategy designed to evoke sympathy from the jury. They presented aspects of his troubled upbringing, delving into his childhood experiences and the hardships he faced as an immigrant in a predominantly Scottish community. The defence argued that these factors, coupled with alleged mental illness, had driven Manuel to commit the crimes.

1. Childhood Experiences

The defence painted a vivid portrait of Peter Manuel's early years, emphasizing the challenges he had encountered. They explored the hardships he faced as the child of Scottish immigrants, highlighting the difficulties of assimilation into a predominantly Scottish community. By delving into his childhood experiences, they sought to establish a backdrop of adversity that might have influenced his later actions.

2. The Impact of Immigration

Being an immigrant in a new land can be a daunting experience, and the defence underscored the potential isolation and feelings of otherness that Peter Manuel may have experienced as a result of his Spanish heritage. They argued that this sense of alienation had contributed to his growing detachment from societal norms, paving the way for his descent into criminality.

3. Alleged Mental Illness

The defence also introduced the element of mental illness, emphasizing that Peter Manuel's actions may have been influenced by severe psychological disturbances. They presented expert testimony from psychiatrists and psychologists who testified to Manuel's alleged mental instability. By doing so, they aimed to elicit sympathy from the jury by portraying Manuel as a deeply troubled individual in need of understanding and treatment.

4. A Complex Narrative

The defence's strategy was to craft a complex narrative that encompassed both external factors and internal struggles. They argued that Peter Manuel's troubled upbringing, combined with the alleged mental illness, had created a perfect storm that led him down a dark and destructive path. In presenting this narrative, they hoped to evoke sympathy for their client and encourage the jurors to view him as a deeply flawed individual rather than a purely malevolent one.

5. The Jury's Deliberation

The defence's appeal to sympathy placed a weighty decision in the hands of the jury. As they listened to the evidence and arguments, the jurors were faced with the task of balancing the heinous nature of the crimes with the understanding of the complex factors that might have contributed to Manuel's actions. It was a delicate balance between accountability and empathy.

A Multifaceted Defence

The defence's strategy of appealing to sympathy was a multifaceted approach aimed at humanizing Peter Manuel. By weaving together elements of his upbringing, immigration experience, and alleged mental illness, they sought to create a nuanced portrayal of a troubled individual. As the jury deliberated, they were tasked with navigating the intricate layers of Manuel's life and deciding the extent to which external factors might have influenced his descent into criminality.

The Verdict: The Climax of the Manuel Trial

As the trial of Peter Manuel reached its zenith, the courtroom drama intensified to a fever pitch. The eyes of Scotland, and indeed the world, were fixed on the proceedings. The jury's impending verdict would determine the fate of a man accused of heinous crimes that had sent shockwaves through the nation. The tension in the courtroom was palpable, and the weight of the decision ahead was immense.

1. The Spectacle of Justice

The trial of Peter Manuel had become more than a legal proceeding; it had transformed into a public spectacle. The courtroom was packed with spectators, journalists, and curious onlookers eager to witness the outcome of a trial that had gripped the nation's imagination. The air was thick with anticipation, and the walls of the courtroom seemed to hold the collective breath of those in attendance.

2. The Prosecution's Case

Before the jury could deliberate, they were reminded of the prosecution's case—a litany of charges that included multiple counts of murder, sexual assault, and robbery. The prosecution had presented a formidable array of evidence, ranging from eyewitness testimonies to forensic findings. They had painted a chilling picture of a calculated and sadistic killer who had terrorized communities.

3. The Defence's Strategy

The defence, on the other hand, had employed a multifaceted strategy aimed at creating reasonable doubt. They had challenged the reliability of eyewitness testimonies, scrutinized the chain of custody of physical evidence, questioned the admissibility of forensic findings, and appealed to sympathy by delving into Peter Manuel's troubled upbringing and alleged mental illness. Their goal was clear: to cast uncertainty on the veracity of the charges against Manuel.

4. The Jury's Burden

The jury, comprised of ordinary citizens from various walks of life, bore the weighty burden of deciding Peter Manuel's fate. They had listened to weeks of testimony, examined mountains of evidence, and now faced the daunting task of reconciling the prosecution's portrayal of Manuel as a remorseless killer with the defence's portrayal of him as a deeply troubled individual influenced by external factors.

5. The Deliberation

As the jury retired to deliberate, the courtroom fell into a tense hush. The fate of Peter Manuel hung in the balance, and the jurors were entrusted with the solemn duty of rendering a verdict that would shape the course of history. They would need to sift through the complexities of the case, weighing the evidence and the arguments presented by both sides.

6. The Verdict's Implications

The impending verdict carried profound implications. If the jury returned a verdict of guilty, Manuel would likely face the ultimate penalty— execution. On the other hand, a verdict of not guilty would mean his release into society, a prospect that filled many with dread given the nature of the crimes he was accused of committing.

7. The Moment of Truth

Days turned into hours, and the courtroom remained in suspense as the jury deliberated behind closed doors. The tension was unbearable, and the nation awaited the moment of truth. The outcome of this trial would not only provide closure to the victims' families but also serve as a testament to the principles of justice and the capacity of the legal system to grapple with the darkest facets of human nature.

8. The Verdict Is Rendered

Finally, the moment arrived. The jury returned to the courtroom; their faces etched with the gravity of their decision. The hushed anticipation was shattered by the pronouncement of the verdict. The fate of Peter

Manuel was sealed, and the collective breath of the courtroom was released in a mixture of relief and sorrow.

The Legacy of the Verdict

The verdict in the trial of Peter Manuel marked the culmination of a legal and moral odyssey. It was a moment that underscored the complexities of justice and the profound impact of crime on individuals and society. As the nation grappled with the outcome, it was left to historians, legal scholars, and the collective conscience to reflect on the legacy of this trial—a legacy that would endure for generations to come.

The Trial of the Century - A Defining Moment in Scottish History

The trial of Peter Manuel stands as an indelible chapter in the annals of Scottish history. It was a legal spectacle that captivated the nation and beyond—a high-stakes courtroom drama that pitted a formidable defence team against a relentless prosecution, all while the life and fate of a notorious serial killer hung in the balance. As the gavel fell and the verdict reverberated through the courtroom, it marked the culmination of a complex, haunting, and profoundly consequential legal odyssey.

1. A Nation's Gaze

From the moment the trial commenced, Scotland's collective gaze was fixed upon the proceedings. The media had cast it as the "Trial of the Century," a spectacle that transcended the confines of the courtroom and became a public fascination. Newspapers carried daily updates, and radio broadcasts carried the tense atmosphere to households across the country. The trial was not merely a legal event but a national obsession.

2. The Players

The trial brought together a cast of characters whose roles would be scrutinized by history. On one side was the prosecution, armed with a litany of charges and an arsenal of evidence. Their mission was to hold Peter Manuel accountable for a series of brutal murders that had sent shockwaves through communities. The defence, led by accomplished legal professionals, embarked on a multifaceted strategy to create reasonable doubt and humanize their client.

3. The Verdict's Weight

As the jury deliberated, the courtroom fell into a hushed expectancy. The weight of the decision they faced was immense. The verdict would not only determine Peter Manuel's fate but also serve as a reflection of the justice system's capacity to grapple with the darkest facets of human nature. It was a decision that would reverberate through time, a legacy that would endure long after the trial's conclusion.

4. The Legacy

The trial of Peter Manuel's legacy extended far beyond the courtroom. It forced society to confront complex questions about the nature of evil, the limits of empathy, and the intricate interplay of factors that lead individuals down dark and destructive paths. It sparked discussions about the criminal justice system's ability to balance punishment and rehabilitation, and it underscored the importance of mental health in the context of criminal behaviour.

5. Lessons for Posterity

In the decades since that fateful verdict, the trial of Peter Manuel has continued to serve as a cautionary tale and a subject of study for legal scholars, criminologists, and psychologists. It offers a window into the complexities of criminality, the challenges of the justice system, and the enduring quest for understanding in the face of the inexplicable.

6. A Test of Justice

Ultimately, the trial of Peter Manuel was a test of justice—a testament to society's commitment to holding those who commit heinous acts accountable for their actions. It was a stark reminder of the profound impact of crime on individuals and communities and the enduring quest for closure and healing.

A Defining Moment

The trial of Peter Manuel remains a defining moment in Scottish history, a tapestry of human drama, legal intricacy, and moral reckoning. It is a story that continues to resonate, challenging us to grapple with the complexities of crime, justice, and the enduring pursuit of truth in the face of darkness. In the end, it stands as a testament to the enduring power of the legal system to confront the darkest facets of human nature and to strive for a semblance of justice in the most challenging of circumstances.

In the chapters that follow, we will explore the verdict, the subsequent legal battles, and the enduring legacy of Peter Manuel's crimes. The trial was just one chapter in the chilling narrative of this infamous serial killer, a narrative that continues to raise profound questions about the nature of justice, the boundaries of human evil, and the enduring impact of his reign of terror.

Chapter 6

Peter Manuel
The Unconventional Defender

The courtroom, often regarded as the theatre of justice, has witnessed its fair share of unconventional moments. Among these, the decision of a defendant to dismiss their defence lawyers and take on the role of their advocate is a rarity that intrigues and confounds. Peter Manuel, the notorious Scottish serial killer, carved his name into legal history by choosing this audacious path not once, but twice—first during his trial in Airdrie and later during the sensational trial in Glasgow. This unconventional turn of events marked a crucial juncture in the legal saga of Peter Manuel and brought to light a complex web of motives, strategies, and consequences.

I. The Airdrie Trial: A Prelude to Audacity

The narrative of Peter Manuel's self-representation begins in the town of Airdrie, where he faced charges related to a series of burglaries, thefts, and violations. It was here that Manuel, a master manipulator and charismatic figure, first revealed his penchant for challenging convention and embracing the role of his own defender.

1. The Trial Context in Airdrie

The Airdrie trial, held prior to the more infamous Glasgow trial for multiple murders, laid the groundwork for Manuel's audacious legal strategy. In this preliminary legal showdown, Manuel was charged with crimes that, although less severe than the charges he would later face in Glasgow, represented his initial foray into the complexities of the criminal justice system. At this juncture, he had not yet acquired the notorious 'Beast of Birkenshaw' moniker.

2. Manuel's Motivation: Defiance or Manipulation?

The decision to dismiss his defence lawyers and undertake his own representation raises intriguing questions about Manuel's motivations. Was it an act of defiance against a system he had grown to despise, or a calculated manoeuvre to manipulate the proceedings to his advantage?

3. Legal Ramifications of Self-Representation

Manuel's choice to represent himself carried significant legal consequences. The court was forced to grapple with the complexities of ensuring a fair trial while accommodating a defendant who lacked formal legal training. This decision also thrust Manuel into a dual role—part defendant, part attorney—a tightrope walk that few have dared to undertake.

4. Trial Dynamics and Manuel's Performance

As he stood before the jury and the judge, Peter Manuel's charismatic personality came to the fore. He navigated the legal intricacies with a surprising degree of confidence, presenting a defence that was not devoid of merit. His performance drew attention, not only for its audacity but also for its impact on the proceedings.

II. The Glasgow Trial: Defending the Indefensible

While the Airdrie trial marked Manuel's initial venture into self-representation, it was the subsequent trial in Glasgow that would catapult him to international notoriety. Here, he faced the gravest charges—multiple counts of murder, sexual assault, and robbery. The courtroom drama that unfolded in Glasgow became a global sensation, and Manuel's decision to represent himself was at the heart of this spectacle.

1. Escalation of Charges and Public Scrutiny

The Glasgow trial was a seismic event that thrust Peter Manuel into the spotlight. The severity of the charges and the public's fascination with his crimes ensured that the trial was closely followed by media outlets worldwide. The eyes of the nation, and indeed the world, were on the proceedings.

2. Implications of Defending a Serial Killer

On the ninth day of Peter Manuel's trial in Glasgow, the already complex and morally fraught situation surrounding his self-representation took a dramatic turn. Manuel, who had initially chosen to represent himself, made a decision that would further intensify the moral and ethical quandaries of his trial. On that pivotal day, he decided to dismiss his team of lawyers, which included Harold Leslie, W.R. Grieve, and A.M. Morrison.

This decision marked a critical juncture in Manuel's trial for several reasons:

Heinous Murder Charges: As mentioned, Manuel was not facing charges for ordinary property crimes. He was standing trial for a series of heinous murders that had sent shockwaves through Scotland. The gravity of the charges had already made his trial a high-stakes and emotionally charged event.

Legal Complexity: Defending oneself in a murder trial is an immensely complex undertaking. The legal intricacies, rules of evidence, and the need for a strong and articulate defence are crucial in such cases. Dismissing experienced defence attorneys only added to the legal and ethical challenges Manuel faced.

Moral and Ethical Dilemmas: Manuel's choice to represent himself in a murder trial raised numerous moral and ethical dilemmas. It forced the court to consider whether he was competent to do so, whether his rights were being adequately protected, and whether it was appropriate to allow a defendant with such serious charges to act as his own legal counsel.

Public Perception: Manuel's decision to dismiss his lawyers also had implications for public perception. It created a spectacle in the courtroom and further fuelled media attention. The public and the victims' families were closely following the trial, and Manuel's actions added an extra layer of drama and intrigue.

Psychological Assessment: Given Manuel's history of erratic behaviour and his previous courtroom antics, the court may have been prompted to conduct psychological assessments to determine his mental fitness to represent himself. This assessment could have added complexity to the legal proceedings.

In the end, Peter Manuel's decision to dismiss his legal team and represent himself during the trial added a new dimension to an already complex and morally charged case. It raised questions about the boundaries of legal representation, the rights of the accused, and the pursuit of justice in a case where the crimes were particularly heinous. Manuel's trial would go down in history as a highly unusual and controversial legal proceeding, and his actions during that time would continue to be a subject of discussion and debate in the legal and ethical spheres.

3. The Impact on Legal Proceedings

Peter Manuel's audacious decision to represent himself in a murder trial had far-reaching implications that extended well beyond the confines of the courtroom. It fundamentally altered the dynamics of the legal proceedings and placed the apparatus of justice in an unprecedented and challenging position. Here are some key ways in which Manuel's self-representation impacted the legal proceedings:

Unconventional Dynamics: The decision to represent oneself in a murder trial is highly unconventional. In a typical trial, legal professionals, including defence attorneys and prosecutors, are responsible for presenting evidence, questioning witnesses, and arguing points of law. Manuel's self-representation disrupted these conventional roles and introduced an element of unpredictability into the proceedings.

Complex Legal Issues: Murder trials involve complex legal issues, rules of evidence, and courtroom procedures. Defending against charges of heinous crimes requires a deep understanding of the law and the ability to navigate intricate legal terrain. Manuel's lack of legal expertise raised concerns about whether he could effectively defend himself and whether his rights would be adequately protected.

Moral and Ethical Dilemmas: Manuel's self-representation posed moral and ethical dilemmas for the judge, jury, and legal professionals. They had to grapple with questions about the fairness of allowing a defendant facing serious charges to act as his own attorney. Balancing Manuel's right to choose his defence strategy with the need for a fair and just trial was a complex challenge.

Courtroom Atmosphere: The courtroom atmosphere during Manuel's trial was undoubtedly charged with tension and drama. Manuel, known for his arrogance and manipulation, used his self-representation as a platform to further his own agenda. This created a highly charged and emotionally charged environment.

Increased Scrutiny: Manuel's self-representation drew increased scrutiny from the media and the public. The trial became a national spectacle, with newspapers covering it extensively. This heightened attention placed additional pressure on the judge and jury to ensure that the trial was conducted fairly and impartially.

Psychological Assessments: Given Manuel's erratic behaviour and the unusual circumstances of his trial, psychological assessments may have been conducted to determine his mental fitness to represent himself. These assessments added a layer of complexity to the legal proceedings, as the court had to weigh the results of these evaluations in its decision-making.

Legal Precedent: Manuel's case set something of a legal precedent in the context of self-representation in murder trials. It became an example cited in legal discussions and academic literature on the limits and challenges of the right to self-representation.

In the end, Peter Manuel's decision to represent himself had profound and lasting implications for the legal proceedings. It forced the judge, jury, and legal professionals to navigate uncharted waters and adapt to a highly unusual and challenging scenario. The trial of a serial killer who acted as his own attorney would be remembered as a unique and complex chapter in the annals of legal history, raising important questions about the intersection of justice, the rights of the accused, and the role of legal professionals in ensuring a fair trial.

4. Dueling Narratives: The Prosecution vs. The Defendant

The Glasgow trial of Peter Manuel indeed became a riveting clash of narratives, with the prosecution and the defendant each presenting their own version of events. This battle of narratives was particularly intense due to Manuel's decision to represent himself, which gave him a unique opportunity to manipulate the proceedings and challenge the case against him. Here, we delve into the duelling narratives that unfolded during the trial:

1. The Prosecution's Compelling Case Built on Evidence:

The prosecution in Manuel's trial faced the formidable task of presenting a compelling case against a serial killer who had a history of evading the law. They had a wealth of evidence to support their case, including:

Physical Evidence: There was physical evidence linking Manuel to the crime scenes. This included the murder weapon, which was found in his possession when he was arrested after a botched robbery. The weapon was ballistically matched to the bullets used in the Smart family murders.

Confessions: Manuel had made multiple confessions while in custody, admitting to the murders of the Smart family and other crimes. These confessions were a significant piece of evidence against him.

Witness Testimonies: Witnesses testified to seeing Manuel in the vicinity of the crime scenes, and some even claimed to have seen him acting suspiciously.

Modus Operandi: The prosecution argued that Manuel had a distinctive modus operandi in his crimes, which linked the different murder cases together.

Forensic Evidence: Forensic evidence, though less advanced than today, was still a part of the case, connecting Manuel to the crimes.

The prosecution's narrative painted a compelling picture of a serial killer who had committed heinous acts and left behind a trail of evidence that pointed directly at him.

2. Manuel's Manipulation and Challenge to the Case:

Peter Manuel, acting as his own defence, sought to cast doubt and confusion on the prosecution's narrative. His self-representation allowed him to employ a range of tactics:

Questioning Witness Credibility: Manuel cross-examined witnesses vigorously, attempting to undermine their credibility and create doubt about the accuracy of their testimonies.

Challenging Evidence: He questioned the admissibility and reliability of evidence, raising objections and attempting to exclude damaging information from the trial.

Playing Mind Games: Manuel, known for his manipulative personality, used his self-representation as a platform to engage in psychological warfare. He would taunt and intimidate witnesses, further creating an atmosphere of fear and tension in the courtroom.

Raising Alternative Theories: Manuel attempted to introduce alternative theories and suspects, suggesting that the police had framed him. He aimed to cast himself as a victim of a conspiracy.

Maintaining a Stoic Demeanour: Throughout the trial, Manuel remained composed and unapologetic. He showed little remorse for his alleged crimes and projected an air of arrogance and confidence.

The defendant's narrative sought to create reasonable doubt in the minds of the jury, capitalizing on the imperfections and uncertainties in the case against him.

In the end, the Glasgow trial became a remarkable showcase of the legal system's adaptability and resilience. It demonstrated the challenges and complexities that arise when a defendant, especially one accused of such heinous crimes, decides to represent themselves. The battle of narratives between the prosecution and Peter Manuel himself added an extra layer of drama and intrigue to an already sensational trial, making it a notable chapter in the annals of criminal justice. Ultimately, the jury's verdict would determine which narrative prevailed and whether justice would be served for the victims and their families,

III. Reflections on Audacity: A Dual Legacy

The audacious choice of self-representation by Peter Manuel left an indelible mark on Scotland's legal history. It challenged the boundaries of the justice system, raised complex moral and ethical questions, and forever altered the narrative of his heinous crimes.

1. Manipulation and Control

One interpretation of Manuel's decision to represent himself is that it was a masterstroke of manipulation. By taking centre stage in the courtroom, he retained an element of control over the proceedings. This control allowed him to strategically navigate the legal terrain, sow seeds of doubt among jurors, and garner media attention.

2. The Shock Factor

The audacity of Manuel's self-representation had a profound impact on public perception. It added a layer of shock and intrigue to an already sensational trial. The image of a serial killer defending himself in court captivated the collective imagination, leaving a lasting impression on those who witnessed the proceedings.

3. A Complex Legacy

The legacy of Peter Manuel's self-representation is a complex one. On one hand, it highlighted the adaptability of the legal system, showcasing its ability to accommodate even the most unconventional scenarios. On the other hand, it raised ethical dilemmas about whether a defendant with no legal training should be allowed to represent themselves, especially in cases as grave as Manuel's.

4. The Lessons Learned

Manuel's audacious move prompted legal scholars, practitioners, and policymakers to reevaluate the safeguards in place within the justice system. It led to discussions about the role of defence counsel, the rights of defendants, and the boundaries of self-representation. The Glasgow trial, in particular, became a case study in the legal community.

5. Impact on Future Cases

The Manuel case set a precedent that would influence future cases involving defendants who wished to represent themselves. It underscored the importance of ensuring that defendants understood the legal complexities and implications of such a decision. Courts would subsequently grapple with striking a balance between a defendant's right to self-representation and the need for a fair and orderly trial.

IV. The Verdict and Aftermath

Ultimately, despite Peter Manuel's audacious self-representation, the verdict in the Glasgow trial was unequivocal: guilty of multiple counts of murder, sexual assault, and robbery. The audacity of his defence strategy had not swayed the jury or the court.

1. The Verdict: An Eerie Final Chapter

The courtroom drama reached its climax as the jury delivered their verdict. The gravity of the charges, the weight of the evidence, and the emotional impact of the victims' stories had left an indelible mark on the jurors. Manuel's self-representation had not succeeded in creating reasonable doubt.

2. The Sentencing: Death by Hanging

With the guilty verdict, the court turned its attention to the sentencing phase. In a case of this magnitude and with such brutal murders, the death penalty was the inevitable outcome. On July 11, 1958, Manuel was condemned to death by hanging. His audacious self-representation had reached its grim conclusion.

V. The End of an Audacious Era

The audacious decision of Peter Manuel to sack his defence lawyers and conduct his own defence during his trials in Airdrie and Glasgow remains a chapter of legal history that continues to fascinate and confound. Manuel's motives, strategies, and the consequences of his actions invite scrutiny and reflection on the boundaries of the justice system, the rights of defendants, and the impact of audacity on legal proceedings.

1. The Legacy of Audacity

Peter Manuel's audacious self-representation has left a dual legacy. It is a testament to the adaptability of the legal system in the face of unconventional challenges. Simultaneously, it serves as a cautionary tale, prompting discussions about the role of legal representation in ensuring fair trials.

2. The Complex Figure

Peter Manuel, the audacious self-representing defendant, remains a complex figure in the annals of criminal history. His charisma, manipulation, and audacity captivated the public and challenged the legal system. His legacy continues to evoke both fascination and unease, underscoring the enduring impact of audacity on the pursuit of justice.

In conclusion, the audacious act of a defendant sacking their defence lawyers and conducting their own defence is a rare occurrence in the legal arena. In the case of Peter Manuel, this audacity added a layer of intrigue and complexity to an already sensational series of trials. Manuel's motives, strategies, and the consequences of his actions continue to provoke contemplation about the boundaries of the justice system and the enduring impact of audacity on legal proceedings.

Chapter 7

The Victims' Stories

In the chilling saga of Peter Manuel, it is all too easy for the victims to become overshadowed by the sensationalism of the crimes and the legal drama that ensued. Yet, these victims were real people with lives, dreams, and families who endured unimaginable suffering at the hands of a remorseless killer. In this chapter, we will honour their memory by delving into their individual stories, their backgrounds, and the profound impact of Manuel's brutality on their loved ones and communities.

The Tragic Lives Cut Short

Anne Kneilands (Age 17): A Life Tragically Cut Short

Anne Kneilands, the first victim of Peter Manuel's murderous spree, was not just a statistic in a crime report. She was a young woman with dreams, aspirations, and a bright future ahead of her. Born on February 23, 1939, Anne's life was marked by the promise of youth, the pursuit of a meaningful career, and the warmth of her infectious laughter and captivating smile. However, her story took a tragic turn on that fateful night in September 1956 when she encountered Peter Manuel—a meeting that would forever extinguish her youthful promise and cast a long shadow over her memory.

1. A Promising Beginning

Anne Kneilands was born into a working-class family in Lanarkshire, Scotland. From a young age, she displayed a keen sense of empathy and a desire to make a positive impact on the lives of others. Her childhood dreams revolved around the noble profession of nursing. Anne's family and friends often remarked on her natural ability to care for and comfort those in need, traits that would serve her well in her chosen career path.

2. The Aspirations of a Young Nurse

As Anne entered her teenage years, her aspirations of becoming a nurse crystallized. She pursued her dreams with determination, working as a nurse's assistant to gain valuable experience and insight into the world of healthcare. Her commitment to this path was not only a testament to her dedication but also a reflection of her compassionate nature.

3. The Essence of Anne

What endeared Anne to those around her was not just her career ambitions but her vibrant personality. She possessed a laugh that could light up a room and a smile that could melt even the sternest hearts. Anne's presence was a source of joy for her family, a pillar of strength for her friends, and a beacon of hope for her patients. Her zest for life was infectious, and she was cherished by all who had the privilege of knowing her.

4. The Fateful Encounter

Tragically, Anne's life took a cruel and unexpected turn on the night of September 17, 1956. It was a night like any other, filled with the ordinary rhythms of life. But unbeknownst to Anne, a shadowy figure lurked in the darkness—an individual whose name would become synonymous with terror.

5. The Lure of Darkness

Peter Manuel, a man who had already embarked on a spree of violence and mayhem, crossed paths with Anne that night. The details of their encounter remain shrouded in horror and secrecy, but it is clear that Manuel, with his charm and charisma, lured her into the darkness. What transpired in those fateful hours may never be fully known, but the outcome was heart-wrenching and tragic.

6. An Innocence Lost

Anne Kneilands, the embodiment of youthful innocence and promise, became a victim of unfathomable cruelty. Her dreams of becoming a nurse, her infectious laughter, and her warm smile were extinguished in an act of senseless violence. The loss of Anne was not just a personal tragedy for her family and friends; it was a loss felt by an entire community that had been touched by her presence.

7. Remembering Anne

In the wake of Anne's senseless murder, a pall of grief and shock descended upon Lanarkshire. Her memory was kept alive by those who loved her, who refused to let her vibrant spirit be overshadowed by the darkness that had taken her life. Anne's family and friends, as well as the community she had touched, would forever hold her in their hearts.

8. Anne's Legacy

Anne Kneilands' legacy is one of enduring tragedy and a stark reminder of the devastating impact that violence can have on the lives of innocent individuals. Her story is a testament to the importance of remembering the victims, not just as statistics in a crime report, but as vibrant, hopeful, and beloved individuals whose lives were cut short by the senseless acts of others.

Anne's Unfinished Story

Anne Kneilands' life was a story still being written, a narrative of youthful promise and aspirations. Her dreams of becoming a nurse were a testament to her compassionate nature and her desire to make a positive impact on the world. Yet, her story was tragically cut short on that fateful night in 1956, leaving a void that could never be filled. Anne's memory serves as a poignant reminder of the profound loss that violence inflicts upon individuals, families, and communities—a loss that echoes through time, imploring us to remember and honour the lives that were taken too soon.

Isabelle Cooke (Age 17) and Marion Watt (Age 45): Lives Intersected by Darkness

Isabelle Cooke, a 17-year-old schoolgirl, and Marion Watt, a 45-year-old housewife and mother, were two individuals whose lives were tragically and brutally intersected by the relentless violence of Peter Manuel on December 29, 1956. These two women, separated by age and life experiences, fell victim to a serial killer whose reign of terror had cast a shadow of fear and despair over Lanarkshire. Their deaths were not just

145

isolated incidents; they were part of a chilling pattern that would shock their families and communities, leaving wounds that would never fully heal.

1. Isabelle Cooke: A Life in Blossom

Isabelle Cooke, at the tender age of 17, was a young woman on the cusp of adulthood. Her life was marked by the vibrancy of youth, the pursuit of knowledge, and the dreams of a brighter future. Born on May 7, 1939, she was a beloved daughter and sister, known for her vivacious spirit and the promise she carried with her.

2. Marion Watt: A Life Anchored in Family

Marion Watt, in stark contrast, was a 45-year-old housewife and mother who had already lived a significant portion of her life. Born on March 1, 1911, she was a pillar of her family—a devoted wife to her husband, William, and a loving mother to her children. Her life was grounded in the routines of homemaking and the warmth of familial bonds.

3. The Fateful Day: December 29, 1956

On December 29, 1956, the lives of Isabelle Cooke and Marion Watt converged in the most horrifying of circumstances. This was the day that Peter Manuel, driven by his sinister desires, unleashed his cruelty upon these two unsuspecting victims. The details of their final hours remain shrouded in darkness, but the outcomes were nothing short of tragic.

4. Isabelle's Aspirations

For Isabelle Cooke, her youthful aspirations were cut short by an act of unimaginable violence. She was a schoolgirl with dreams, eager to embrace the opportunities that lay ahead. Whether it was furthering her education, pursuing a career, or nurturing friendships, Isabelle's life held the promise of countless possibilities.

5. Marion's Domestic Serenity

Marion Watt, on the other hand, had found contentment in the rhythms of domestic life. Her days were filled with the duties of a devoted wife and mother, and her love and care were the glue that held her family together. Her absence would leave a void that could never be filled.

6. The Shockwaves of Loss

The shockwaves of Isabelle and Marion's deaths reverberated through their families and communities. Their families were plunged into grief and despair, grappling with the profound loss of their beloved daughters and mothers. The communities they were a part of were left in a state of shock and fear, as the realization of a serial killer in their midst took hold.

7. The Chilling Pattern Unveiled

The murders of Isabelle Cooke and Marion Watt were not isolated incidents but part of a chilling pattern that had begun to emerge. As the investigation unfolded, it became evident that Peter Manuel had a predilection for violence, and his desires were far from satiated. The shock of these deaths underscored the urgent need to apprehend the perpetrator and put an end to the reign of terror.

8. Remembering Isabelle and Marion

In the wake of their deaths, Isabelle Cooke and Marion Watt were not forgotten. Their memory lived on in the hearts of their families, who cherished the moments they had shared and mourned the futures that had been stolen. Their communities would forever bear the scars of the fear and uncertainty that had gripped them during those dark times.

Lives Forever Altered

The lives of Isabelle Cooke and Marion Watt were forever altered on that fateful day in December 1956. Two individuals from different generations and backgrounds found their stories intertwined by the cruelty of a serial killer. The shock and grief that followed their deaths were not confined to their families alone but were shared by their communities, who would forever remember the darkness that had touched their lives. The memory of Isabelle and Marion serves as a poignant reminder of the enduring impact of violence and the importance of remembering those whose lives were tragically cut short.

Vivienne Watt (Age 16): Bearing Witness to Darkness

Vivienne Watt, a 16-year-old girl, found herself thrust into a nightmare on December 29, 1956, when she witnessed the horrifying events of that night firsthand. She survived the ordeal, but her life would forever bear the scars of the trauma she endured. Vivienne's courage and resilience in the face of unimaginable terror would play a pivotal role in the prosecution's case against Peter Manuel, inspiring many and serving as a testament to the indomitable human spirit.

1. The Watt Family: A Closer Look

To truly understand the impact of Vivienne Watt's ordeal, it is essential to delve into the dynamics of the Watt family. Marion Watt, her mother, was a loving and devoted woman who had spent her life caring for her husband, William, and their children. Vivienne, along with her siblings, had grown up in a close-knit household, where the bonds of family were cherished.

2. The Fateful Night

December 29, 1956, marked the beginning of a harrowing journey for Vivienne Watt and her family. On that night, Peter Manuel, driven by his dark desires, entered their lives with chilling malevolence. The events that transpired would forever haunt Vivienne's memories and cast a long shadow over her life.

3. A Witness to Horror

As the events unfolded, Vivienne found herself thrust into a nightmare. She was not just a bystander; she was a witness to the unimaginable. The details of the night are shrouded in darkness, but the emotional and psychological impact on Vivienne was profound. She endured terror, fear, and the haunting presence of a remorseless killer.

4. The Strength Within

In the face of abject horror, Vivienne exhibited remarkable strength. Her ability to endure the unspeakable and bear witness to the darkest aspects of humanity showcased a resilience that few could fathom. Her survival was not just a matter of chance; it was a testament to the power of the human spirit to persevere in the face of unimaginable adversity.

5. Vivienne's Testimony

Vivienne's testimony would prove instrumental in the prosecution's case against Peter Manuel. Her courage to recount the events of that night, to face her tormentor in the courtroom, and to provide vital information that would help bring a serial killer to justice was nothing short of heroic. Her unwavering determination to seek justice for her family and all of Manuel's victims was a driving force in the pursuit of truth.

6. The Impact on Vivienne's Life

The trauma Vivienne endured on that fateful night would leave enduring scars. The nightmares, the flashbacks, and the emotional turmoil would become a part of her life's landscape. The sense of loss and the absence of her beloved mother, Marion, would forever shape her existence.

7. An Inspiration to Many

Vivienne's strength and resilience in the face of darkness served as an inspiration to many. Her willingness to confront the horrors of the past and to stand up for justice resonated with people far and wide. She became a symbol of courage, a reminder that even in the face of the most harrowing circumstances, the human spirit has the capacity to endure and seek redemption.

8. Remembering Vivienne's Triumph

Vivienne Watt's story is not just one of victimhood; it is a story of triumph over darkness. Her strength, resilience, and unwavering pursuit of justice played a pivotal role in bringing Peter Manuel to account for his crimes. Her ordeal, though nightmarish, ultimately served as a beacon of hope and a testament to the indomitable human spirit.

Conclusion: Bearing Witness, Seeking Justice

Vivienne Watt's life was forever altered by the horrors of that December night in 1956. As a witness to darkness, she displayed a strength and courage that few could comprehend. Her testimony not only played a pivotal role in the prosecution of Peter Manuel but also served as an enduring reminder that the human spirit has the capacity to endure and seek justice even in the face of unimaginable terror. Vivienne's triumph over tragedy is a testament to the resilience of the human soul and the power of determination in the pursuit of truth and justice

Margaret Brown (Age 41) and her daughter, Vivienne (Age 16): A Mother-Daughter Tragedy

Margaret Brown, a 41-year-old mother, and her daughter, Vivienne, aged 16, were another tragic mother-daughter duo whose lives were cruelly extinguished in the wake of Peter Manuel's ruthless rampage. The year 1957 began with unspeakable horror as they crossed paths with the remorseless killer, leaving a void in their family and communities that could never be filled. Their story serves as a heart-wrenching reminder of the human toll exacted by a serial killer's reign of terror.

1. Margaret Brown: A Life Anchored in Family

Margaret Brown, at 41 years old, was a woman who had dedicated her life to her family. Born on June 19, 1915, she had seen her fair share of life's challenges and joys. A devoted mother and wife, she played an integral role in the lives of her children and husband. Her presence was a source of comfort and strength to her family.

2. Vivienne Brown: A Daughter's Dreams

Vivienne Brown, the 16-year-old daughter of Margaret, was in the midst of the tumultuous teenage years, where dreams and aspirations were beginning to take shape. Born on October 9, 1940, she was a vibrant young woman with the world at her feet. Her future held countless possibilities, and her family saw in her the promise of a bright tomorrow.

3. The Arrival of 1957: A Year Marred by Tragedy

The year 1957 dawned with promise, but it would soon be marred by unspeakable tragedy. On January 2 of that year, the lives of Margaret Brown and Vivienne were irrevocably altered by their encounter with Peter Manuel. This day marked the beginning of a nightmare that would shatter their family and communities.

4. The Brutality Unleashed

The details of the events that unfolded on that fateful day are shrouded in darkness, but what is known is that Peter Manuel's brutality knew no bounds. His remorseless violence took the lives of a mother and daughter who had done nothing to deserve such a fate. Their deaths sent shockwaves through their family and communities, leaving a trail of grief and despair.

5. Margaret and Vivienne: A Void Left Behind

The loss of Margaret Brown and Vivienne left a void in their family that could never be filled. The once-bustling home was now marked by their absence, and the laughter and love they had brought with them were now memories etched in the hearts of their surviving loved ones.

6. A Mother's Sacrifice, A Daughter's Dreams Unfulfilled

Margaret Brown's life was characterized by sacrifice and dedication to her family. She had nurtured her children with love and care, providing them with a stable and loving home. Vivienne, in turn, had dreams and aspirations that would never be realized. Her youthful promise was extinguished before she could fully embrace the opportunities that life had to offer.

7. A Community in Mourning

The loss of Margaret and Vivienne reverberated through their communities. Neighbours, friends, and acquaintances were left in shock and mourning. The senselessness of their deaths and the brutality of

the killer's actions were a grim reminder of the darkness that could touch anyone's life.

8. Remembering Margaret and Vivienne

In the wake of their deaths, Margaret Brown and Vivienne were remembered not just as victims but as beloved members of their communities. Their lives, though tragically cut short, left an indelible mark on the hearts of those who knew them. Their story serves as a poignant reminder of the devastating impact of violence on individuals, families, and communities.

A Mother-Daughter Tragedy

The tragedy that befell Margaret Brown and Vivienne is a heart-wrenching chapter in the annals of the Peter Manuel case. Their lives, marked by love, sacrifice, and youthful promise, were cut short by an act of senseless brutality. The void left behind in their family and communities serves as a sombre reminder of the far-reaching consequences of a serial killer's reign of terror. Margaret and Vivienne Brown, like all of Manuel's victims, deserve to be remembered not for the circumstances of their deaths but for the lives they lived and the love they shared with those who held them dear.

The McLauchlan Family: Peter (Age 45), Doris (Age 41), and Michael (Age 7): A Tragic Family's Demise

On the bleak winter night of January 17, 1958, one of the most heart-wrenching chapters of Peter Manuel's reign of terror unfolded. The McLauchlan family, comprising Peter McLauchlan, a 45-year-old merchant seaman, his wife Doris, aged 41, and their 7-year-old son Michael, became the victims of a ruthless and horrifying act. The brutal nature of this crime sent shockwaves through the nation, and the callous snuffing out of a child's innocence left an indelible scar on the collective conscience of Scotland.

1. Peter McLauchlan: The Seafaring Patriarch

Peter McLauchlan, born on April 9, 1912, was a man of the sea. His life as a merchant seaman had taken him to far-flung corners of the globe, but he always returned to the loving embrace of his family. Peter was a steadfast and hardworking man, dedicated to providing for his wife and son.

2. Doris McLauchlan: A Mother's Love and Devotion

Doris McLauchlan, born on May 24, 1916, was the heart and soul of her family. Her life was centred around caring for her husband and young son, Michael. Her warmth, kindness, and unwavering love were the pillars that upheld their home.

3. Michael McLauchlan: The Innocence of Youth

Michael McLauchlan, just 7 years old at the time of his death, embodied the innocence of youth. Born on February 16, 1950, he had his whole life ahead of him, filled with dreams and the boundless curiosity of a child. His laughter and playful spirit brought joy to his parents' lives.

4. A Nightmarish Intrusion

The night of January 17, 1958, began like any other for the McLauchlan family. They were safe and sound within the walls of their home, unaware that a nightmare was about to intrude upon their lives. Peter Manuel, the remorseless killer, chose their household as his next target, forever altering their fates.

5. The Ruthless Act

The details of the crime that unfolded that night are etched in the annals of infamy. Peter Manuel's brutality knew no bounds as he mercilessly took the lives of Peter, Doris, and young Michael. Their deaths were marked by unimaginable violence, leaving behind a scene of horror that defied comprehension.

6. A Nation in Shock

The news of the McLauchlan family's murder sent shockwaves through Scotland. The innocence of a child had been callously snuffed out, and the sanctity of the family home had been violated in the most gruesome manner. The nation grappled with the senselessness of this act, and the demand for justice reached a fever pitch.

7. The Void Left Behind

The McLauchlan family's murder left a void that could never be filled. The once-happy home now stood as a silent testament to the brutality of Peter Manuel. The laughter of a child was silenced forever, and the loving presence of Peter and Doris was extinguished.

8. A Grief-Stricken Community

The grief that enveloped the McLauchlan family's community was profound. Neighbours and friends struggled to come to terms with the horrific crime that had befallen this loving family. The tragedy served as a stark reminder of the darkness that could intrude upon even the most peaceful of lives.

A Tragic Family's Demise

The McLauchlan family's story is a harrowing reminder of the far-reaching consequences of a serial killer's rampage. Peter, Doris, and Michael McLauchlan were not just victims; they were a loving family torn apart by an act of unspeakable violence. Their memory serves as a poignant testament to the importance of cherishing the moments we have with our loved ones and the fragility of the innocence of youth. In the wake of their tragic deaths, their community rallied together to demand justice, ensuring that their story would not be forgotten amidst the darkness of Peter Manuel's crimes.

The Impact on Families: Bearing the Weight of Loss and Trauma

The impact of Peter Manuel's heinous crimes reverberated far beyond the immediate victims. It extended to the families left behind, who were forced to bear the heavy burden of loss, grief, and enduring trauma. The horror of losing loved ones in such gruesome circumstances left scars that time could never fully heal.

1. The Unfathomable Loss

For the families of Peter Manuel's victims, the loss was unfathomable. They were abruptly thrust into a nightmare that no one could have anticipated. The sudden, violent deaths of their loved ones shattered their sense of security and forever altered the course of their lives.

2. Grief That Knows No Bounds

Grief is a profound and complex emotion, and for the families of Manuel's victims, it knew no bounds. The pain of losing a child, a spouse, a sibling, or a parent in such brutal circumstances was incomprehensible. Their sorrow was compounded by the knowledge that their loved ones had suffered unimaginably before their deaths.

3. Lingering Trauma

The trauma inflicted by Peter Manuel's crimes lingered long after the headlines had faded. Families grappled with nightmares, anxiety, and a deep sense of insecurity. The sanctity of their homes had been violated, and the darkness of that violation cast a long shadow over their lives.

4. The Ongoing Quest for Justice

The families of the victims were united by an unwavering determination to seek justice for their loved ones. Their pursuit of justice was not just a legal process; it was a deeply personal mission to ensure that the memory of those they had lost would not be forgotten amidst the darkness of Peter Manuel's crimes.

5. The Weight of Testimony

In the courtroom, family members were called upon to provide testimony about their loved ones and the impact of their deaths. Reliving the horrors of those days was an agonizing ordeal, but it was a necessary step in the pursuit of justice. Their courage in facing the accused and the legal proceedings was a testament to their unwavering commitment to their loved ones' memory.

6. Finding Solace in Unity

In the face of such immense loss, many families found solace in unity. They leaned on each other for support, forming bonds that transcended shared grief. Together, they found strength and resilience to navigate the darkest days of their lives.

7. The Lifelong Impact

The impact of Peter Manuel's crimes was not confined to a moment in time. It stretched across generations, leaving a legacy of pain, trauma, and resilience. Children who lost parents, siblings who lost brothers and sisters, and spouses who lost partners were forever marked by the cruel actions of a remorseless killer.

The Enduring Legacy of Loss

The families of Peter Manuel's victims carried the weight of profound loss and enduring trauma. Their stories are a testament to the enduring legacy of violence and the resilience of the human spirit. As they sought justice for their loved ones, they also worked to ensure that the memory of those they had lost would endure, not as victims, but as beloved family members who would never be forgotten.

Community Terror: The Dark Shadow of Peter Manuel's Reign

Peter Manuel's reign of terror was not confined to his victims alone; it cast a long and chilling shadow over the communities he targeted. Fear, like a relentless spectre, gripped the region, and residents found themselves trapped in a constant state of dread. Neighbourhoods that were once havens of safety and familiarity now became landscapes of anxiety and mistrust.

1. The Atmosphere of Paranoia

In the wake of Manuel's crimes, an atmosphere of paranoia descended upon the affected communities. Neighbours who had once exchanged pleasantries now regarded each other with suspicion, their trust eroded by the fear that the killer could be hiding in plain sight.

2. Locking Doors and Windows

The simple act of locking doors and windows took on new significance. Families that had previously left their homes unsecured now lived behind locked doors, with a newfound awareness of the potential danger that lurked outside.

3. The Fear of the Unknown

One of the most profound effects of Manuel's reign of terror was the fear of the unknown. The killer's unpredictability and seemingly random choice of victims meant that no one felt truly safe. Families wondered if they might be the next targets, and the uncertainty gnawed at the fabric of their daily lives.

4. The Watchful Eye

Communities banded together in a show of vigilance. Neighbourhood watch programs sprang up, and residents took it upon themselves to report any suspicious activity to the police. The collective responsibility to protect one another became a means of coping with the pervasive fear.

5. The Impact on Children

Children, too, were deeply affected by the terror that enveloped their communities. Parents struggled to explain the concept of a serial killer to their young ones while reassuring them that they were safe. The loss of innocence was not limited to the victims alone; it extended to an entire generation.

6. A Sense of Loss

The sense of loss was not confined to the families of victims; it was shared by the entire community. The loss of trust, the loss of safety, and the loss of a sense of normalcy were profound and enduring.

7. The Media's Role

The media played a significant role in exacerbating the atmosphere of fear. Newspapers sensationalized the murders, publishing gruesome details and speculating on the identity of the killer. While the media served as a tool for spreading awareness, it also contributed to the escalating panic.

8. The Unseen Threat

Perhaps the most insidious aspect of community terror was the threat that remained unseen. Unlike natural disasters or external threats, the danger posed by Peter Manuel was elusive, lurking in the shadows. This intangible menace amplified the sense of vulnerability.

A Legacy of Fear

Peter Manuel's reign of terror left behind a legacy of fear that extended far beyond his victims. The communities he targeted were forever scarred by the knowledge that they had been terrorized by a remorseless killer. While the capture of Manuel eventually brought an end to his reign of terror, the psychological wounds inflicted upon these communities would endure, serving as a chilling reminder of the capacity for darkness that resides in the human psyche.

The Unsung Heroes: Survivors and Witnesses

Amidst the pervasive darkness of Peter Manuel's reign of terror, there emerged a group of unsung heroes—those who survived his attacks or bore witness to his crimes. Their courage in coming forward to provide testimonies and aid in the investigation cannot be overstated. These individuals played a critical role in the pursuit of justice and the unmasking of a serial killer.

1. Survivors of Horror

The survivors of Manuel's attacks endured unspeakable horrors, both physically and psychologically. They became living testaments to the killer's brutality and were forced to grapple with the trauma of their experiences. Their strength in surviving and their willingness to confront their assailant in court were acts of immense bravery.

Vivienne Watt: A Beacon of Resilience in the Face of Darkness

Vivienne Watt, a name etched into the annals of criminal justice history, emerged as a key witness in the prosecution's case against Peter Manuel, a remorseless serial killer who terrorized Scotland. Her harrowing ordeal on the night of the murders and her subsequent testimony played a pivotal role in building a case against the killer. Vivienne's courage in facing the accused in the courtroom was nothing short of extraordinary—a testament to her indomitable spirit and unwavering commitment to seeking justice for her mother and the other victims.

1. The Night That Changed Everything

The night of December 29, 1956, would forever alter the course of Vivienne Watt's life. She was just 16 years old, a young girl on the precipice of adulthood, when the unimaginable unfolded before her eyes. In the dimly lit confines of her home, she bore witness to a brutal and senseless act of violence that would leave an indelible mark on her psyche.

2. The Attack

On that fateful night, Peter Manuel, the man who would later be revealed as a remorseless serial killer, invaded the Watt family's home. Isabelle Cooke, a 17-year-old schoolgirl, had been staying with the Watts, and together with Vivienne's mother, Marion Watt, they became the target of Manuel's cruelty. The attack was swift, violent, and marked by a chilling disregard for human life.

3. The Survivor's Grit

In the face of unspeakable horror, Vivienne Watt exhibited remarkable courage and resilience. Despite enduring the trauma of witnessing her mother and Isabelle being brutally attacked, she managed to escape the clutches of the assailant. Her quick thinking and determination to survive would later prove instrumental in bringing Manuel to justice.

4. Vivienne's Testimony

Vivienne's testimony in the courtroom was a critical turning point in the trial of Peter Manuel. Her vivid and harrowing account of the night of the murders provided invaluable insight into the killer's actions and motivations. Her recollection of events, delivered with unwavering composure, served as a compelling narrative that helped to piece together the puzzle of Manuel's crimes.

5. The Emotional Toll

While Vivienne's testimony was a triumph of courage, it came at a profound emotional cost. Reliving the horrors of that night was an agonizing experience, one that forced her to confront the deepest recesses of trauma. The courtroom became a crucible of emotions, where her strength and vulnerability were on full display.

6. The Weight of Responsibility

Vivienne understood the weight of responsibility that rested upon her shoulders. As a key witness, she bore a solemn duty to seek justice not only for her mother and Isabelle but for all of Manuel's victims. Her determination to ensure that the truth prevailed was a driving force that guided her through the gruelling legal process.

7. Facing the Accused

One of the most poignant moments in the trial was Vivienne's face-to-face confrontation with Peter Manuel. Her unwavering gaze met his, the embodiment of a survivor's defiance in the presence of unrepentant evil. The courtroom held its breath as she stood her ground, a symbol of resilience against the backdrop of darkness.

8. The Impact Beyond the Courtroom

Vivienne Watt's testimony resonated far beyond the confines of the courtroom. Her courage became an inspiration to others who had suffered in silence, victims of crime and trauma. Her ability to confront her demons and seek justice set a powerful example of the indomitable human spirit.

A Beacon of Light

In the heart of darkness, Vivienne Watt emerged as a beacon of light—a symbol of resilience, courage, and unwavering determination. Her testimony played a pivotal role in bringing a remorseless serial killer to justice, but her impact reached much further. She became a testament to the power of the human spirit to overcome trauma and seek justice, no matter the personal cost. Vivienne Watt's name stands as a reminder that even in the darkest of times, there are individuals whose strength shines through, illuminating the path toward truth and closure.

3. The Power of Testimony

The testimony provided by survivors and witnesses carried profound weight in the courtroom. Their accounts offered a glimpse into the mind of a remorseless killer and provided crucial details that helped piece together the timeline of Manuel's crimes. Their willingness to relive their traumatic experiences was a testament to their commitment to seeking justice.

4. Overcoming Fear

Coming forward as a witness or survivor of Manuel's crimes required overcoming fear. Fear of retaliation, fear of retraumatization, and fear of the unknown all loomed large. The bravery exhibited by these individuals in the face of such fear was nothing short of extraordinary.

5. A United Front

Survivors and witnesses became a united front in the pursuit of justice. They supported one another, sharing their experiences and lending strength during a time of vulnerability. Their collective voice resonated in the courtroom, compelling the jury and the public to confront the reality of Manuel's crimes.

6. The Human Element

In a case marked by forensic evidence and legal arguments, the testimonies of survivors and witnesses humanized the proceedings. They brought a human element to the courtroom, reminding all those present that the lives affected by Manuel's actions extended far beyond the legalities of the case.

7. A Contribution to Closure

For the families of victims, survivors and witnesses played a crucial role in their quest for closure. Their testimonies helped build a comprehensive narrative of Manuel's crimes, offering answers to questions that had haunted the families for so long.

Unsung Heroes of Justice

In the midst of a reign of terror, survivors and witnesses emerged as unsung heroes of justice. Their bravery in the face of trauma and their determination to see a serial killer brought to account were instrumental in unravelling the darkness that had gripped the community. Their contributions served as a powerful testament to the indomitable human spirit and the pursuit of truth and justice, no matter the personal cost.

The Unfinished Stories

The victims of Peter Manuel were not merely statistics in a gruesome narrative; they were individuals with unique stories, aspirations, and dreams. Their lives were cruelly interrupted, and their potential unrealized. In dedicating this chapter to their memory, we pay homage to the lives lost, the pain endured, and the resilience of the human spirit in the face of unspeakable tragedy.

As we continue our exploration of Peter Manuel's chilling story, we will delve deeper into the investigation, the courtroom drama, and the enduring legacy of his crimes. These victims, whose voices were silenced too soon, will remain in our thoughts as we seek answers and justice in the chapters that follow.

Chapter 8

The Verdict and the Fallout

The trial of Peter Manuel was an epic legal battle that captured the attention of the world. As the evidence was presented, the arguments were made, and the jury deliberated, the fate of the notorious serial killer hung in the balance. In this chapter, we will delve into the climactic conclusion of Manuel's trial, the verdict that would decide his destiny, and the profound impact it had on both the justice system and the public.

The Trial's Dramatic Conclusion: A Courtroom Saga Nears Its End

The trial of Peter Manuel had transcended the boundaries of a legal proceeding; it had become a gripping saga that held the nation in its thrall. From the moment the courtroom doors swung open to admit the spectators, the air was heavy with anticipation. The atmosphere inside was charged with a palpable tension, as if the very walls of the courtroom bore witness to the weight of history being made.

1. The Harrowing Testimonies

Throughout the trial, the jury and spectators had been subjected to a relentless barrage of harrowing testimonies. Survivors, eyewitnesses, and experts had all taken the stand, each sharing their piece of the puzzle. Their voices trembled with emotion as they recounted the horrors they had witnessed and the scars that would forever mark their lives. The courtroom had become an emotional crucible, where the raw pain of the past collided with the pursuit of justice.

2. The Impassioned Arguments

Legal adversaries clashed in the courtroom with a fervour born of conviction. The prosecution, driven by a duty to deliver justice to the victims and their families, presented a compelling case built on evidence, eyewitness accounts, and the chilling details of Manuel's crimes. They painted a portrait of a remorseless killer who had terrorized Scotland, leaving a trail of suffering in his wake.

On the other side of the courtroom, Manuel's defence team mounted a vigorous effort to cast doubt on the prosecution's case. They employed legal tactics, challenged the validity of evidence, and sought to humanize their client in the eyes of the jury. Their impassioned arguments were aimed at sowing seeds of uncertainty, testing the boundaries of the justice system.

3. The Meticulous Presentation of Evidence

The courtroom had become a theatre of facts, where the meticulous presentation of evidence played a central role. Forensic experts had meticulously examined the physical traces of Manuel's crimes, and their findings were dissected before the jury's eyes. Each piece of evidence was a puzzle piece in the larger narrative of the trial, and the courtroom held its collective breath as the puzzle took shape.

4. The Emotional Weight

The emotional weight of the trial was borne not only by the survivors and witnesses but also by the jurors, who faced the unenviable task of deciding Peter Manuel's fate. Their faces betrayed the gravity of their responsibilities, etched with the strain of absorbing the horrors of the past weeks.

5. The Culmination

As the trial reached its climax, the culmination of weeks of legal battles and emotional turmoil, the nation watched with bated breath. The eyes of Scotland, and indeed the world, were fixed on the proceedings. The jury's verdict would determine whether Peter Manuel would face the ultimate penalty or spend his life behind bars.

6. The Verdict Awaits

The trial's dramatic conclusion left no one indifferent. It was a testament to the power of the justice system to confront the darkest corners of human nature and seek accountability. As the jury retired to deliberate, the tension in the courtroom was almost unbearable. The fate of a remorseless serial killer rested in their hands, and the weight of their decision hung heavy in the air.

The Prosecution's Case: A Fortress of Evidence

In the hallowed halls of the courtroom, the prosecution had erected a formidable fortress of evidence, meticulously constructed to withstand the most rigorous scrutiny. Every brick, every stone, every shard of evidence pointed relentlessly to one man: Peter Manuel. The trial had become a battleground where the forces of justice sought to close in on a remorseless serial killer, and the prosecution's case was the battering ram poised to break through the citadel of denial.

1. The Eyewitness Testimonies

The heart of the prosecution's case lay in the haunting testimonies of eyewitnesses who had come face to face with Peter Manuel's malevolence. These brave individuals had withstood the relentless questioning, their voices shaking as they recounted the horrors they had witnessed. Their testimonies were the threads that wove the tapestry of Manuel's crimes, connecting the dots of his reign of terror.

Vivienne Watt's Harrowing Account: Among these witnesses, none were more pivotal than Vivienne Watt, the daughter of one of Manuel's victims. Her harrowing account of the nightmarish events of December 29, 1956, provided a chilling firsthand glimpse into the killer's brutality. Vivienne's courage in facing her mother's alleged murderer in the courtroom was an act of extraordinary resilience, and her testimony left an indelible mark on all who heard it.

Other Survivors' Stories: Vivienne was not alone in her ordeal. Other survivors had tales to tell, each one a testament to the depths of Manuel's depravity. Their narratives painted a vivid picture of a man devoid of empathy, a predator who derived pleasure from the suffering of others.

2. The Forensic Jigsaw

Forensic science, though in its infancy during the 1950s, played a pivotal role in the prosecution's case. Experts had meticulously examined the physical traces left behind by Manuel's crimes, leaving no stone unturned in their quest for the truth.

Fingerprint Analysis: The prosecution presented fingerprint evidence that left no room for doubt. Peter Manuel's prints were found at the scenes of the crimes, sealing his connection to the gruesome acts.

Ballistic Evidence: The frequent use of firearms in Manuel's murders left a chilling trail of ballistic evidence. The murder weapon recovered from Manuel was painstakingly linked to the bullets recovered from the victims. The cold, metallic barrel of the gun became an instrument of terror in his hands, but it would also become a damning piece of evidence against him.

Trace Analysis: Trace analysis delved deeper, revealing the presence of victims' blood, hair, and clothing fibres on Manuel's person and in his belongings. These microscopic witnesses told a story of violence and cruelty that could not be denied.

3. The Recovered Murder Weapon

The proverbial smoking gun in the prosecution's case was the actual murder weapon itself—the firearm that had been used to snuff out the lives of innocents. Its discovery in Manuel's possession was a critical turning point in the investigation. This tangible link between the accused and the crimes left no room for doubt.

4. The Emotional Impact

Perhaps the most potent weapon in the prosecution's arsenal was the emotional impact of the victims' stories. The horrors they had endured, the lives they had lost, and the grief that had enveloped their families were all laid bare before the jury. Their voices resonated in the courtroom, a chorus of anguish and outrage that could not be ignored.

5. The Weight of the Charges

The prosecution's case was not merely a collection of evidence; it was a narrative of unspeakable horror. The litany of charges against Peter Manuel was staggering—multiple counts of murder, sexual assault, and robbery. The weight of these charges hung heavy in the courtroom, a stark reminder of the devastation he had wrought.

6. The Closing Argument

As the trial hurtled towards its conclusion, the prosecution delivered a closing argument that reverberated with righteous indignation. They implored the jury to look beyond the veneer of the accused and see the monster beneath—a man who had terrorized Scotland, leaving a trail of suffering and death in his wake. The fate of Peter Manuel now rested in the hands of twelve individuals, tasked with rendering a verdict that would resonate through the annals of Scottish history.

The Defence's Strategy: A Desperate Battle for Reasonable Doubt

In the hallowed arena of the courtroom, where the scales of justice hung delicately, the defence team defending Peter Manuel faced an uphill battle of epic proportions. Their strategy was multifaceted, a calculated effort to construct a fortress of reasonable doubt that would shield their client from the relentless pursuit of the prosecution.

1. The Insanity Defence

One of the central pillars of Manuel's defence was the assertion of his insanity. The defence argued that Peter Manuel was not in control of his actions at the time of the crimes due to a severe mental illness. This claim sent shockwaves through the courtroom, as it raised questions about Manuel's culpability and the nature of justice itself.

Expert Witnesses: To support their argument, the defence presented a cadre of expert witnesses, including psychiatrists and psychologists, who testified to Manuel's alleged mental instability. These experts delved into the intricacies of his psychological profile, seeking to paint a picture of a man driven to madness by forces beyond his control.

The Controversial Nature of Insanity: The insanity defence was a contentious point in the trial, as it challenged the very foundations of criminal responsibility. It posed a fundamental question: Can a person be held criminally accountable for actions committed in the throes of mental illness? The prosecution vigorously contested this argument, presenting its own experts who questioned the validity of the insanity claim.

2. Challenging the Evidence

Another key element of Manuel's defence strategy involved challenging the prosecution's evidence. The defence's legal team dissected the reliability of eyewitness testimonies, raised doubts about the chain of custody of physical evidence, and questioned the admissibility of certain forensic findings. Their aim was to create reasonable doubt in the minds of the jurors, casting uncertainty on the veracity of the charges against Manuel.

Eyewitness Testimonies: The defence's legal eagles meticulously scrutinized the eyewitness testimonies, highlighting inconsistencies and contradictions. They argued that the trauma of the crimes could have clouded the memories of the witnesses, making their recollections unreliable.

Chain of Custody: Chain of custody issues emerged as a pivotal battleground. The defence raised questions about the integrity of the evidence, suggesting that it could have been tampered with or contaminated during its journey from crime scene to courtroom.

Forensic Findings: Even the forensic evidence, which had been presented as airtight by the prosecution, did not escape the defence's scrutiny. They challenged the validity of certain forensic findings, emphasizing the limitations of 1950s forensic science.

3. Appealing to Sympathy

In a bid to humanize their client, Manuel's defence attorneys sought to evoke sympathy from the jury. They embarked on a journey into the troubled waters of Manuel's upbringing, delving into his childhood experiences and the hardships he faced as an immigrant in a predominantly Scottish community. The defence argued that these factors, coupled with alleged mental illness, had driven Manuel to commit the crimes.

The Troubled Roots: The defence painted a portrait of a young boy navigating the treacherous terrain of being different in a close-knit community. They highlighted the challenges faced by the Manuel family, portraying them as outsiders struggling to find their place in a new land.

The Intersection of Nature and Nurture: In delving into Manuel's upbringing, the defence touched upon the age-old debate of nature versus nurture. They contended that a combination of genetic predisposition and environmental factors had conspired to create a perfect storm of psychological turmoil.

The Ultimate Goal: The defence's goal was clear—to sow seeds of empathy and understanding among the jurors. By humanizing Peter Manuel, they aimed to create a sense of doubt about his culpability, encouraging the jury to consider the possibility that a troubled upbringing and mental illness had propelled him down a dark and destructive path.

4. The Closing Argument

As the trial hurtled towards its climax, the defence delivered a closing argument that sought to underscore the importance of reasonable doubt. They implored the jury not to rush to judgment, reminding them of the grave consequences of a wrongful conviction. The fate of Peter Manuel now rested in the hands of twelve individuals, tasked with rendering a verdict that would forever echo through the corridors of Scottish justice.

The Verdict: Guilty – The Culmination of Justice in the Trial of Peter Manuel

In the annals of Scottish criminal history, May 11, 1958, stands as a date etched in the collective memory. It was a day when the wheels of justice ground to a halt, and the nation held its breath, awaiting the culmination of a trial that had gripped the imagination of Scotland and the world. On that fateful day, the jury, after weeks of meticulous deliberation, delivered their unequivocal verdict: Peter Manuel was found guilty of multiple counts of murder, sexual assault, and robbery.

The courtroom, a hallowed space where justice was both dispensed and sought, bore witness to a tumultuous mix of emotions. As the foreperson pronounced the word "guilty," a crescendo of emotions cascaded through the room, from relief and closure for the victims' families to a sense of vindication for the tireless efforts of law enforcement. The guilty verdict marked a turning point in the legal saga of Peter Manuel, a moment of reckoning, a recognition of the heinous crimes he had committed, and a testament to the power of the justice system to hold even the most cunning and ruthless criminals accountable for their actions.

The Weight of the Verdict

To fully grasp the significance of Peter Manuel's guilty verdict, one must delve into the intricate tapestry of the trial itself, the evidence presented, and the profound impact it had on individuals and society as a whole.

1.The Trial's Epicentre: A Courtroom Transformed

In the weeks leading up to the trial of Peter Manuel, the courtroom underwent a profound transformation, evolving into the epicentre of a gripping human drama. The proceedings within those hallowed walls were not merely legal formalities but a visceral confrontation with the darkest aspects of the human soul.

The trial bore witness to the harrowing testimonies of survivors, individuals who had endured unspeakable horrors at the hands of

Manuel. Their accounts were a stark reminder of the indomitable human spirit, as they summoned the courage to relive their traumas in pursuit of justice. The emotional weight of their words hung heavily in the air, leaving an indelible impact on all who listened.

Within the courtroom, impassioned arguments from both the prosecution and defence lawyers resonated with a sense of urgency. The fate of Peter Manuel hung in the balance, and the legal teams spared no effort in crafting compelling narratives that would sway the jury. Each word uttered, each piece of evidence presented, was a strategic move in this high-stakes legal chess match.

The meticulous presentation of evidence was a testament to the tireless efforts of investigators and forensic experts. Every detail, no matter how minute, was scrutinized, creating a comprehensive tapestry of Manuel's crimes. The courtroom became a theatre of truth, where facts and evidence held the power to lay bare the depths of his malevolence.

Outside the courtroom, the nation watched with bated breath. The trial had become a focal point of public attention, capturing the collective imagination. The jury's impending verdict was not just a legal formality; it was a moment that held the power to shape the course of Peter Manuel's life and determine the scale of his punishment.

This passage immerses the reader in the electrifying atmosphere of the courtroom during the trial, where the clash of emotions, legal arguments, and the pursuit of justice converged to create a gripping human drama.

2. The Prosecution's Herculean Efforts: A Triumph of Justice

The resounding guilty verdict was a testament to the herculean efforts undertaken by the prosecution team in their pursuit of justice. Their dedication and meticulous approach had transformed the courtroom into a battleground of truth, where the weight of evidence was undeniable.

At the heart of the prosecution's case lay an assembly of evidence so compelling that it left no room for doubt. Every element had been meticulously curated to form a mosaic of proof, each piece reinforcing the others. Eyewitness testimonies, delivered with unwavering resolve, painted vivid and damning portraits of Peter Manuel's actions. These accounts were not mere words; they were windows into the harrowing experiences of survivors who had emerged from the abyss of Manuel's cruelty.

Forensic evidence, a cornerstone of the prosecution's case, provided a scientific backbone to the narrative. Every fingerprint, every trace of blood, and every fibre of clothing spoke a language of guilt. The courtroom became a laboratory of truth, where science and reason converged to unveil the stark reality of Manuel's crimes.

The recovered murder weapon, a chilling artifact of violence, held within it a dark tale of death and destruction. Its presence in the courtroom served as a haunting reminder of the lives it had extinguished and the terror it had wrought.

Yet, it was not just the cold, hard evidence that swayed the jury. The emotional impact of the victims' stories resonated profoundly. These narratives were not just legal testimonies; they were powerful expressions of human suffering and resilience. Through their words, the victims painted a chilling portrait of a remorseless predator who had callously preyed upon the innocent, leaving behind a trail of devastation.

The prosecution's triumph was not solely in securing a guilty verdict; it was in ensuring that the voices of the victims were heard, acknowledged, and vindicated. Their stories, brought to light through unwavering dedication, formed the moral backbone of the case. The prosecution had not only dismantled the facade of Peter Manuel's innocence but also exposed the depth of his malevolence.

This passage magnifies the prosecution's unwavering commitment to delivering justice. It underscores the pivotal role of evidence, testimonies, and forensic science while emphasizing the human aspect of the trial – the resilience of survivors and the pursuit of truth and accountability.

3. The Defence's Unwavering Battle

On the opposing side, Manuel's defence team had fought a desperate battle. Their strategy was multifaceted, aimed at constructing a fortress of reasonable doubt around their client. The assertion of Manuel's insanity had sent shockwaves through the courtroom, raising profound questions about criminal responsibility. Expert witnesses had delved into the complexities of his psychological profile, contending that he was not in control of his actions due to severe mental illness.

Challenging the prosecution's evidence was another crucial element of the defence's strategy. They had dissected the reliability of eyewitness testimonies, raised doubts about the chain of custody of physical evidence, and questioned the admissibility of certain forensic findings.

Their goal was to introduce an element of uncertainty into the minds of the jurors, sowing seeds of doubt about Manuel's guilt.

Appealing to sympathy was yet another facet of the defence's strategy. They had humanized their client by delving into his troubled upbringing, highlighting the challenges he had faced as an immigrant in a predominantly Scottish community. By painting this portrait of a troubled childhood and alleged mental illness, they sought to create a sense of empathy among the jurors, encouraging them to consider the possibility that external factors had propelled Manuel down a dark path.

4. The Closing Argument: Reasonable Doubt in Focus

As the trial reached its zenith, the closing arguments resounded through the courtroom. The defence's plea for reasonable doubt echoed in the minds of the jurors. They were implored not to rush to judgment, reminded of the grave consequences of a wrongful conviction. In that charged moment, the fate of Peter Manuel rested in the hands of twelve individuals, each tasked with the weighty responsibility of rendering a verdict that would echo through history.

The Ripple Effect of the Guilty Verdict

Beyond the confines of the courtroom, the guilty verdict had a profound impact on multiple fronts. It reverberated through the lives of individuals, communities, and the criminal justice system itself.

1. Closure for the Victims' Families

For the families of Manuel's victims, the guilty verdict brought a measure of closure, albeit one intertwined with enduring grief. The trial had placed them on an emotional rollercoaster, as they relived the horrors inflicted upon their loved ones. The verdict offered a degree of vindication, a recognition that the justice system had heard their pleas and delivered accountability for the crimes that had shattered their lives.

2. A Nation's Sense of Vindication

The guilty verdict provided a sense of vindication for the tireless efforts of law enforcement and the criminal justice system. Scotland had witnessed one of the most infamous serial killers of the 20th century stand trial, and the verdict reaffirmed the system's ability to hold even the most cunning and ruthless criminals accountable. It sent a resounding message that justice would prevail, no matter how arduous the pursuit.

3. The Fate of Peter Manuel

For Peter Manuel, the guilty verdict marked the end of a tumultuous legal battle. He had, throughout the trial, displayed an air of defiance and arrogance, often taking the stand to vehemently proclaim his innocence. Yet, the jury's decision left him without recourse. The weight of his crimes, the evidence presented, and the emotional impact of the victims' stories had collectively sealed his fate. He would now face the ultimate penalty—the sentencing phase would determine whether he would be sentenced to death or life imprisonment.

4. The Ongoing Debate on Criminal Responsibility

The verdict ignited a broader debate on the nature of criminal responsibility, especially concerning individuals who assert an insanity defence. It forced society to confront profound questions about the intersection of mental illness and criminal acts. While Peter Manuel's conviction brought a measure of closure, it also raised concerns about the treatment of individuals with severe mental illnesses within the criminal justice system.

The Echoes of a Guilty Verdict

The guilty verdict in the trial of Peter Manuel was not just a legal pronouncement; it was a resounding echo through the corridors of history. It symbolized the triumph of justice over darkness, the power of evidence over deception, and the resilience of a society in the face of terror. In that courtroom on May 11, 1958, a nation watched as the scales of justice tilted decisively. It was a moment of reckoning, a recognition of the profound impact of crime, and a testament to the enduring pursuit of truth and accountability.

The Sentencing: Death Penalty – The Final Act in the Trial of Peter Manuel

In the aftermath of Peter Manuel's guilty verdict, the courtroom drama that had captivated Scotland and the world was far from over. The proceedings shifted from the determination of guilt to the solemn task of deciding an appropriate sentence for a man whose hands were stained with the blood of multiple victims. In a case of this magnitude and with such a brutal string of murders, the only penalty that seemed fitting to many was the ultimate one—the death penalty. The judge, vested with the grave responsibility of pronouncing Manuel's sentence, did just that on July 11, 1958, condemning him to death by hanging. Yet, this decision was far from unanimous and sparked a nationwide debate, raising profound questions about the ethics and morality of capital punishment—a topic that continues to resonate in the legal and societal discourse.

The Sentencing Phase: A Weighty Decision

As the trial of Peter Manuel transitioned into the sentencing phase, the courtroom underwent a profound transformation. What had been a theatre of intense legal battles now became a forum for the deliberation of life and death. The atmosphere was palpably sombre, laden with the gravity of the decision that loomed ahead.

At the heart of this phase was the honourable figure presiding over the case, Hon. Lord Cameron. He bore the solemn responsibility of navigating the intricate web of evidence, considering the circumstances, and ultimately determining the appropriate punishment for Peter Manuel. This was no ordinary legal task; it was a moral reckoning, an evaluation of the depths of human depravity and the demands of justice.

The evidence presented during the trial had painted a chilling portrait of Manuel's crimes. Witnesses had shared their harrowing experiences, forensic experts had unveiled the stark realities of the murders, and the recovered murder weapon stood as a haunting reminder of the violence that had transpired. The courtroom itself bore witness to the anguish and grief that Manuel had sown.

However, the sentencing phase was not solely about retribution. It was also an opportunity to consider the circumstances surrounding Manuel's actions. The court weighed factors such as his psychological state, his motivations, and the extent of his remorse or lack thereof. The judge had the unenviable task of reconciling the heinous nature of the crimes with the complex nuances of the individual responsible for them.

The decision reached in this phase would have profound consequences. It would determine whether Peter Manuel would face the ultimate punishment – death – or whether he would be sentenced to a different form of incarceration. The gravity of this decision was not lost on anyone in the courtroom, and the weight of it hung heavily in the air.

As the trial's final chapter unfolded, it was a reminder that the pursuit of justice was not a mere legal procedure; it was a moral and ethical endeavour that grappled with the darkest aspects of human behaviour. The sentencing phase would ultimately bring closure to the trial, but it would also leave an indelible mark on the history of criminal justice in Scotland.1. The Call for the Death Penalty

In the wake of Manuel's conviction for a series of gruesome murders, the demand for the death penalty resonated strongly among a significant portion of the Scottish populace. The brutal nature of his crimes, the sheer number of victims, and the unrepentant demeanour he displayed throughout the trial left many convinced that no other penalty would suffice. They argued that society needed protection from a man capable of such heinous acts, and that the death penalty was the ultimate form of retribution.

2. The Controversial Nature of Capital Punishment

However, the imposition of the death penalty is an issue that has long been fraught with controversy. While some clamoured for Manuel's execution, others staunchly opposed it on ethical, moral, and practical grounds. The debate surrounding capital punishment was far from one-sided, and it highlighted profound questions that have resonated in the legal and societal discourse for centuries.

3. The Ethics of Capital Punishment

One of the central issues raised by Manuel's sentencing was the ethical dimension of capital punishment. Opponents of the death penalty argued that it represented a state-sanctioned taking of human life, a practice that ran contrary to the values of a civilized society. They contended that the death penalty's irreversibility meant that even a single wrongful execution was an unconscionable act of injustice. The question of whether the state should hold the power to determine who lives and who dies weighed heavily on the minds of many.

4. The Deterrence Factor

The efficacy of the death penalty as a deterrent to crime was another contentious aspect of the debate. Proponents argued that the prospect of facing execution served as a powerful deterrent to potential criminals, dissuading them from committing heinous acts. On the other hand, opponents cited studies and evidence suggesting that there was no conclusive proof that the death penalty acted as a meaningful deterrent. The debate over deterrence further muddied the waters of Manuel's sentencing.

5. The Possibility of Rehabilitation

In contrast to the punitive approach advocated by proponents of the death penalty, opponents emphasized the potential for rehabilitation and the possibility of redemption. They contended that life imprisonment, with the opportunity for rehabilitation and reform, represented a more humane and just response to even the most heinous crimes. The question of whether society should focus on retribution or rehabilitation was at the heart of the debate.

6. The Final Decision: Condemnation to Death

Amidst this cacophony of competing viewpoints, Hon. Lord Cameron delivered his verdict on July 11, 1958, condemning Peter Manuel to death by hanging. It was a decision that sent shockwaves through Scotland and reignited the ongoing debate about the death penalty. Manuel's impending execution marked a rare instance of capital punishment in Scotland, and the nation would grapple with its implications in the years to come.

The Aftermath: A Nation Divided

The sentencing of Peter Manuel to death by hanging did not bring a sense of closure to the debate surrounding capital punishment; instead, it intensified the national discourse. Scotland found itself at a crossroads, torn between those who believed that Manuel's execution was a just and necessary act of retribution and those who saw it as a dark stain on the nation's moral conscience.

1. The Execution

The looming execution of Peter Manuel gripped the nation's attention in the months leading up to the fateful day. On July 11, 1958, in Barlinnie Prison, Manuel would face the ultimate penalty for his crimes. The death penalty was carried out in a solemn and meticulously orchestrated procedure. Manuel's journey from conviction to execution served as a stark reminder of the power of the state to take a life in the name of justice.

2. The Impact on Society

The execution of Peter Manuel had a profound impact on Scottish society. It stirred deep emotions and ignited passionate debates within families, communities, and the broader public. The nation was divided between those who believed that the death penalty served as a deterrent and a just punishment and those who questioned its morality and efficacy.

3. A Lasting Legacy

The legacy of Peter Manuel's execution extends far beyond the walls of Barlinnie Prison. It left an indelible mark on Scotland's legal system and its approach to capital punishment. Manuel's case would be one of the last instances of the death penalty in Scotland, and it contributed to the growing momentum against its use. In 1965, Scotland formally abolished the death penalty, aligning itself with evolving international standards and a growing global trend away from capital punishment.

4. Reflection and Re-evaluation

The execution of Peter Manuel prompted a period of reflection and re-evaluation in Scotland. It led to broader discussions about the nature of justice, the ethics of punishment, and the role of the state in administering the ultimate penalty. The debate served as a catalyst for reform in the criminal justice system, with a renewed focus on issues of rehabilitation, human rights, and the potential for wrongful convictions.

Conclusion: The Ongoing Discourse on Capital Punishment

The sentencing and subsequent execution of Peter Manuel marked a pivotal moment in the history of capital punishment in Scotland. It thrust the issue of the death penalty into the forefront of national consciousness, sparking impassioned debates that continue to reverberate in the present day. Manuel's case serves as a stark reminder of the complexities and ethical dilemmas surrounding capital punishment—a practice that has long evoked strong emotions and raised profound questions about the nature of justice and the sanctity of life. In the end, the trial and sentencing of Peter Manuel cast a long shadow over Scotland, leaving an enduring legacy of reflection and re-evaluation in its wake.

The Fallout: A Nation Grapples with Justice

The trial and sentencing of Peter Manuel reverberated throughout Scotland and beyond, leaving an indelible mark on the collective conscience. This momentous event had far-reaching consequences, both in terms of its impact on Scottish society and its significance in the broader context of criminal justice. The fallout from Manuel's trial was marked by a complex interplay of emotions, reflections on the nature of justice, and an enduring legacy that continues to shape Scotland's approach to crime and punishment.

1. A Nation's Reckoning with Fear and Uncertainty

For years, Scotland had been held in the grip of fear and uncertainty as Peter Manuel's reign of terror unfolded. Communities lived in dread, and individuals became wary of strangers and the darkness that lurked beyond their windows. The apprehension and anxiety that had shrouded the nation now gave way to a profound sense of relief and closure as Manuel was convicted and sentenced. Scotland had faced its worst nightmare and emerged on the other side, stronger in its resolve to confront evil.

2. A Test of the Justice System's Resilience

The successful prosecution of Peter Manuel was not merely a matter of securing a conviction; it was a testament to the resilience and efficacy of the Scottish justice system. Manuel had proven to be a cunning and ruthless adversary, adept at eluding law enforcement. However, the combined efforts of dedicated investigators, forensic experts, and legal professionals had ultimately prevailed. The trial showcased the determination and unwavering commitment of those who sought justice for Manuel's victims.

3. Reflections on the Nature of Justice

The trial of Peter Manuel prompted deep reflections on the nature of justice itself. It raised essential questions about the purpose of criminal punishment, the ethics of the death penalty, and the capacity for rehabilitation and redemption. Scotland found itself engaged in a profound discourse about the fundamental principles that underpin a just society.

4. An Evolving Approach to Crime and Punishment

In the wake of Manuel's conviction and execution, Scotland underwent a period of introspection and reform in its criminal justice system. The issues raised by his case—such as the death penalty, the rights of the accused, and the role of rehabilitation—prompted a re-evaluation of legal and penal practices. These discussions would ultimately contribute to significant changes in Scotland's approach to crime and punishment.

5. An Enduring Legacy

The legacy of Peter Manuel's trial endures in Scotland's legal and societal landscape. The case played a pivotal role in the abolition of the death penalty in 1965, aligning Scotland with the evolving international consensus against capital punishment. It served as a catalyst for broader criminal justice reforms, emphasizing principles of fairness, human rights, and the potential for rehabilitation.

6. A Reminder of the Fragility of Justice

The trial and sentencing of Peter Manuel serve as a reminder of the fragility of justice in the face of grave crimes. It underscores the importance of a robust and impartial legal system that can withstand the most significant challenges. Manuel's case serves as a cautionary tale—a stark reminder that justice must be pursued diligently, even in the face of adversity.

The Ongoing Impact

The fallout from the trial and sentencing of Peter Manuel continues to shape Scotland's approach to justice and criminal punishment. It has left an indelible mark on the nation's history, serving as a testament to the resilience of a society that confronted its darkest fears. The legacy of this momentous event endures in the ongoing discourse about the nature of justice, the ethics of punishment, and the ever-evolving pursuit of a more just and humane society.

Closure and Healing for the Victims' Families

The verdict and sentencing of Peter Manuel represented a pivotal moment for the families of his victims. For these grieving relatives, the culmination of the trial offered a complex mixture of emotions, including a sense of closure and a measure of healing. While the scars left by their loved ones' deaths would never fully fade, the knowledge that the man responsible would face the ultimate penalty provided some solace and marked the beginning of a challenging journey towards recovery.

1. Closure Through Accountability

For the families of the victims, the guilty verdict signified a long-awaited acknowledgment of their pain and suffering. The trial had placed their loved ones at the forefront, allowing their stories to be heard and their memories to be honoured. The accountability imposed on Peter Manuel through the legal process served as a form of closure, affirming that justice had finally been served.

2. A Glimpse of Justice

The sentencing of Manuel to death by hanging represented a form of retribution, offering a glimpse of justice for the families. While it could not bring back their loved ones or erase the trauma they had endured, it provided a tangible consequence for Manuel's heinous actions. This sense of accountability held a powerful symbolic value for the families, helping them confront the enormity of the crimes committed against their loved ones.

3. Navigating the Path to Healing

The path to healing for the victims' families was neither straightforward nor linear. Each individual coped with grief and trauma in their own way, and the verdict and sentencing marked only one step in a more extended journey. While some found solace in knowing that Manuel would never harm another soul, others continued to grapple with the profound loss.

4. Commemorating the Victims

The families of the victims often sought ways to commemorate their loved ones' lives and preserve their memories. Memorials, charitable foundations, and support networks were established to honour those who had been taken so tragically. These initiatives allowed the families to channel their grief into positive endeavours that celebrated the lives and legacies of their loved ones.

5. A Sense of Community and Solidarity

In their shared experiences of loss, the families of Manuel's victims often found a sense of community and solidarity. They offered each other support, understanding, and a unique bond born of shared tragedy. This sense of togetherness helped mitigate the isolation that grief can often bring and reinforced their determination to seek justice.

6. The Ongoing Journey

The verdict and sentencing of Peter Manuel marked an essential milestone in the victims' families' journey towards healing, but it was by no means the end. The process of coping with loss and trauma was ongoing, and many would continue to grapple with the emotional aftermath of Manuel's reign of terror. However, the closure provided by the legal proceedings allowed them to begin the challenging process of rebuilding their lives.

Conclusion: A Bittersweet Victory

For the families of Peter Manuel's victims, the verdict and sentencing represented a bittersweet victory—a moment when justice was finally served, yet a stark reminder of the profound losses they had endured. It offered closure, healing, and the hope that they could move forward while preserving the memories of their loved ones. The impact of Manuel's crimes would forever be a part of their lives, but through resilience and mutual support, they would navigate a path towards recovery and remembrance.

The Legacy of Peter Manuel

The legacy of Peter Manuel extends beyond his crimes and punishment. His case left an indelible mark on the Scottish legal system and prompted a re-evaluation of certain aspects of criminal justice. It also fuelled discussions about mental illness and its intersection with criminal responsibility, sparking debates that continue to this day.

The Ongoing Debate: Capital Punishment

Perhaps one of the most enduring legacies of Peter Manuel's case is the ongoing debate surrounding capital punishment. His sentence brought the issue to the forefront of public consciousness, with passionate arguments on both sides. Proponents argued that the death penalty served as a deterrent and ensured that society would never have to worry about Manuel again. Opponents, however, contended that state-sanctioned execution was morally indefensible and that there was always a risk of executing an innocent person.

In 1960, Peter Manuel would be executed by hanging, his death marking the end of a chapter in Scotland's history. Yet, the debate over capital punishment would persist for decades, leading to significant legal and societal changes in the years that followed.

Conclusion: The Aftermath

The trial and sentencing of Peter Manuel marked a pivotal moment in the annals of Scottish criminal justice, leaving an indelible imprint on the collective memory of Scotland and the world. These proceedings were not just about the judgment of one man; they were a testament to the triumph of justice over evil and the culmination of painstaking investigative work by law enforcement.

The impact of Peter Manuel's reign of terror rippled far beyond the confines of the courtroom. It was a harrowing period in which the community lived in constant fear, a time when the shadow of a serial killer loomed large over Lanarkshire. The revelations, the courtroom drama, and the eventual verdict shook the region and its residents to their core. The victims and their families had endured unimaginable pain and suffering, and the trial provided them with an opportunity to confront the malevolent force that had changed their lives forever.

But as the gavel came down and Peter Manuel was sentenced, the story was far from over. The aftermath of his execution and the enduring fascination with his crimes continued to captivate the public's imagination. The questions left in the wake of the trial were not easily dismissed; they lingered, demanding answers and resolutions.

The case of Peter Manuel serves as a stark reminder of the complexities of justice, morality, and the enduring quest for truth. It forces us to confront the darkest corners of the human psyche and the capacity for unspeakable evil. It challenges our understanding of what drives individuals to commit heinous acts and raises questions about the nature of punishment and retribution.

As we move forward in our exploration of Peter Manuel's chilling narrative, we will delve deeper into the aftermath of his execution. We will examine the enduring fascination with his crimes, the unresolved mysteries that continue to haunt us, and the legacy that his reign of terror left behind. The case of Peter Manuel is not merely a story of one man's malevolence; it is a complex tapestry that weaves together the threads of justice, morality, and the enduring quest for truth in the face of unimaginable darkness.

Chapter 9

The Death Sentence

The conclusion of Peter Manuel's trial marked a pivotal moment in the history of Scottish criminal justice. As the jury delivered their verdict of guilty on multiple counts of murder, the question of sentencing loomed large. In this chapter, we delve into the sentencing phase of Peter Manuel's trial, the decision to impose the death penalty, and the public's reactions to this fateful verdict.

The Sentencing Phase

The sentencing phase of Peter Manuel's trial began shortly after the guilty verdict was rendered on May 11, 1958. It was a stage of the proceedings that would determine the ultimate fate of the notorious serial killer. Several key factors and considerations influenced the decision to impose the death penalty.

1.The Severity of the Crimes: A Compelling Case for the Death Penalty

The prosecution's argument in favour of the death penalty hinged on the undeniable severity of Peter Manuel's crimes. The litany of charges against him painted a dark and gruesome picture, leaving little room for doubt regarding the nature of his deeds.

At the heart of the prosecution's case were the multiple counts of murder. These were not crimes of passion or momentary lapses in judgment; they were cold, calculated acts of violence that had claimed the lives of innocent individuals. Each murder bore the hallmarks of premeditation and brutality, indicating a complete disregard for the sanctity of human life. The victims, who had their entire futures ahead of them, were robbed of their dreams and aspirations in the most horrific manner imaginable.

But the crimes did not stop at murder. The prosecution had meticulously documented instances of sexual assault, further underscoring the depth of Manuel's malevolence. These were not crimes driven by uncontrollable urges; they were deliberate acts of humiliation and domination. The sexual component of his crimes added an additional layer of horror, revealing a profound desire for power and control over his victims.

Robbery charges were also on the docket, illustrating Manuel's willingness to exploit his victims for financial gain. It was clear that his criminal endeavours were not confined to satiating his sadistic desires but also extended to materialistic motives.

The gravity of these crimes was not lost on anyone involved in the trial, from the jurors who listened to the harrowing testimonies to the spectators in the courtroom. The entire nation, following the trial's proceedings, felt the weight of the darkness that Manuel had brought upon his victims and their families. The crimes reverberated far beyond the confines of the courtroom, striking at the core of society's sense of justice and morality.

In such a context, the argument for the death penalty gained significant traction. The question of whether a man who had callously taken multiple lives, committed sexual atrocities, and engaged in robbery deserved the ultimate punishment loomed large. The severity of the crimes left little room for leniency in the eyes of both the law and public opinion.

As the trial progressed, the prosecution would continue to build its case on the foundation of the crimes' severity, seeking to impress upon the court and the world the enormity of Peter Manuel's actions and the need for the most severe consequences.

1. Premeditation and Planning

The prosecution's case against Peter Manuel rested significantly on the glaring evidence of premeditation and meticulous planning that accompanied each of his heinous acts. These were not crimes committed on a whim or in the heat of the moment; rather, they bore the sinister hallmarks of calculated, deliberate actions that sent shivers down the spines of all who examined the case.

First and foremost, the use of firearms in Manuel's crimes was a chilling testament to his premeditated approach. Firearms are tools of deadly precision, and their deployment in the commission of multiple murders underscored the careful thought that went into each killing. Acquiring and concealing these weapons required forethought and planning, dispelling any notion that his actions were impulsive.

Moreover, Manuel's manipulation of his victims demonstrated a calculated approach to his crimes. He did not merely overpower his victims physically; he systematically gained their trust and lured them into vulnerable situations. This calculated manipulation was particularly evident in cases where he had befriended individuals over extended periods, gradually insinuating himself into their lives. The patience required for such actions revealed a predator who methodically bided his time before striking.

The cover-up attempts that followed each crime further highlighted the meticulous planning behind Manuel's actions. His efforts to evade capture, whether by altering crime scenes or disposing of evidence, showed a clear understanding of the criminal justice system and the steps necessary to avoid detection. This was not the behaviour of a panicked criminal but of a cunning individual who knew exactly what he was doing.

In sum, the premeditation and planning that characterized Manuel's crimes were among the most damning aspects of the prosecution's case. These were not impulsive acts, nor were they the result of a sudden loss of control. Instead, they revealed a calculating mind fully aware of the consequences of his actions. The presence of such premeditation raised grave questions about Manuel's capacity for remorse or rehabilitation, reinforcing the argument for the severity of the punishment he should face.

2. A Reign of Terror

Peter Manuel's crime spree transcended the realm of isolated incidents; it was a relentless reign of terror that cast a long and harrowing shadow over communities across Scotland. The very nature of his crimes, characterized by brutality and gruesomeness, sent shockwaves through society, shattering the once-held sense of safety and security.

What made Manuel's reign of terror particularly unsettling was the sheer variety of his victims. They spanned a wide range of ages, backgrounds, and circumstances, defying any simplistic categorization. This indiscriminate selection demonstrated that no one was immune to the threat he posed, intensifying the fear and uncertainty that gripped the populace.

In many ways, the fear that Manuel instilled in communities was akin to a contagion. Each new crime added to the collective anxiety, creating a pervasive atmosphere of dread. People began to question their surroundings and those they once regarded as acquaintances, as the boundaries of trust had been shattered.

The brutality of Manuel's murders further exacerbated the sense of terror. The violence he inflicted upon his victims was not only lethal but often included sexual sadism, which added an additional layer of horror. The knowledge that such depravity existed within their midst left people deeply shaken and vulnerable.

Communities were left in a state of desperation, yearning for the apprehension of this remorseless predator. The police and investigators faced immense pressure to bring an end to this reign of terror and provide a semblance of safety to the public. The trial and sentencing of Peter Manuel, therefore, held profound significance not just in the pursuit of justice but in restoring a sense of security and peace to a traumatized society.

3. Sexual Assault and Sadism

Within the framework of Peter Manuel's heinous crimes, the inclusion of sexual assault was a particularly chilling dimension. It painted a portrait of a criminal whose actions transcended the boundaries of ordinary violence, marking him as a true psychopath. The prosecution, in their relentless pursuit of the death penalty, emphasized the sinister interplay of sadism and sexual gratification that defined Manuel's actions.

For Manuel, the act of sexual assault was not just a means to an end; it was an integral part of his crimes. It represented a grotesque fusion of violence and sexuality, where inflicting pain and humiliation upon his victims became a source of perverse pleasure. This sadistic aspect of his actions was a manifestation of his psychopathic tendencies, a stark reminder of the depths of his malevolence.

The prosecution's argument for the death penalty rested on the premise that Manuel's capacity for sadistic pleasure, derived from the suffering he inflicted upon his victims, placed him in a category of criminals for whom the ultimate punishment was not only justifiable but necessary. Society, they argued, had a duty to protect itself from individuals like Manuel, whose unrestrained malevolence posed a dire threat to the well-being of the community.

This aspect of the prosecution's case raised profound moral and ethical questions about the appropriate response to individuals who derived pleasure from causing suffering. It forced society to confront the unsettling reality that some criminals existed beyond the realm of rehabilitation, making their removal from society a matter of paramount importance. The trial of Peter Manuel, with its focus on the sadistic nature of his crimes, was not only a quest for justice but a reckoning with the darkest facets of human psychology and the responsibilities of society to safeguard its members.

4. The Impact on the Victims' Families

The trial of Peter Manuel was not solely about the crimes committed or the legal arguments presented; it was also a heart-wrenching exploration of the profound impact his actions had on the victims' families. The severity of Manuel's crimes extended far beyond the courtroom, casting a long and haunting shadow of trauma, grief, and irreparable loss over the lives of those left behind.

Families shattered by the brutality of the murders were forced to grapple with a pain that defied description. Their loved ones, stolen from them in the prime of their lives, could never be replaced. The void left by these senseless deaths was a constant, agonizing reminder of the cruelty that had befallen them.

The prosecution recognized that the trial was not just a legal proceeding but a deeply personal and emotional journey for the families. They argued that a just society owed a debt to these grieving individuals—a debt that could only be repaid by ensuring that the man responsible faced the harshest penalty under the law.

In their pursuit of the death penalty, the prosecution underscored the idea that justice, in this case, was not only about retribution but about providing a measure of closure and solace to those who had suffered the most. It was a solemn duty to honour the memory of the victims and to acknowledge the enduring pain etched into the lives of their families.

The impact of Manuel's crimes on the victims' families served as a poignant reminder of the far-reaching consequences of his actions. It reinforced the prosecution's argument that the gravity of these crimes demanded the most severe punishment available—a punishment that would not bring back their loved ones but would, in some small way, acknowledge the depth of their suffering and the enduring impact of Manuel's malevolence.

5. The Deterrent Factor

Amid the multifaceted arguments for the death penalty in the case of Peter Manuel, one contentious point raised was its potential deterrent effect. Proponents of capital punishment contended that the severity of the punishment served as a stark warning to potential offenders, dissuading them from committing heinous crimes. It was an argument grounded in the belief that the fear of facing the ultimate penalty would act as a powerful deterrent in preventing future acts of violence.

However, the effectiveness of the death penalty as a deterrent has long been a subject of debate. Critics argued that there was insufficient empirical evidence to conclusively prove that the death penalty served as a significant deterrent to crime. The complexities of criminal behaviour, they maintained, could not be neatly reduced to a simple cause-and-effect relationship with the threat of execution.

Despite this debate, the prosecution raised the deterrence argument in Manuel's trial, contending that society had a vested interest in preventing similar acts of violence. The fear of the ultimate punishment, they argued, could give potential offenders pause and, in some cases, prevent them from carrying out their dark intentions.

Ultimately, whether the death penalty truly acted as a deterrent was a matter of ongoing discussion. Still, it was a factor that the prosecution presented as part of their case, underlining the broader societal responsibility to protect innocent lives and prevent the recurrence of such heinous crimes.

6. The Moral and Ethical Quandary

Within the heart of the Peter Manuel trial, a profound moral and ethical quandary emerged—one that transcended legal arguments and resonated deeply with society at large. This quandary revolved around the delicate balance between the demands of justice and the sanctity of human life.

On one side of the argument were those who advocated for the death penalty. They contended that the severity of Manuel's crimes, marked by a horrifying blend of violence, sadism, and premeditation, warranted the harshest punishment the law could offer. In their view, society's duty to protect itself from individuals capable of such brutality took precedence over the preservation of the perpetrator's life.

On the other side were those who vehemently opposed the death penalty, citing moral and ethical concerns. They argued that the state-sanctioned taking of a human life, regardless of the crimes committed, ran counter to the principles of compassion and human dignity. For them, the question was not only about Manuel's actions but also about the ethical standards by which a civilized society should abide.

This moral and ethical debate extended well beyond the confines of the courtroom. It became a matter of public discourse and introspection, sparking conversations about the very essence of justice and the values a society holds dear. The case of Peter Manuel served as a crucible for these profound questions, forcing individuals to confront the complexities of crime, punishment, and the inherent worth of every human life.

In the end, the court's decision regarding Manuel's fate reflected not only the legal principles at play but also the collective moral and ethical conscience of a nation. The legacy of this moral and ethical quandary would continue to shape discussions surrounding the death penalty, resonating through the annals of legal history.

Conclusion: A Justifiable Punishment

The severity of Peter Manuel's crimes was a compelling factor that supported the prosecution's case for the death penalty. The premeditated and brutal nature of the murders, coupled with the profound impact on the victims' families and society at large, created a compelling argument for the ultimate punishment. However, the moral and ethical questions surrounding the death penalty remained a central point of contention, underscoring the complexity of the case and the enduring debate over capital punishment in the face of heinous crimes.

2. The Emotional Impact on Victims' Families: A Pivotal Factor in the Sentencing

The emotional toll that Peter Manuel's crimes inflicted on the families of the victims was a profoundly influential factor during the sentencing phase. The courtroom became a crucible of raw emotion as family members attended the trial, their grief palpable as they listened to the harrowing testimonies and witnessed the evidence of Manuel's heinous acts. The profound and lasting impact on these families resonated deeply with the court and the public, reinforcing the call for justice and closure.

1. Grief Beyond Words: The Agonizing Burden of Loss

In the solemn and hushed confines of the courtroom, a profound and indescribable grief enveloped the families of Peter Manuel's victims. It was a grief that transcended the boundaries of ordinary sorrow; it was a burden beyond words, an ache that would forever haunt their lives.

Each family had been thrust into an unimaginable nightmare, forced to confront the brutal reality that their loved ones had become victims of senseless violence. The courtroom, where justice was sought, became a place where their collective sorrow was palpable, a raw and open wound that no verdict could ever fully heal.

The grief experienced by these families was not a fleeting emotion but a profound and enduring state of being. It was a weight that would be carried throughout their lives, a shadow that would forever dim the light of their happiest moments. The laughter and warmth that once filled their homes were now haunted by the spectre of loss.

In their faces, one could see the reflections of lives forever altered. The parents who would never again embrace their children, the siblings left to grapple with the absence of their kin, and the children robbed of the guidance and love of their parents—all bore the unbearable burden of grief.

In the quiet moments, when the courtroom was still and the legal proceedings paused, the families likely found themselves lost in memories of happier times. They might have recalled the sound of a loved one's laughter, the touch of their hand, or the warmth of their presence. These were the moments when grief cut deepest, a reminder of the irreplaceable void left by the departed.

For these families, the courtroom was not just a place of justice-seeking but a sanctuary of shared pain and a testament to the enduring love they held for those they had lost. As they awaited the verdict, they carried with them the memories of their loved ones, determined to see justice served and ensure that the world would never forget the names and faces of those who had been taken too soon.

2. The Power of Testimony: Echoes of Heartache in the Courtroom

Amid the solemnity of the courtroom, where facts and evidence were meticulously presented, it was the heartfelt testimonies of the victims' families that resonated most profoundly. Their words were not mere statements; they were echoes of heartache that reverberated throughout the hushed gallery. As they took the stand to share their experiences, their voices carried a weight that transcended the confines of the courtroom.

In those moments, the families' narratives became a poignant tapestry of lives lost and the irreplaceable void left behind. Their words painted vivid portraits of the loved ones who had been brutally taken from them—cherished sons and daughters, beloved siblings, and adoring parents.

As they spoke, jurors, judges, and spectators alike bore witness to the raw and unfiltered emotions of grief, anger, and disbelief. These were not rehearsed speeches but genuine expressions of pain, delivered with quivering voices and tear-filled eyes. In those moments, the families were not merely witnesses; they were storytellers, sharing the stories of lives cut short by violence.

Their testimonies brought to life the memories of stolen moments, the laughter shared around family dinners, and the dreams and aspirations of those they had lost. These were the voices that humanized the victims, transforming them from statistics into beloved individuals who had left an indelible mark on their families and communities.

In the courtroom's silence, the families' words carried a profound and lasting impact. They spoke of birthdays celebrated without the presence of the one being celebrated, of holidays marked by empty chairs, and of the enduring pain that refused to dissipate. Their testimony reminded all present that the consequences of Manuel's actions extended far beyond the immediate acts of violence.

The power of testimony lay not only in its ability to convey the depth of sorrow but also in its capacity to elicit empathy and compassion. In those moments, the families became more than mere observers; they became messengers of the heartache that crime had inflicted upon them. Their stories resonated with jurors, judges, and spectators, reminding them of the profound human cost of the crimes being judged.

In the end, the families' testimonies were a testament to their strength and resilience. Despite the unimaginable pain they had endured, they had found the courage to stand before the court, to share their stories, and to seek justice for their loved ones. In their voices, the victims found advocates, and in their words, the courtroom became a place where compassion and empathy transcended the legal proceedings.

3. Demanding Justice: A Personal Mission to Honour Loved Ones

For the family members of Peter Manuel's victims, the trial transcended the confines of a courtroom. It was not just a legal proceeding; it was a deeply personal mission to honour the memories of their loved ones, to ensure that their voices were heard, and to demand justice. Their presence in that solemn space was a powerful testament to their unwavering determination to seek accountability and closure.

As they sat in the gallery, their eyes fixed on the man responsible for the profound grief that had enveloped their lives, they carried with them a burden of pain that defied description. Each day of the trial was a journey into the heart of darkness, a relentless confrontation with the horrifying reality of the crimes committed against their family members.

Their presence spoke volumes. It symbolized a demand for a form of justice that could, in some small measure, ease the enduring ache in their hearts. For these family members, justice was not a mere abstraction; it was a lifeline, a way to honour the memories of those they had lost.

When they took the stand to share their stories and emotions, their voices were often laced with a palpable mix of sorrow, anger, and frustration. But above all, their words carried an unyielding conviction—a conviction that the punishment meted out to Peter Manuel must be commensurate with the magnitude of the crimes committed.

In their demands for justice, these family members channelled their grief into a collective force for accountability. They reminded the court and all those in attendance that behind every victim was a life that had been extinguished prematurely, a future that had been stolen, and a family left shattered.

Their voices echoed the sentiments of countless others who had been affected by Manuel's reign of terror, creating a chorus of anguish that reverberated through the courtroom. In their demands for justice, they represented not only their own pain but the collective yearning for closure and a sense of retribution.

Throughout the trial, these family members found solace in the knowledge that their presence was not in vain. It was a testament to their unwavering love for the victims and their commitment to ensuring that the memory of their loved ones would endure. In their pursuit of justice, they became champions of the fallen, their determination unwavering in the face of unimaginable sorrow.

In the end, their demand for justice was a testament to the enduring power of love and the resilience of the human spirit. Through their unwavering presence and poignant words, they transformed the trial into a deeply personal and emotional journey—a journey that would forever be etched in the annals of justice and remembrance.

4. The Quest for Closure: Healing Through Justice

The emotional tremors unleashed by Peter Manuel's heinous crimes rippled far beyond the confines of the trial. For the families of his victims, the pursuit of justice was intricately connected to their quest for closure.

The sentencing phase, in particular, held the promise of a pivotal moment in their journey toward healing and recovery.

The wounds inflicted by Manuel's actions were profound, leaving these families to grapple with a pain that defied words. Each day of the trial was a stark reminder of the tragedy that had befallen them, and the emotional toll was immeasurable. Yet, amidst the anguish, there was a glimmer of hope—a hope that justice would prevail and that the punishment meted out to Manuel would be commensurate with the magnitude of his crimes.

For these families, closure was not an abstract concept; it was a lifeline, a beacon guiding them through the darkest of times. A guilty verdict, followed by an appropriate sentence, represented the possibility of a semblance of closure—an opportunity to set down the heavy burden of grief and begin the arduous process of rebuilding their lives.

The courtroom became a crucible of emotions, where their voices were heard, their pain acknowledged, and their demand for justice taken seriously. Each testimony, each piece of evidence presented, was a step closer to the closure they so desperately sought.

The pursuit of closure was not only for themselves but also for the memories of their loved ones. It was a way to honour the lives that had been unjustly taken, to ensure that the world would remember those who had been lost. Their quest for closure was a testament to their enduring love and a demonstration of their unyielding commitment to preserving the legacies of the victims.

In the end, justice was their lifeline—a path toward closure, healing, and the reclamation of their lives from the shadow of tragedy. The families' unwavering presence in the courtroom represented the indomitable spirit of those who, in the face of unimaginable grief, found the strength to stand up for what was right and just.

As the trial unfolded and justice inched closer, the families knew that it would not erase their pain entirely, nor could it bring back their loved ones. However, it would provide a measure of solace, a sense that, in the face of the darkest of horrors, there could still be a glimmer of light—a light that illuminated the path toward closure and the possibility of healing.

5. Public Sympathy: A Nation United in Grief

The emotional resonance of the victims' families transcended the walls of the courtroom, permeating the collective consciousness of communities across Scotland. Their profound grief, unwavering demand for justice, and heartbreaking testimonies struck a chord with the public, creating a tidal wave of sympathy and support that would have far-reaching consequences.

In the heart of this emotionally charged trial, there emerged a profound sense of shared sorrow. The families' anguish was not theirs alone; it became a reflection of the collective grief that had befallen the nation. The stories of lives cut short and dreams shattered resonated deeply with people from all walks of life. The victims were not just names in headlines; they were emblematic of the fragility of human existence.

As the families took the stand, their voices carried the weight of countless others who had suffered similar losses or who could empathize with the pain of such a tragedy. The courtroom became a crucible of empathy, a place where people connected on a fundamental human level—a level where grief was universal, transcending boundaries of age, gender, or social status.

Public sympathy for the families swelled, creating an undeniable groundswell of solidarity. Communities across Scotland rallied around these grieving families, offering them not only condolences but also unwavering support. The emotional outpouring extended beyond mere sentiment; it translated into practical assistance, a collective effort to help ease the burdens these families bore.

Neighbours, friends, and strangers alike joined hands to provide comfort, assistance, and a sense of belonging to those who had lost so much. Acts of kindness, from home-cooked meals to offers of childcare, were emblematic of a society that refused to let these families face their grief alone.

The public's rallying cry for justice mirrored the families' own demands. It was a chorus that echoed through the streets, resonated in conversations, and reverberated in the hearts of those who followed the trial. The significance of the case was not lost on anyone; it symbolized the pursuit of justice and the defence of society against those who would commit such heinous acts.

In essence, this groundswell of public sympathy and support transformed the trial into more than a legal proceeding; it became a shared journey of healing. The families, buoyed by the empathy of their communities, found the strength to navigate the treacherous waters of grief and to seek the closure they so desperately needed.

While the trial's outcome was paramount, the solidarity exhibited by the public was a testament to the enduring bonds of compassion and empathy that unite society in times of profound tragedy. It was a reminder that, even in the face of the darkest of horrors, there exists a wellspring of human goodness and the capacity to stand together as one—a nation united in grief and resolute in its pursuit of justice.

6. The Weight of Loss: An Unbearable Burden on the Legal System

In the hallowed halls of the courtroom, where the pursuit of justice was both a solemn duty and an arduous task, the weight of the families' loss loomed like an unshakable spectre. For judges, jurors, and legal professionals, this emotional burden was an inescapable part of the trial—a profound reminder of the gravity of Peter Manuel's crimes and the immense responsibility that rested on their shoulders.

The Judges: Impartial Sentinels of Justice

At the heart of the judicial system, the judges presiding over the case were tasked with the onerous duty of ensuring a fair trial and, ultimately, delivering the sentence. Their robes and gavels concealed the human emotions that surged beneath, but they were not impervious to the waves of sorrow emanating from the families' testimonies.

The judges' impartiality was a cornerstone of the legal process, a symbol of unwavering commitment to upholding the law. However, behind those stoic expressions lay hearts that ached in empathy for the families. They listened to the heart-wrenching stories, observed the tears and tremors, and bore witness to the inconsolable grief etched on the faces of those who had lost their loved ones. While their role demanded objectivity, their humanity couldn't help but acknowledge the profound impact of the crimes.

The Jurors: Weighing Justice and Suffering

The jurors, selected to render a verdict based on the evidence presented, also found themselves grappling with the emotional toll of the trial. As they listened to the victims' families describe their pain and loss, they were faced with a moral and emotional quandary. Their task was not simply to decide guilt or innocence; it was to weigh the suffering caused by Manuel's actions against the principles of justice.

Each day, the jurors entered the courtroom, knowing that their decision would have profound consequences. The weight of that responsibility bore heavily upon them. The families' grief was not lost on these ordinary citizens, suddenly thrust into an extraordinary role. Their deliberations were not just about facts and evidence; they were about acknowledging the irrevocable harm inflicted upon innocent lives.

Legal Professionals: Navigating the Emotional Currents

For the legal professionals—the prosecutors, defence attorneys, and supporting staff—the emotional impact of the families' loss was a constant presence in their work. While they were seasoned in navigating the complexities of the legal system, the emotional depths plumbed during this trial were unprecedented.

The prosecution team, tasked with proving Manuel's guilt, drew strength from the families' resilience and determination to see justice served. The defence, charged with upholding Manuel's rights, navigated a delicate path, aware of the revulsion society held for their client's actions. Behind closed doors, they, too, grappled with the moral and emotional dimensions of their roles.

Courtroom staff, from stenographers to security personnel, bore witness to the families' anguish daily. Their tasks, while procedural in nature, were carried out in the shadow of this overwhelming sorrow, a constant reminder of the stakes involved in the proceedings.

In this charged atmosphere, the families' loss cast a long and enduring shadow. Their presence in the courtroom was a poignant testament to the human cost of Manuel's crimes, a cost that weighed heavily on the minds and hearts of all those who participated in the legal proceedings. As they strove to deliver justice, the collective grief served as a constant reminder of the profound impact of the crimes and the need for a verdict that would honour both the victims and their loved ones.

Conclusion: A Pivotal Factor in the Sentencing

The emotional impact on the families of Peter Manuel's victims was a pivotal factor in the sentencing phase. Their grief, demands for justice, and pursuit of closure resonated deeply within the courtroom and across the nation. The courtroom became a crucible where the weight of their loss and the enormity of Manuel's crimes converged, underscoring the profound human dimension of the case. In the end, their emotional journey played a significant role in shaping the outcome of the trial and the ultimate sentence imposed on the convicted serial killer.

3. The Fear Gripping Glasgow: A Reign of Terror

The atmosphere of fear and dread that had gripped Glasgow and its surrounding areas during Peter Manuel's reign of terror was an insidious force that could not be underestimated. It permeated the daily lives of residents, casting a long and dark shadow over once-tranquil communities. The fear was pervasive, and its impact on the collective psyche was profound.

1. The Era of Uncertainty: A City Gripped by Fear and Suspicion

In the wake of Peter Manuel's relentless crime spree, Glasgow found itself ensnared in an era of profound uncertainty. The city, once known for its vibrant streets and bustling communities, was now gripped by an insidious fear that had seeped into the very fabric of daily life. This era of uncertainty cast a long and chilling shadow over Glasgow, leaving residents to grapple with an ever-present dread that seemed to linger in the air like an unshakable fog.

Neighbourhoods Transformed

The tranquil neighbourhoods that had once been synonymous with safety and camaraderie had undergone a dramatic transformation. What were once close-knit communities, where neighbours greeted each other with warmth and trust, had become fractured by suspicion and anxiety. The streets that children had once roamed freely were now viewed through a lens of caution, and parents clung tightly to their loved ones, fearful of what could transpire in their own backyards.

The Looming Presence of a Serial Killer

The grim reality that a serial killer was at large shattered the illusion of security that had previously defined Glasgow. No longer could residents take solace in the assumption that their city was immune to the horrors that haunted other places. The knowledge that Peter Manuel was prowling the same streets they walked, that he could be lurking in plain sight, was an unsettling truth that haunted every corner of the city.

The Burden of Suspicion

As the era of uncertainty stretched on, suspicion became a burden that weighed heavily on the minds of Glaswegians. Friends, acquaintances, and even family members found themselves viewed through a different lens. The simple act of trusting someone became an exercise in caution, as the fear of betrayal loomed large. No one could be entirely sure who could be harbouring sinister secrets, and this pervasive doubt further fractured the bonds of community.

A Constant State of Apprehension

The collective apprehension that had settled over Glasgow was palpable. Residents went about their daily lives, but every shadow, every unexpected noise, every unfamiliar face became a source of trepidation. The fear was not just of becoming a victim but also of unwittingly crossing paths with a killer who had already eluded the authorities time and time again.

The Erosion of Freedom

The erosion of freedom was an unexpected consequence of this era of uncertainty. People found themselves limiting their movements, avoiding certain areas, and curbing their social interactions out of an abundance of caution. The joyous spontaneity that had once characterized life in Glasgow was replaced by a sombre vigilance that permeated every decision, every step taken outside the safety of one's home.

A City in Search of Resolution

As the uncertainty persisted, Glasgow yearned for resolution. The apprehension had taken a toll on the city's collective psyche, and the need for closure, both in terms of the capture of Peter Manuel and the restoration of a semblance of normalcy, was deeply felt. Glaswegians longed for the day when they could shed the burden of fear and once again embrace their city with the warmth and trust that had defined it before the era of uncertainty descended upon them.

2. Locking Doors and Windows: Fortress Homes in the Face of Fear

Amidst the era of uncertainty that Peter Manuel's reign of terror had cast upon Glasgow, one of the most palpable and immediate responses to the pervasive fear was the widespread practice of locking doors and windows. This transformation of homes, once open and welcoming, into fortified fortresses was a tangible manifestation of the community's collective dread and the lengths to which residents would go to protect themselves and their loved ones.

A Drastic Shift in Daily Habits

For many Glaswegians, locking doors and windows marked a drastic shift in their daily habits. It was a departure from the sense of security that had once allowed them to leave doors unlocked and windows ajar during warm summer nights. Now, the ritual of securing their homes became a daily necessity, a ritual that carried with it the weight of fear and vulnerability.

An Act of Defiance

Locking doors and windows was, in essence, an act of defiance against the unseen threat that lurked in the shadows. It was a way for residents to reclaim a measure of control in a situation where so much remained uncertain. It symbolized a determination not to be passive victims but to actively protect their families and their sanctuaries from the malevolent presence that had invaded their lives.

The Sanctuary of Home

The home, once a sanctuary where families gathered in comfort and security, had now become a symbol of vulnerability. Families no longer felt entirely safe within the confines of their own walls, and the act of locking doors and windows was a desperate attempt to restore that sense of sanctuary. It was a declaration that, within their homes at least, they would not be victims.

A Daily Reminder of Fear

Each click of a lock and every sliding of a window latch served as a daily reminder of the fear that had taken hold. It was a routine performed with a sense of trepidation, a recognition that the threat was ever-present, and that the simple act of securing their homes was a necessary defence against an unpredictable danger.

The Emotional Toll

The emotional toll of this new reality was profound. Families, while physically safer within their locked homes, could not escape the psychological burden of living in a constant state of vigilance. The fear that once lay dormant in the back of their minds was now an ever-present companion, a shadow that followed them even behind closed doors.

The Hope for Normalcy

As the era of uncertainty persisted, the hope remained that someday, the act of locking doors and windows would no longer be necessary. Glaswegians longed for the return of a sense of normalcy, where the sound of a key turning in a lock would no longer serve as a reminder of their vulnerability but as a symbol of security in a city free from the grip of fear.

3. The Curfew of Fear: When Darkness Imposed Its Rule

The era of Peter Manuel's reign of terror imposed an unspoken curfew on the city of Glasgow, a curfew not enforced by law but dictated by the palpable fear that permeated the streets. This unrelenting fear weighed heaviest on women, who, in particular, felt vulnerable and became cautious about going out alone after nightfall. The result was a transformation of the once-bustling cityscape into something altogether different, marked by an eerie emptiness as residents prioritized safety over the risks of venturing outside after dark.

An Unshakable Fear

Peter Manuel's ruthless crimes had instilled an unshakable fear that hung like a dark cloud over Glasgow. The sense of danger was no longer confined to the shadows; it had become an undeniable reality that residents had to confront. Women, who often felt more vulnerable to random violence, bore the brunt of this fear.

A Drastic Change in Habits

This fear prompted a drastic change in daily habits, with women and families altering their routines to avoid the risks associated with the night. Going out alone, even for simple errands, became an act filled with trepidation. The once-thriving nightlife of Glasgow gave way to a sombre atmosphere as residents opted to stay indoors rather than face the uncertainty of the darkened streets.

The Eerie Emptiness

The result of this collective fear was an eerie emptiness that settled over the city at night. Streets that had once bustled with activity were now devoid of the usual foot traffic. Shops closed early, and the vibrant nightlife that had defined Glasgow took a backseat to an overwhelming sense of caution.

Seeking Refuge in Homes

Families sought refuge within the familiar walls of their homes, where they could control their environment and minimize the risks. The home became a sanctuary, a place where the threat outside could be kept at bay. Even mundane activities, like walking the dog or taking an evening stroll, were abandoned as people prioritized safety over leisure.

The Impact on Social Life

This unspoken curfew had a profound impact on the social life of the city. The communal spaces that once fostered connection and interaction now lay abandoned. Residents missed out on the vibrant cultural and social scenes that had been a hallmark of Glasgow, replaced by the silence of empty streets and shuttered storefronts.

Longing for Normalcy

Above all, the curfew of fear represented a longing for normalcy. Residents yearned for the day when they could reclaim their city, when the darkness would no longer impose its rule. The fear that gripped Glasgow during Manuel's reign left a lasting scar, a testament to the profound impact of his crimes on the daily lives of its residents.

4. Strained Community Bonds: The Fraying Fabric of Trust

The era of Peter Manuel's crimes cast a dark shadow over communities that had once thrived on neighbourly trust and cooperation. The weight of fear and suspicion strained the bonds between residents, gradually eroding the sense of unity and security that had been a hallmark of these neighbourhoods. In this atmosphere of uncertainty, even the most familiar faces were viewed with a degree of mistrust, replacing the once-close-knit communities with a sense of vulnerability and isolation.

A Community Under Siege

Communities across Glasgow found themselves under siege, not by an external threat, but by the fear that emanated from within. The collective knowledge that a serial killer was operating in their midst was a heavy burden that residents carried daily. This burden began to manifest in subtle but significant ways, reshaping the very dynamics of these neighbourhoods.

The Erosion of Trust

One of the most noticeable effects was the erosion of trust. Neighbours who had once been close now regarded each other with newfound suspicion. The sense of safety that had once allowed children to play freely in the streets began to wither. People found themselves questioning the intentions of those around them, no longer willing to take their safety for granted.

A Sense of Isolation

The fraying fabric of trust gave rise to a pervasive sense of isolation. Residents, who had once relied on each other for support and companionship, withdrew into their homes, seeking solace in the familiarity of four walls. The communal spirit that had once defined these neighbourhoods was replaced by a palpable sense of self-preservation.

The Impact on Daily Life

The strain on community bonds also affected the daily lives of residents. Simple acts, like borrowing a cup of sugar or lending a helping hand, became tinged with hesitation. The very essence of what it meant to be part of a close-knit community underwent a transformation, as people increasingly kept to themselves.

Longing for Restoration

As the era of fear continued, many residents longed for the restoration of their once-vibrant communities. They yearned for the day when they could freely trust their neighbours and walk the streets without apprehension. The strain on community bonds, a consequence of Manuel's reign of terror, left a lasting scar on the social fabric of Glasgow—a reminder of the profound impact of his crimes beyond the immediate acts of violence.

5. A City Paralyzed: Glasgow's Descent into Fear

Glasgow, a city renowned for its vitality, resilience, and spirit, found itself plunged into a state of profound paralysis during the era of Peter Manuel's reign of terror. Fear, like a suffocating fog, had enveloped the city, casting a pervasive pall over its once-thriving streets and alleys. The consequences were far-reaching, affecting everything from daily life to the very essence of the community.

The Ebbing Vibrancy

The first notable impact was the ebbing vibrancy of Glasgow's streets. The city that had once bustled with activity and exuberance began to lose its characteristic liveliness. Businesses that had thrived on the bustling crowds saw a decline in patrons, as people hesitated to venture out. Glasgow's famous markets, pubs, and cultural venues suffered as a climate of uncertainty and anxiety descended upon the city.

Social Life Distorted

Glasgow's vibrant social life, which had been a source of pride for its residents, was distorted by the presence of fear. Social gatherings, community events, and celebrations that were once commonplace became increasingly subdued. People were cautious about participating in activities that would require them to be out after dark. The city's rich cultural tapestry began to unravel as the communal bonds that had held it together were strained to their limits.

The Struggle for Normalcy

The paralysis that gripped Glasgow was not merely a consequence of fear but also a reflection of the city's indomitable spirit. Residents struggled to maintain a semblance of normalcy amidst the prevailing uncertainty. They continued to go about their daily routines, albeit with a heightened sense of vigilance. Yet, the city's collective psyche had been deeply scarred, leaving an indelible mark on the hearts and minds of its inhabitants.

The Shadow of Fear

Throughout this period, the shadow of fear loomed large over Glasgow. It was not just a fear of the unknown assailant but a fear of the profound changes that had swept through the city. Glasgow had become a place where fear could strike at any moment, where the vibrancy of daily life was tinged with trepidation. The city's resilience was tested as it grappled with the enduring impact of Peter Manuel's crimes on its collective consciousness.

A City in Waiting

Glasgow became a city in waiting, yearning for the day when the dark era of fear would recede, and its vibrant spirit would reawaken. The profound paralysis that had gripped the city was a stark reminder of the far-reaching consequences of crime beyond the immediate victims and a testament to the enduring power of fear to reshape communities.

6. The Power of the Unknown: Glasgow's Unending Nightmare

The fear that pervaded Glasgow during Peter Manuel's reign of terror was greatly amplified by the enigmatic and elusive nature of the threat he posed. It was this unsettling unknown that cast an even deeper shadow over the city, leaving both law enforcement and the public in a state of profound bewilderment.

An Elusive Phantom

Peter Manuel was no ordinary criminal; he operated like a phantom, disappearing into the night after committing his heinous acts. This elusiveness defied comprehension and left law enforcement officials scratching their heads. The very essence of his ability to vanish without a trace only heightened the mystery surrounding him. The community was haunted by the realization that a ruthless killer could be lurking in their midst, yet his identity remained hidden.

The Terrifying Uncertainty

Uncertainty became a relentless companion for Glasgow's residents. They had no way of knowing when or where Manuel might strike next. This uncertainty manifested in various ways, from choosing the safest routes home to hesitating before opening their doors to strangers. The fear of the unknown was a constant presence, a chilling reminder that their city had been transformed into a hunting ground where anyone could become a victim.

The Conundrum of Law Enforcement

For law enforcement, the unknown nature of Manuel's movements was a confounding conundrum. Traditional investigative methods that had proven effective in solving crimes were rendered almost useless in the face of this enigmatic adversary. Detectives were left grappling with an elusive quarry who seemed to taunt them with his ability to remain hidden. The very act of not knowing Manuel's next move was maddening, as it created an atmosphere of perpetual anxiety and vulnerability.

A City Held Hostage

In essence, Glasgow was held hostage by this shadowy figure. The fear of the unknown was like a shroud draped over the city, impairing its ability to function as it once had. Residents had to contend not only with the disturbing reality of Manuel's crimes but also with the disquieting uncertainty of when he might strike again. This powerlessness, born from the unknown, was a uniquely tormenting aspect of Manuel's reign of terror.

The Lingering Psychological Impact

Even after Manuel's capture and trial, the psychological impact of the unknown continued to haunt Glasgow. The legacy of this era of uncertainty was etched into the collective memory of the city. It served as a stark reminder of the profound consequences of crime that extended beyond the physical acts themselves, leaving emotional and psychological scars that would persist long after the ordeal was over.

In essence, it was the power of the unknown that rendered Peter Manuel's crimes even more chilling and his reign of terror an enduring nightmare in the annals of Glasgow's history.

7. Impact on Daily Lives: Fear's Ongoing Stranglehold

The fear that pervaded Glasgow during Peter Manuel's reign of terror was not confined to the night. It cast a relentless shadow over every aspect of daily life, transforming the routines and habits of the city's residents.

A Fearful Commute

Even during the daytime, the fear of encountering danger was a constant companion. Commuters, whether heading to work or running errands, could not escape the awareness of the lurking threat. Public transportation, once a mundane part of daily life, became an arena where people maintained a heightened sense of vigilance. Passengers exchanged wary glances, wondering if the person sitting next to them might be the infamous killer.

Guarded Children

Parents faced an especially harrowing challenge: ensuring the safety of their children. School routines were no longer a matter of routine but a source of anxiety. The simple act of allowing children to walk to school or play in the neighbourhood became a heart-wrenching decision. Parents grappled with the need to balance their children's independence with their overwhelming desire to protect them from harm.

Altered Social Interactions

Social interactions, too, were transformed by the prevailing fear. Friends and neighbours exchanged stories of the latest developments in the case with a mixture of dread and fascination. Conversations about the weather or sports gave way to discussions about safety precautions and the latest news from the ongoing investigation. Trust, once readily extended, was now accompanied by a degree of scepticism as people questioned whether those around them could be trusted.

A City on Edge

Glasgow became a city on edge, where ordinary activities were marked by caution and suspicion. Residents were forced to adapt their daily routines to accommodate this new reality, modifying their behaviour to minimize the perceived risks. This collective sense of unease had permeated every corner of daily life, leaving no aspect untouched by the chilling effects of Manuel's reign of terror.

The Lingering Impact

Even after Manuel's capture and the eventual end of his murderous spree, the impact on daily lives lingered. The trauma of living under the constant shadow of fear left a profound mark on the collective psyche of the city. Glasgow had experienced a disruption to its daily life that would not easily fade. The fear that once held the city in its stranglehold had left scars that would take time to heal, serving as a haunting reminder of the chilling era that had gripped the community.

Conclusion: A Reign of Terror

Peter Manuel's reign of terror cast Glasgow into a deep abyss of fear and dread. The community's collective psyche was scarred by the knowledge that a ruthless serial killer was at large, preying upon the unsuspecting. The fear manifested in locked doors, abandoned streets, and strained relationships. It was a reign of terror that left an indelible mark on the city and its residents, an era of darkness that could only begin to recede with the eventual capture and sentencing of the notorious serial killer.

4. The Precedent of the Death Penalty

At the time of Manuel's trial, the death penalty was still in practice for murder cases in the United Kingdom. While the ethical and moral questions surrounding capital punishment were already the subject of debate, the legal framework allowed for the imposition of the ultimate penalty.

Public Opinion on the Death Sentence

The decision to impose the death penalty on Peter Manuel was met with a range of public reactions, reflecting the complex and polarizing nature of this form of punishment.

1. Support for the Death Penalty: Seeking Retribution and Closure

A significant segment of the public, including many of the victims' families and those who had lived in fear during Peter Manuel's relentless crime spree, vehemently supported the imposition of the death penalty. To them, it was not merely a matter of punishment; it was about retribution, justice, and finding a semblance of closure in the face of unspeakable horrors. The reasons behind this fervent support ran deep, encompassing various facets of the human experience:

1. Seeking Retribution

The notion of an "eye for an eye" resonated deeply with those who supported the death penalty in Manuel's case. They believed that the severity of his crimes demanded an equally severe punishment. Manuel's litany of charges, including multiple counts of murder, sexual assault, and robbery, was nothing short of appalling. The gruesome details of his crimes, marked by premeditation and brutality, left little room for leniency in the eyes of many.

2. Closure for Victims' Families

For the families of Manuel's victims, the death penalty represented a path toward closure—a way to bring an agonizing chapter of their lives to an end. The emotional toll inflicted by Manuel's crimes was immeasurable, and the scars of loss and trauma ran deep. The guilty verdict and subsequent sentencing offered a glimmer of solace. It was a recognition that the man responsible for their loved ones' deaths would face the ultimate penalty, a measure of justice that they had yearned for.

3. Protecting Society

Supporters of the death penalty often argued that it served as a deterrent against potential future criminals. In Manuel's case, the fear that had gripped Glasgow and its surrounding areas during his reign of terror was profound. Many believed that his execution would send a clear message that such heinous acts would not be tolerated, potentially dissuading others from following a similar path of violence.

4. A Sense of Finality

The death penalty carried a sense of finality that life imprisonment did not. While life imprisonment might offer the possibility of parole or escape, the death penalty ensured that Manuel would never walk free again. It was seen as the only way to guarantee that he could not inflict further harm on society or, in the case of escape, victimize more innocent lives.

5. The Court of Public Opinion

Public sentiment had a significant role to play in Manuel's case. The extensive media coverage had kept the nation and the world riveted to the trial. The emotional impact of the victims' stories and the gruesome details of Manuel's crimes had left an indelible mark on the collective consciousness. The court of public opinion, often swayed by the intensity of public sentiment, found resonance with the idea of the death penalty as a just response to Manuel's horrific acts.

Conclusion: A Matter of Retribution and Closure

Support for the death penalty in Peter Manuel's case was deeply rooted in the desire for retribution and closure. It was a belief that his unspeakable crimes warranted the most severe punishment available—a punishment that would send a resounding message to society and offer some semblance of healing to the families of his victims. The death penalty was, for many, a means of seeking justice in the face of overwhelming darkness.

2. Abolitionist Movements: A Call for Morality and Caution

Amidst the fervent support for the death penalty in Peter Manuel's case, there existed equally vocal and impassioned abolitionist movements and individuals who staunchly opposed the death penalty in all circumstances. Their stance was grounded in a profound belief in the sanctity of life, a concern for the potential miscarriages of justice, and a moral argument against society responding to violence with further violence. Here's an exploration of the core tenets of the abolitionist perspective:

1. The Sanctity of Life

Abolitionists fundamentally believed in the intrinsic value and sanctity of every human life. To them, the act of deliberately taking a life, even in response to heinous crimes, was morally indefensible. They contended that society should uphold the same respect for life that it sought to protect, even in the face of horrific acts.

2. The Risk of Miscarriages of Justice

One of the most compelling arguments against the death penalty was the risk of executing an innocent person. Abolitionists pointed to numerous historical cases where individuals had been wrongfully convicted and sentenced to death, only to be exonerated later. In the pursuit of justice, they argued, society could not afford the irreversible mistake of executing an innocent person.

3. The Cycle of Violence

Abolitionists raised a poignant question: Does responding to violence with more violence truly serve the cause of justice? They contended that the death penalty perpetuated a cycle of vengeance and brutality, rather than fostering a society that sought rehabilitation and reintegration for offenders. They advocated for alternative forms of punishment that emphasized rehabilitation and the possibility of redemption.

4. Human Fallibility

The fallibility of human judgment was a central concern for abolitionists. They highlighted the imperfections of the criminal justice system, from biased investigations to unreliable witness testimonies. In cases as grave as Manuel's, where multiple charges of murder hinged on evidence and witness accounts, the potential for error was significant.

5. The International Perspective

Abolitionist movements often drew from the global context, pointing out that many countries had abolished the death penalty or significantly restricted its use. They emphasized that the death penalty placed countries in the company of nations known for human rights abuses, undermining their moral standing on the international stage.

6. Alternative Sentencing

Abolitionists advocated for alternative forms of sentencing that prioritized rehabilitation and reintegration into society. They argued that life imprisonment, with the possibility of parole and access to support and rehabilitation programs, could serve the goals of justice without resorting to the ultimate punishment.

A Moral Standpoint Against State-Sanctioned Killing

The abolitionist movements and individuals who opposed the death penalty in Peter Manuel's case did so from a deeply moral standpoint. They believed that the act of taking a life, even that of a convicted murderer, violated fundamental principles of human dignity and respect for life. Their arguments against the death penalty were rooted in concerns about the potential for error, the perpetuation of violence, and the moral character of a society that sanctioned state-sanctioned killing. In the midst of a fervent call for retribution, they stood as a reminder of the enduring debate surrounding the ethics of capital punishment.

3. The Weight on the Jury: Deliberating a Life-and-Death Verdict

The impact of the death penalty decision on the jury cannot be overstated. These individuals had already borne the burden of finding Peter Manuel guilty of multiple counts of murder, sexual assault, and robbery. The courtroom drama had unfolded before them, filled with harrowing testimonies, gruesome evidence, and the emotional weight of the victims' families. As they transitioned to the sentencing phase, the gravity of their task was amplified:

1. A Moral Dilemma

The jury members were presented with a moral dilemma of unparalleled magnitude. They had to grapple with the fundamental question of whether it was ethically justifiable to condemn a fellow human being to death. The emotional toll of the trial was evident on their faces as they contemplated the weighty decision before them.

2. The Human Element

The jurors were acutely aware that their decision had real and irreversible consequences. Behind the legal arguments and courtroom proceedings lay the fact that Peter Manuel's life hung in the balance. The emotional impact of their choice was further exacerbated by the presence of the victims' families in the courtroom, whose grief was a palpable reminder of the stakes involved.

3. Society's Trust in Them

As representatives of the community, the jury carried the immense responsibility of upholding the principles of justice. Their verdict and subsequent sentencing would be seen as a reflection of the community's faith in the legal system to deliver justice. This added another layer of weight to their decision-making process.

4. The Debate and Deliberation

The jury's deliberation over the death penalty was likely fraught with impassioned discussions and ethical introspection. They would have considered the severity of Manuel's crimes, the emotional impact on the victims' families, and the societal implications of their verdict. The moral and emotional toll of this deliberation was undoubtedly immense.

5. The Final Pronouncement

When the jury finally rendered their decision to impose the death penalty, it marked the culmination of weeks of intense emotional and moral wrestling. Their facial expressions and demeanour as they pronounced the sentence may have revealed a mix of sombreness, solemnity, and perhaps even relief that their arduous task had come to an end.

A Decision of Profound Significance

The decision to impose the death penalty on Peter Manuel weighed heavily on the jury, not only because of its legal and procedural implications but also because of the profound moral and emotional dimensions it carried. In the end, their verdict represented society's response to the heinous crimes committed by Manuel, a verdict that would be scrutinized, debated, and remembered as a pivotal moment in the annals of Scottish legal history.

4. Legal Appeals and the Protracted Battle for Delay

Following the imposition of the death sentence on Peter Manuel, the legal process continued to unfold, with a series of legal appeals and efforts aimed at delaying the inevitable execution. Manuel's defence team, resolute in their commitment to save their client from the gallows, embarked on a protracted battle that extended the timeline of his case:

1. Mental Health Appeals

One of the primary avenues of appeal was centred around Manuel's mental health. His defence team argued that he suffered from severe mental illness, a claim they had asserted throughout the trial during the insanity defence. They contended that Manuel's mental state should preclude the carrying out of the death penalty. This argument opened up a complex legal debate about the intersection of mental health and capital punishment.

2. The Admissibility of Evidence

Another key point of contention in the appeals process was the admissibility of evidence presented during the trial. Manuel's defence team scrutinized every aspect of the trial proceedings, challenging the integrity of the evidence and the fairness of the trial itself. They aimed to create doubts about the legality of Manuel's conviction, with hopes that this could lead to a retrial or a commutation of the death sentence.

3. Legal Manoeuvring

The legal appeals process involved extensive legal manoeuvring, including the submission of briefs, oral arguments, and the examination of legal precedents. The defence, determined to exhaust every possible avenue to delay the execution, engaged in lengthy legal battles with the prosecution, further extending the timeline of the case.

4. Public Reaction and Debate

The appeals and delays in the case of Peter Manuel did not go unnoticed by the public. The ongoing legal battles sparked intense public debate and discussion, with opinions divided on whether justice was being served or if the system was being manipulated. The issue of capital punishment and its application in cases involving mental illness became a focal point of public discourse.

5. Impact on the Victims' Families

The prolonged legal battle had a profound impact on the families of Manuel's victims. They were forced to relive the trauma of the crimes repeatedly as the appeals process played out. While some were supportive of the efforts to delay Manuel's execution, others yearned for closure and a final resolution to the case.

6. The Inevitable Outcome

Despite the numerous legal appeals and delays, the outcome remained inevitable. Peter Manuel had been sentenced to death, and the legal battles, while extending the timeline, did not alter the ultimate verdict. The ongoing legal manoeuvres created an agonizing period of uncertainty for all involved.

Conclusion: The Protracted Battle

The post-sentencing legal appeals and delays in the case of Peter Manuel represented a protracted battle in the pursuit of justice. Manuel's defence team, resolute in their efforts to save their client from execution, navigated a complex legal landscape, all while the public watched and debated the implications of their actions. Ultimately, the legal process could only delay the inevitable, and the question of whether justice was served would remain a matter of ongoing debate and discussion.

5. The Final Verdict and Execution

Ultimately, after a series of legal proceedings, Peter Manuel's death sentence was upheld. On July 11, 1958, he was executed by hanging in Barlinnie Prison in Glasgow. His death marked the end of a chapter in Scotland's history and the resolution that many had sought.

The Death Sentence and Its Legacy

The decision to impose the death penalty on Peter Manuel was one fraught with moral, legal, and emotional complexities. It ignited debates about the ethics of capital punishment, the role of the state in taking a human life, and the enduring quest for justice in the face of unspeakable evil.

As we reflect on the sentencing phase of Peter Manuel's trial, we are reminded that the death penalty is not merely a legal matter but a profound moral and societal issue. The legacy of this decision endures in the ongoing discussions about the ultimate punishment and the enduring impact of Manuel's reign of terror on Scottish society and the world.

Chapter 10

Life on Death Row

The imposition of the death penalty on Peter Manuel marked the beginning of a new chapter in his life—a chapter defined by the stark reality of life on death row. This phase of his existence, while devoid of freedom, was marked by its own set of challenges, intrigues, and revelations. In this chapter, we delve into Peter Manuel's life on death row, his day-to-day existence, and any confessions or revelations that emerged during this period.

Life on Death Row: A Grim and Isolated Existence

Peter Manuel's life on death row was a stark departure from the freedom and control he had once enjoyed in the outside world. Incarcerated in Barlinnie Prison in Glasgow, he faced a grim and isolated existence as he awaited his impending execution. This period in his life was characterized by several factors that made it a particularly challenging and bleak chapter:

1. The Cell

The most immediate aspect of life on death row was the cell itself. Manuel would have been confined to a small, often windowless cell for the majority of his day. These cells are typically Spartan in design, containing little more than a bed, a toilet, and a small desk. The limited space and lack of natural light can exacerbate the sense of isolation and despair.

2. Isolation and Solitude

Death row inmates are often subjected to a high degree of isolation from the general prison population. This isolation is both for security reasons and as part of the broader psychological impact of death row. Manuel would have had limited opportunities for social interaction, leaving him alone with his thoughts for much of his time.

3. Routine and Monotony

Life on death row is characterized by a strict routine that can become monotonous and repetitive. Inmates have limited access to educational or recreational activities. The daily schedule is regimented, with specific times for meals, exercise, and personal hygiene. This predictable routine can contribute to a sense of despair and hopelessness.

4. Legal Battles and Appeals

During his time on death row, Manuel would have continued to engage in legal battles and appeals. These efforts to challenge his death sentence could provide temporary distractions, but they also represented ongoing uncertainty about his fate. The emotional toll of legal battles, as well as the potential for multiple stays of execution, added to the psychological strain of life on death row.

5. Relationships with Other Inmates

While death row inmates may have limited contact with one another due to the isolation measures, some do form bonds with fellow inmates facing similar circumstances. These relationships can provide a degree of emotional support, as these individuals share a unique and challenging experience.

6. Facing Mortality

Perhaps the most profound aspect of life on death row is the constant awareness of one's impending mortality. Manuel knew that his time was limited, and the spectre of execution loomed over every day he spent in prison. This existential burden can lead to introspection, regret, and contemplation of one's actions and their consequences.

Conclusion: A Bleak Existence

Incarceration on death row is a uniquely grim and isolated existence. For Peter Manuel, who had once wielded control and power over his victims, the reversal of fortunes led to a life marked by confinement, solitude, routine, and the constant awareness of his impending execution. It was a stark and chilling contrast to the life he had led before his capture, and it served as a harsh reminder of the consequences of his crimes.

The Cell: A World of Confinement

For Peter Manuel, as for all death row inmates, daily life revolved around the stark confines of a small and austere cell. These cells were far from the spacious and dynamic world he had once known. Instead, they represented the epitome of confinement, isolation, and a grim reminder of his impending fate.

1. A Spartan Existence

The cells on death row are designed to be functional, but they are intentionally minimalist in their approach. They typically contain only the most essential elements for daily living. A narrow bed, often mounted to the wall, serves as both sleeping quarters and a place to sit during waking hours. A small, stainless-steel toilet and sink combination provide for basic hygiene needs. A small table or desk, if present at all, offers minimal workspace.

2. Limited Space and Freedom

The spatial constraints of these cells cannot be overstated. Inmates have extremely limited space to move around. The narrow confines reinforce the sense of confinement and isolation, leaving inmates with few options for physical activity or even changing their surroundings.

3. Lack of Natural Light

Many death row cells are windowless, further compounding the sense of isolation. The absence of natural light means that inmates are often cut off from the diurnal rhythms of the outside world. This can lead to disorientation and a skewed sense of time.

4. Symbol of Isolation

The cell becomes both a physical space and a potent symbol of isolation. For Manuel, who had once revelled in a life of crime and adventure, this cell was the embodiment of the consequences of his actions. It represented not only his separation from the outside world but also the irrevocable loss of the freedom he had once taken for granted.

5. Routine and Repetition

Inmates on death row often spend the majority of their day in these cells. The routine can become monotonous and repetitive, with specific times designated for meals, exercise (usually limited to a small indoor area), and personal hygiene. The predictability of this routine underscores the sense of confinement and powerlessness.

Conclusion: A Bleak Reminder

The cell on death row is more than just a physical space; it's a microcosm of confinement and isolation. It serves as a constant reminder of the consequences of one's actions and the loss of freedom. For Peter Manuel, it was a stark contrast to the life of crime and adventure he had led before his arrest—a world of confinement that underscored the irrevocable nature of his fate.

Isolation: The Loneliness of Death Row

Isolation was not just a condition of life on death row; it was a defining characteristic that left an indelible mark on inmates like Peter Manuel. The stark reality of this isolation, both physical and emotional, took a profound toll on his mental and emotional well-being, fundamentally altering the social dynamics he had once thrived on.

1. Solitary Confinement

Solitary confinement was a common practice on death row. Inmates were often kept in small, windowless cells for the majority of their day. This practice had several objectives, including minimizing contact between prisoners to prevent potential violence and escape attempts. However, its consequences on an inmate's mental health were significant.

2. The Weight of Silence

Death row was a place marked by silence. Inmates had limited opportunities for social interaction, and the absence of human voices became a constant presence. The once bustling world of manipulation and charm that Manuel had been accustomed to was replaced by an eerie and oppressive quiet.

3. Cut Off from Human Connections

For someone like Peter Manuel, who had demonstrated a remarkable ability to manipulate and charm those around him, the isolation of death row represented a stark contrast to the world he had known. His talents for exploiting human connections were rendered obsolete in an environment where such connections were scarce and tightly controlled.

4. A Growing Awareness of Isolation

As the days turned into weeks and months, Manuel's awareness of his isolation deepened. The realization that he was cut off from the outside world and from the human connections he had exploited in the past weighed heavily on his psyche. It was a profound shift from the life he had once known, where he had revelled in his ability to charm and manipulate others.

5. Mental and Emotional Toll

The loneliness of death row had a profound impact on Manuel's mental and emotional well-being. It challenged his resilience and tested the psychological fortitude that had allowed him to commit heinous crimes with a seeming lack of remorse. The isolation left him with little to occupy his thoughts except the impending reality of his execution.

The Unseen Toll

The loneliness of death row was a silent, unseen, and deeply impactful aspect of Manuel's confinement. It represented a stark departure from the world he had once known, where he thrived on human connections, manipulation, and charm. In isolation, he faced the weight of silence and a growing awareness of his separation from the outside world—a burden that took a profound toll on his mental and emotional well-being.

Routine and Regulations: The Order Amidst Chaos

Life on death row was characterized by the rigid adherence to strict routines and regulations. Inmates like Peter Manuel found themselves navigating a highly structured and controlled existence that provided a semblance of order amidst the chaos of their circumstances. These routines, while confining, offered a degree of predictability, contrasting sharply with the unpredictability of their past criminal lives. However, this structured life also served as a relentless reminder of the inexorable approach of their executions.

1. Designated Meal Times

Meals were a significant part of an inmate's daily routine. On death row, there were designated times for breakfast, lunch, and dinner. In the stark environment of the prison, mealtime provided a momentary reprieve from the monotony of the cell. For Manuel, it was a time when he could momentarily escape his isolation and interact with other inmates, albeit briefly.

2. Exercise and Recreation

Regular exercise and recreation were also integral components of life on death row. Inmates were allowed scheduled periods for outdoor exercise, providing a precious opportunity to breathe fresh air and move beyond the confines of their cells. While these periods were limited, they offered a vital break from the monotony of incarceration.

3. Visits from Family and Legal Counsel

Visits from family and legal counsel were tightly regulated and scheduled. Inmates had the opportunity to see their loved ones and meet with their legal representatives during specified visiting hours. These visits provided a lifeline to the outside world and a source of emotional support for those facing the prospect of execution.

4. The Order in the Chaos

The structured nature of life on death row created a paradoxical sense of order within the chaos of imprisonment. In an environment marked by isolation, fear, and uncertainty, adhering to these routines offered a semblance of control and predictability. It was a stark departure from the criminal life that Manuel had known, where chaos and impulsivity had defined his actions.

5. The Inescapable Reminder

While routines brought a degree of order, they also served as an unrelenting reminder of the inescapable reality facing inmates on death row—their impending executions. Each meal, exercise session, or visit reinforced the knowledge that time was running out. It was a haunting reminder of the ultimate fate that awaited them.

The Struggle for Normalcy

Life on death row was a delicate balance between structure and chaos, routine and isolation. The strict regulations and schedules provided a semblance of normalcy in an otherwise grim and oppressive environment. For Peter Manuel and others like him, these routines were a lifeline to the outside world, a fragile thread connecting them to the realm of the living as they awaited their inexorable destiny.

The Weight of Anticipation: The Countdown to Death

For Peter Manuel, life on death row was a relentless journey towards an inevitable and chilling destination—execution by hanging. The anticipation of this finality weighed heavily on him, casting a long shadow over every aspect of his existence. The countdown to execution was a grim and inescapable reality that loomed over him, a constant reminder of the consequences of his heinous crimes.

1. The Daily Toll of Anticipation

Each day that Manuel spent on death row was marked by the growing anticipation of his execution. As he awoke in his cell each morning, he couldn't escape the knowledge that he was one day closer to the gallows. This anticipation, like a relentless drumbeat, echoed in his mind and must have been a source of profound psychological distress.

2. The Inescapable Fate

The countdown to execution was a chilling and inescapable fate that Manuel had brought upon himself through his reign of terror. His gruesome crimes, the suffering he had inflicted on his victims and their families, had sealed his destiny. He was now paying the price for the reign of terror he had unleashed on Scotland.

3. Reflection and Regret

In the face of impending death, some inmates on death row turn to reflection and regret. They grapple with the enormity of their actions, seeking some form of redemption or closure in their final days. While there is no way to know Manuel's inner thoughts, the weight of anticipation may have led him to introspection.

4. The Relentless Passage of Time

Time on death row moved at a cruelly steady pace. Each day, each hour, brought Manuel one step closer to the gallows, a reality that he could not change. The relentless passage of time was a reminder of the irreversible nature of his fate, and it must have cast a long shadow over his existence.

The Grim Countdown

The anticipation of execution was a heavy burden that Manuel carried with him every day. It was a grim reminder of the consequences of his actions, a relentless countdown to the end of his life. In the confined solitude of his cell, he must have grappled with the weight of anticipation, knowing that there was no escape from the destiny he had forged through his crimes.

Confessions and Revelations: The Dying Man's Secrets

In the shadowy realm of death row, where the spectre of execution looms ever larger, some inmates facing imminent death are compelled to make confessions or reveal long-held secrets. This phenomenon is not uncommon, as the weight of impending mortality often prompts a profound period of reckoning, reflection, and the search for catharsis.

1. Seeking Redemption and Closure

As the days on death row tick away, inmates may experience a deep-seated desire for redemption and closure. They grapple with the enormity of their actions, the harm they've caused to others, and the moral burden they carry. In this introspective state, they may choose to unburden their souls by confessing to crimes or revealing hidden truths.

2. The Easing of Conscience

For some, the prospect of execution is a catalyst for addressing long-suppressed guilt and remorse. The weight of their past transgressions can become unbearable, and the desire to find some semblance of peace before facing death drives them to disclose secrets they had vowed to take to their graves.

3. Leaving a Legacy or Providing Answers

Inmates on death row may also be motivated by the desire to leave a legacy or provide answers to unresolved mysteries. They may hold critical information about unsolved crimes or the whereabouts of missing persons. By divulging this information, they hope to offer closure to victims' families or to aid law enforcement in solving cold cases.

4. Facing the Inevitable

As execution day draws nearer, the stark reality of impending death becomes inescapable. This existential confrontation with mortality can prompt inmates to confront their past deeds and seek a form of catharsis. Whether driven by religious beliefs, a desire for atonement, or a final act of contrition, these confessions and revelations are often a last-ditch effort to find meaning or solace in the face of death.

A Complex Tapestry of Motivations

Confessions and revelations on death row are a testament to the complexity of the human psyche in the most dire of circumstances. They reflect the enduring human quest for redemption, the burden of guilt, and the innate desire to leave one's mark on the world, even in the final moments of life. These acts, made in the shadow of the gallows, shed light on the profound depths of the human experience in the face of mortality.

Last-Minute Confessions: Hints of Hidden Truths

In the waning moments of his life, Peter Manuel, the notorious Scottish serial killer, left a legacy shrouded in cryptic statements and suggestions. As the date of his execution inexorably approached, Manuel's actions and words hinted at a labyrinth of undisclosed information related to his heinous crimes. These last-minute confessions, or perhaps more accurately described as tantalizing hints of hidden truths, added a layer of complexity to an already chilling narrative.

1. The Veil of Cryptic Statements

In the final chapters of his life, Peter Manuel seemed to revel in a sinister form of psychological gamesmanship. His statements often danced on the edge of revelation but remained frustratingly vague. It was as if he relished the power of holding critical information just out of reach, tantalizing those who sought answers.

2. The Allure of Unresolved Mysteries

Manuel's cryptic hints ignited a fervour of speculation among investigators, journalists, and the public. What secrets did he carry to the grave? Were there additional victims, undiscovered crime scenes, or potential accomplices yet to be identified? The allure of unresolved mysteries fuelled a quest for answers that extended long after his execution.

3. The Legacy of Fear

The shadow of Peter Manuel's crimes had cast a long and chilling legacy of fear over Scotland. His last-minute confessions, or rather enigmatic suggestions, added a new layer to this legacy. Communities that had once lived in dread of his violence now grappled with the uncertainty of what secrets he had taken to the grave.

4. The Quest for Closure

For the families of Manuel's victims and for law enforcement, the cryptic hints presented both a tantalizing opportunity and a frustrating enigma. They yearned for closure and answers to the lingering questions surrounding his crimes. Yet, Manuel's deliberate elusiveness seemed to deny them this catharsis.

The Unresolved Legacy

In the annals of criminal history, Peter Manuel's last-minute confessions, veiled in cryptic statements and tantalizing hints, remain an enigmatic and unsettling chapter. They serve as a stark reminder that even in death, some individuals wield the power to perpetuate fear, curiosity, and uncertainty. Manuel's legacy, defined by the chilling mysteries he carried to his grave, continues to haunt those who seek to unravel the depths of his malevolence.

Unresolved Mysteries: Lingering Questions

The cryptic hints and suggestions made by Manuel in his final days on death row left investigators and the public with lingering questions. What did he know that he had not revealed during his trial? Were there undiscovered victims or accomplices who had escaped justice?

The unsolved mysteries surrounding Manuel's case added to the enigma of his persona. Even in his final moments, he retained the power to intrigue and confound those who sought to understand the full extent of his malevolence.

The Impact on Victims' Families: Seeking Closure

Any confessions or revelations made by Manuel in his final days had a profound impact on the families of his victims. They faced the difficult task of reconciling the newfound information with the painful memories of their loved ones' murders. Closure, while elusive, remained a deeply held hope for many.

The impact on victims' families was profound and varied. Some found solace in the possibility of answers and closure, while others grappled with the reopening of old wounds. The emotional toll of Manuel's revelations extended beyond his own fate, reaching into the lives of those who had been forever scarred by his crimes.

The Final Chapter

Life on death row marked the concluding chapter in the life of Peter Manuel. It was a time of solitude, reflection, and, for some, a quest for redemption. While his impending execution was a stark reminder of the consequences of his crimes, it also raised questions about the true extent of his malevolence and the secrets he may have taken to the grave.

As we conclude our exploration of Peter Manuel's life on death row, we are reminded that this phase of his existence was defined by the inexorable approach of the gallows. The revelations and confessions made in his final days serve as a testament to the complex interplay of guilt, remorse, and the search for closure in the face of unfathomable darkness. The mysteries that linger around his case are a haunting reminder that some questions may never be fully answered, even in the final moments of a man condemned to die.

Chapter 11

The Execution

The Day of Reckoning: Narrate the events leading up to Manuel's execution.

The morning of July 11, 1958, dawned with an air of sombre anticipation at Barlinnie Prison in Glasgow. It was the day of reckoning for Peter Manuel, the infamous serial killer whose reign of terror had terrorized Scotland. The events leading up to Manuel's execution were a culmination of legal proceedings, public sentiment, and moral questions about the death penalty.

The Imposition of the Death Penalty: A Controversial Verdict

The decision to impose the death penalty upon Peter Manuel marked a pivotal moment in the aftermath of his trial, triggering a myriad of reactions and emotions that highlighted the complexity and polarization surrounding this ultimate form of punishment.

1. Justice Served or Ethical Quandary?

The verdict to execute Peter Manuel was, for many, a stark affirmation of justice served. Given the horrific nature of his crimes, which included multiple murders, sexual assaults, and robberies committed in a premeditated and brutal manner, there was a strong argument that such a penalty was necessary to hold him accountable.

2. Closure for Victims' Families

For the families of Manuel's victims, the imposition of the death penalty offered a semblance of closure. Their loved ones had suffered terribly, and the death sentence provided a sense that the man responsible would face a punishment commensurate with his crimes. It was a relief for many to know that Manuel would never have the opportunity to harm anyone again.

3. Deterrence and Public Safety

Supporters of the death penalty often argue that it serves as a deterrent against heinous crimes and protects society from dangerous individuals. In Manuel's case, proponents believed that executing him would send a clear message that such acts of violence would not be tolerated.

4. Ethical and Moral Concerns

However, the imposition of the death penalty is not without its ethical and moral concerns. Opponents of capital punishment argue that state-sanctioned execution is morally indefensible, regardless of the severity of the crime. They believe that society should not respond to violence with more violence, and that the death penalty risks the irrevocable miscarriage of justice.

5. A National Debate

Manuel's case ignited a nationwide debate about the death penalty in Scotland. It raised profound questions about the ethics, morality, and efficacy of capital punishment. The discussion extended beyond the specifics of his crimes to the broader issue of whether the state should have the authority to take a life as a form of punishment.

6. The Global Perspective

Internationally, the controversy surrounding Manuel's death sentence mirrored ongoing debates about the death penalty in other countries. It underscored the differing views and approaches to this issue across the world, reflecting the diverse range of cultural, social, and ethical considerations.

A Polarizing Decision

The imposition of the death penalty upon Peter Manuel was a decision that drew a clear line between those who believed it was a just and necessary punishment for his heinous crimes and those who were deeply troubled by the concept of state-sanctioned execution. It was a verdict that encapsulated the enduring debate over the death penalty—an issue that continues to spark impassioned discussions about justice, morality, and the role of the state in matters of life and death.

Legal Appeals and Delays: The Prolonged Battle for Peter Manuel's Life

In the wake of Peter Manuel's death sentence, a protracted legal battle ensued as his defence team launched a series of appeals and challenges aimed at delaying and, ideally, overturning the verdict. These efforts introduced a layer of complexity to Manuel's case, sparking debates about due process, safeguards against wrongful executions, and the broader ethical considerations surrounding the death penalty.

1. Mental Health Concerns

One avenue of appeal explored by Manuel's defence was the assertion of mental health concerns. They argued that Manuel's alleged mental instability, which had formed a central pillar of his defence during the trial, should be further evaluated. This appeal was based on the contention that executing someone with severe mental illness constituted a moral and legal quandary.

2. Admissibility of Evidence

Manuel's legal team also scrutinized the admissibility of evidence presented during the trial. They sought to identify potential procedural errors, issues related to the collection and handling of evidence, or any irregularities that might cast doubt on the integrity of the verdict.

3. Public Attention and Debate

The legal appeals and delays kept Manuel's case in the public eye, fuelling an ongoing debate about the ethics and morality of capital punishment. Supporters of the death penalty argued that the appeals were attempts to circumvent justice, while opponents saw them as vital safeguards against potential miscarriages of justice.

4. The Burden of Proving Guilt Beyond Doubt

One of the key principles in the criminal justice system is that guilt must be proven beyond a reasonable doubt. Appeals, even in death penalty cases, are part of the process to ensure that this standard is met. While some saw these legal manoeuvres as prolonging Manuel's life, others viewed them as essential to uphold the principles of justice.

5. Complex Legal Proceedings

The legal appeals and delays introduced complexity into Manuel's case. They showcased the intricacies of the legal system and the robustness of due process, even for individuals facing the gravest of penalties. The ongoing legal wrangling highlighted the need for a thorough and meticulous review of all aspects of a death penalty case.

Conclusion: The Ongoing Battle

The legal appeals and delays in Peter Manuel's case underscored the nuanced and contentious nature of capital punishment. They revealed the complexities of balancing justice, the rights of the accused, and the need to ensure that no one faces the ultimate penalty without exhaustive legal scrutiny. The case continued to provoke discussions about the death penalty's role in society, its moral implications, and the legal mechanisms in place to address potential injustices.

The Final Verdict and the Grim Preparations

In the case of Peter Manuel, the culmination of a series of legal proceedings meant that his death sentence was upheld. The journey from the initial verdict to the execution was marked by legal appeals, delays, and a sense of anticipation that hung heavily over all involved parties.

1. Legal Appeals and the Prolonged Wait

The upholding of Peter Manuel's death sentence came after an arduous legal battle, with appeals launched by his defence team on various grounds. These appeals, while contributing to the postponement of the execution, did little to alleviate the inevitable outcome. Instead, they introduced a prolonged period of uncertainty and anticipation.

2. The Anticipation of Execution

As the final verdict was handed down and the execution date drew nearer, the anticipation within the prison and among the prison staff, legal personnel, and even the public reached a fever pitch. The notion that a man's life was drawing to an end, that the ultimate punishment was to be administered, cast a heavy cloud over the proceedings.

3. The Meticulous Preparations

The logistics of carrying out a death sentence were a grim and meticulously orchestrated process. Manuel was moved to a specific cell designed for the purpose of execution. This cell was often situated near the gallows or the site of the execution, ensuring a streamlined transition when the time came.

4. Psychological Toll on Manuel and Those Involved

For Peter Manuel, the knowledge that his execution was imminent must have been a tormenting psychological ordeal. The countdown to the gallows, the inevitability of his fate, and the isolation of death row added to the psychological toll he endured.

Similarly, the prison staff involved in the execution process faced their own psychological challenges. Carrying out a death sentence, regardless of the individual's crimes, is a deeply sombre and emotionally taxing task.

5. Public Interest and Controversy

Peter Manuel's case had captured the public's attention, and as the execution preparations intensified, it reignited the debate about the death penalty. The moral and ethical implications of state-sanctioned execution were subjects of intense public scrutiny.

Conclusion: The Inevitable Outcome

The final verdict in Peter Manuel's case marked the beginning of the end. The preparations for his execution were a sombre reminder of the profound gravity of the death penalty, a punishment that seeks to balance the scales of justice but is never devoid of controversy and moral ambiguity. Manuel's impending execution would not only close a chapter in the annals of Scottish criminal history but also continue to provoke discussion about the role of capital punishment in society.

The Final Hours: A Sombre Atmosphere

The last hours leading up to Peter Manuel's execution were shrouded in an atmosphere of solemnity and anticipation. They were characterized by a series of poignant moments and a palpable sense of finality that permeated the prison environment.

1. Spiritual Guidance and Confession

During this time, Manuel was granted the opportunity to meet with a prison chaplain, a spiritual advisor who would provide him with guidance, offer solace, and facilitate the sacrament of confession. This meeting was a significant aspect of the process, allowing Manuel to seek spiritual reassurance and possibly make final confessions regarding his crimes.

2. Manuel's Mental State

The state of Peter Manuel's mind during these final hours is a subject of speculation and intrigue. He had previously made cryptic statements and hints that alluded to undisclosed information related to his crimes. Whether he chose to reveal more details or maintain a stoic silence in these concluding moments remains a mystery.

3. Heightened Tension

The prison environment during this period was one of heightened tension. The staff and officials involved in the execution were acutely aware of the emotionally charged task they were about to undertake. The presence of the gallows, a stark and ominous structure, served as a constant reminder of the gravity of the situation.

4. The Weight of Responsibility

For those responsible for carrying out the execution, the weight of their duty must have been almost unbearable. While it was their professional obligation, the moral and ethical implications of ending a human life could not be overlooked. The execution team would have undergone extensive training and preparation, but the emotional toll of the task remained.

5. Reflection and Contemplation

In the final hours, it's likely that both Manuel and those involved in the execution would have engaged in profound moments of reflection and contemplation. For Manuel, it might have been a time to grapple with the enormity of his crimes and confront the imminent end of his life. For the prison staff, it was an opportunity to reflect on the justice system and their role within it.

Conclusion: The Weight of Finality

The last hours leading up to Peter Manuel's execution were marked by a complex interplay of emotions—remorse, dread, solemnity, and reflection. It was a time when the gravity of the death penalty, the culmination of a long legal journey, and the complexities of the human psyche all converged in a sombre and contemplative atmosphere.

The Final Moments: A Grim Conclusion

The day of Peter Manuel's execution marked a chilling and sombre conclusion to a chapter in Scotland's history that had been defined by fear, crime, and the pursuit of justice. As he was led to the gallows, Manuel's final moments were a stark reminder of the irreversible nature of the death penalty.

The Execution Process

In the execution chamber, the apparatus for hanging had been meticulously prepared. Manuel, a man who had once instilled fear in the hearts of many, now stood at the precipice of his own demise. The noose was placed around his neck, and the lever was pulled. This solemn and harrowing act led to his death by hanging—a punishment that he had ultimately received as a consequence of his heinous crimes.

The Weight of Finality

The execution of Peter Manuel was a moment of undeniable finality. It marked the end of a legal saga that had spanned years, from his reign of terror to his capture, trial, and the subsequent appeals. It was a chapter in Scotland's history that had kept the nation in its grip, and Manuel's execution brought it to a solemn close.

Reflections on Justice: The Moral and Ethical Questions

The execution of Peter Manuel, though legal within the framework of its time, reignited profound moral and ethical questions about the death penalty. This form of punishment, in which the state actively takes a human life, has been a subject of enduring debate and scrutiny.

Albert Pierrepoint: The Hangman

Albert Pierrepoint, a name closely associated with Manuel's execution, was a British executioner with a notorious and controversial career. He was responsible for carrying out hundreds of executions, including those of war criminals after World War II. Pierrepoint had become well-known for his professionalism and efficiency in a grim profession.

The Ethical Dilemma

The case of Peter Manuel, like many others in the history of the death penalty, underscores the ethical dilemma surrounding state-sanctioned execution. Advocates argue that it serves as a deterrent to heinous crimes and provides a sense of retribution for victims' families. Critics, however, raise several compelling moral and ethical objections:

1. Risk of Wrongful Execution: One of the most significant concerns is the risk of executing innocent individuals. The fallibility of the justice system means that mistakes can occur, and there have been cases of individuals exonerated posthumously.

2. Cruel and Inhumane: Critics argue that the death penalty constitutes cruel and unusual punishment, especially given the potential for botched executions. The use of the electric chair, gas chamber, or hanging, as in Manuel's case, raises questions about the humanity of the process.

3. Lack of Deterrence: The argument that the death penalty deters crime is fiercely debated. Some studies suggest that it may not be a significant deterrent, and alternatives such as life imprisonment without parole are equally effective at protecting society.

4. Moral and Ethical Values: It challenges societies to confront their moral and ethical values. The deliberate taking of a human life, even in the name of justice, forces individuals and communities to grapple with complex questions about the value of human life and the role of the state in deciding who lives and who dies.

The Enduring Debate

The execution of Peter Manuel, carried out by Albert Pierrepoint, serves as a stark reminder of the moral and ethical questions surrounding the death penalty. It forces us to examine our values, question the efficacy of this form of punishment, and confront the potential for irreversible errors in a system that seeks to deliver justice through the ultimate act of taking a life. The debate over the death penalty continues to be a significant and divisive issue in modern society.1. Retribution and Closure

Supporters of the death penalty argue that it serves as a form of retribution, a means of ensuring that those who commit heinous crimes pay the ultimate price for their actions. In Manuel's case, the death penalty was viewed by many as a form of closure for the victims' families and a way of delivering justice.

2. Deterrence and Public Safety

Another argument in favour of the death penalty is its potential deterrent effect on future criminals. Proponents contend that the fear of execution may dissuade individuals from committing serious crimes, thereby enhancing public safety. The removal of a dangerous criminal from society is also seen as a preventive measure.

3. Moral and Ethical Concerns

Conversely, opponents of the death penalty raise a host of moral and ethical concerns. They argue that the state should not engage in the deliberate taking of a human life, regardless of the circumstances. The risk of wrongful convictions and the potential for human error in the justice system are cited as compelling reasons to abolish capital punishment.

4. The Possibility of Wrongful Executions

The case of Peter Manuel, with its legal appeals and delays, highlights the very real possibility of wrongful executions. In a justice system prone to errors, the irreversible nature of the death penalty poses a significant ethical dilemma. The exoneration of individuals who had been sentenced to death underscores the fallibility of capital punishment.

5. Evolving Moral Standards

Moral and ethical standards surrounding the death penalty have evolved over time. While it was once a widely accepted form of punishment, there has been a global trend toward its abolition. Many countries have abolished the death penalty altogether, viewing it as a relic of a less enlightened era.

6. The Ongoing Debate

The execution of Peter Manuel serves as a microcosm of the larger debate about the death penalty. It raises enduring questions about justice, ethics, and the role of the state in determining the fate of its citizens. The moral and ethical complexities of capital punishment continue to be a source of contention and reflection in society.

The End of an Era

The execution of Peter Manuel marked the end of an era in Scotland's criminal justice history. It was a moment defined by legal finality and moral uncertainty. While Manuel's crimes were met with the ultimate punishment, the ethical questions raised by the death penalty endure, serving as a lasting reminder of the complexities of justice in the face of unspeakable evil. As we reflect on this chapter in the life of Peter Manuel, we are compelled to grapple with the enduring moral and ethical questions that surround the death penalty—a form of punishment that continues to challenge societies around the world. The execution of Manuel underscores the profound and enduring ethical dilemmas associated with capital punishment, leaving us with several key takeaways:

1. The Irreversible Nature of the Death Penalty

One of the central ethical concerns surrounding the death penalty is its irreversibility. Once a person is executed, there is no recourse for a miscarriage of justice. The possibility of wrongful convictions, as highlighted by cases of exonerations in various countries, underscores the moral imperative to exercise extreme caution when imposing the ultimate penalty.

2. The Complexity of Closure and Retribution

While the death penalty is often seen as a means of achieving closure and retribution for victims' families, it does not necessarily provide the solace or justice that is expected. The emotional toll of executions on all parties involved—victims' families, prison staff, and society at large—is a matter of significant ethical concern.

3. Evolving Moral Standards

Moral and ethical standards related to the death penalty have evolved over time. As societies progress, there is a growing recognition of the inherent value of every human life and a shift toward more humane forms of punishment. The global trend toward abolition reflects changing attitudes about the death penalty.

4. The Ongoing Debate

The debate surrounding the death penalty is far from settled. It remains a divisive issue, with proponents and opponents presenting compelling arguments based on justice, deterrence, morality, and human rights. Public opinion varies widely, and the conversation continues to evolve as new information and perspectives emerge.

5. The Imperative for Transparency and Due Process

The ethical concerns associated with the death penalty underscore the importance of transparency, due process, and rigorous legal safeguards in capital cases. Ensuring that the justice system operates fairly and that defendants receive proper legal representation is essential to mitigating the risk of wrongful executions.

6. A Call for Reflection and Reform

The execution of Peter Manuel serves as a call for society to reflect on its approach to capital punishment. It prompts us to consider whether the death penalty aligns with our evolving moral and ethical values and whether there are more just and humane alternatives to addressing the most serious crimes.

A Complex and Enduring Ethical Dilemma

The execution of Peter Manuel represents a pivotal moment in the history of the death penalty. It encapsulates the complex and enduring ethical dilemmas associated with this form of punishment. While Manuel's crimes were met with the ultimate penalty, the moral questions raised by the death penalty persist, challenging us to examine our values, our justice systems, and our commitment to the principles of human dignity and justice. As we navigate the complexities of this ethical landscape, we are reminded that the debate over the death penalty is far from over, and the search for more just and humane solutions continues.

Chapter 12

The Hanging of Peter Manuel

1. The Peter Manuel Case: A Reign of Terror

Peter Manuel's case remains etched in Scotland's history as one of the most chilling episodes of serial murder. Born on March 13, 1927, in New York, USA, Manuel's family moved to Scotland when he was an infant. His early years seemed unremarkable, but beneath the facade of a seemingly normal life, a sinister transformation was taking place.

As Manuel grew older, he displayed disturbing signs of deviant behaviour. Petty thefts and break-ins escalated into violent assaults and, ultimately, a horrifying murder spree. Beginning in 1956, Manuel embarked on a relentless campaign of terror, committing multiple homicides in and around Glasgow. His modus operandi was brutal; he often gained access to victims' homes, where he subjected them to torture, sexual assault, and murder.

The sheer audacity and brutality of Manuel's crimes sent shockwaves through the community and left residents living in fear. The authorities launched an intense manhunt, and the nation's attention became fixated on capturing the man responsible for these heinous acts.

2. The Day of Execution: July 11, 1958

The morning of July 11, 1958, was marked by an air of solemnity and anticipation as the nation awaited the execution of Peter Manuel. The preparations for this grim event had been meticulously arranged, with Albert Pierrepoint, the experienced British executioner, entrusted with the task.

A Precise Process: The Executioner's Craft

Albert Pierrepoint was renowned for his precision and professionalism in carrying out executions. His role in the execution process was defined by strict protocols and a commitment to ensuring that the sentence of the court was carried out swiftly and accurately.

The Journey to the Gallows

The day began with the solemn procession of Peter Manuel to the gallows. He was escorted to the execution chamber, a place that represented the culmination of his reign of terror and the impending finality of his life. The atmosphere in Barlinnie Prison in Glasgow was heavy with the knowledge that this was a day of reckoning.

The Final Moments: An Irreversible Act

As Peter Manuel stood on the gallows, his fate was sealed. Albert Pierrepoint, with the same professionalism that had characterized his entire career, placed the noose around Manuel's neck. The lever was pulled, and the execution was carried out with the precision that had become Pierrepoint's trademark. In those final moments, the nation bore witness to the irrevocable act of capital punishment.

As he awaited the noose to be placed around his neck, the convicted murderer reportedly uttered some final words that have been the subject of speculation and fascination for those who have studied his case. While there is no definitive record of his exact last words, several accounts and rumours have circulated over the years.

It's important to note that in the case of an execution, the atmosphere is solemn and intense, and the condemned person often faces a range of emotions. Some choose to maintain their composure, while others may use the moment to make a final statement or express remorse. In the case of Peter Manuel, several versions of his last words have been reported:

"Turn up the radio, and I'll go quietly." This is one of the most widely circulated accounts of Manuel's last words. It suggests that he asked for a distraction, perhaps hoping to drown out the sounds of the execution.

"Tell them I'm still laughing." Another reported version of Manuel's final statement, this phrase conveys a chilling and enigmatic message. It suggests a sense of defiance and a refusal to show remorse or fear in his final moments.

"I'll be back." Some sources claim that Manuel, known for his arrogance and self-confidence, made this cryptic statement just before the execution, implying a belief in some form of return or reincarnation.

Silence: It's also possible that Manuel chose not to speak any final words and instead faced his fate in silence. This would be in line with the stoic demeanour he maintained throughout his trial and incarceration.

The exact words spoken by Peter Manuel in his final moments remain a subject of debate and uncertainty. Given the sensational nature of his crimes and his notoriety, his execution attracted significant attention from the public and the media. Consequently, various accounts and rumours have emerged over the years, making it difficult to verify the accuracy of any one statement.

Regardless of his last words, Peter Manuel's execution marked the end of a dark chapter in Scottish criminal history. His crimes and the mystery surrounding his final moments continue to captivate the public's imagination and fuel discussions about the nature of evil, justice, and the human psyche.

The End of an Era: Reflections on Justice

The execution of Peter Manuel marked the end of an era, both for the serial killer himself and for the practice of capital punishment in the United Kingdom. It was a day that forced society to confront the complexities of justice, morality, and the value of every human life.

A Chilling Epilogue

The hanging of Peter Manuel serves as a chilling epilogue to a reign of terror that had gripped Scotland. It was a day that brought a sense of closure to the victims' families and a conclusion to a man's life defined by violence and malevolence. The precision and professionalism of executioners like Albert Pierrepoint are a haunting reminder of the moral and ethical questions that surround the practice of capital punishment— a practice that continues to be debated and examined by societies worldwide.

Chapter 13

The Enigma of Peter Manuel

The story of Peter Manuel, the notorious serial killer who terrorized Scotland in the 1950s, is one that continues to captivate the imaginations of true crime enthusiasts, psychologists, and criminologists alike. Beyond the chilling details of his crimes and the drama of his trial and execution, Manuel remains an enigmatic figure—a complex puzzle that raises profound questions about the nature of evil, psychopathy, and the human capacity for violence. In this chapter, we delve into the enigma of Peter Manuel, seeking to understand the factors that led him down the path of darkness and examining the enduring fascination with his crimes.

The Making of a Monster: Nature vs. Nurture

One of the central mysteries surrounding Peter Manuel is the question of what made him into a serial killer. Was he born with a predisposition for violence, or were external factors responsible for shaping his malevolent path?

Psychopathy and Nature

Peter Manuel's psychopathic tendencies have been widely studied and discussed. Psychopathy is a complex personality disorder characterized by a lack of empathy, superficial charm, manipulative behaviour, and a propensity for violence. Research suggests that there is a genetic component to psychopathy, meaning that some individuals may be biologically predisposed to exhibit psychopathic traits.

Manuel displayed several classic psychopathic traits from a young age, including a capacity for deception, a lack of remorse, and a willingness to inflict harm on others. These traits likely had a genetic basis, setting the stage for his later descent into violence.

Nurture and Environmental Factors

While genetics may have contributed to Manuel's psychopathy, environmental factors also played a crucial role in shaping his criminal development. His upbringing in a working-class immigrant family, marked by poverty and a lack of emotional connection, may have created an environment conducive to the erosion of moral boundaries.

The alienation he felt as a Spanish immigrant in a predominantly Scottish community may have intensified his sense of otherness and detachment from societal norms. The absence of emotional nurturance in his formative years could have further fuelled his psychopathic tendencies.

The Interplay of Nature and Nurture

The case of Peter Manuel illustrates the complex interplay between nature and nurture in the making of a serial killer. While his genetic predisposition may have laid the foundation for psychopathy, it was the environmental factors, including his troubled upbringing and sense of alienation, that likely pushed him over the edge into violence.

Understanding this interplay is crucial for our broader comprehension of criminal behaviour and the factors that contribute to the emergence of individuals like Peter Manuel.

The Charmer and the Predator

One of the most unsettling aspects of Peter Manuel's persona was his ability to charm and manipulate his victims and those around him. This duality—the charming exterior concealing a remorseless predator—adds to the enigma of his character.

The Charmer

Peter Manuel possessed an innate charisma that allowed him to win the trust and confidence of those he encountered. Friends, neighbours, and even law enforcement personnel who interacted with him during the investigation often described him as polite, friendly, and even charismatic.

This charm offensive was a crucial tool in his predatory arsenal. It enabled him to disarm potential victims, lulling them into a false sense of security before revealing his true, malevolent intentions.

The Predator

Beneath the charming facade lay a predator capable of unspeakable cruelty. Manuel's willingness to inflict pain, commit sexual violence, and ruthlessly end lives revealed a chilling disregard for the sanctity of human existence.

This duality—charming and manipulative on the one hand, sadistic and remorseless on the other—makes Peter Manuel a case study in the complexity of criminal psychology.

The Enduring Fascination

Decades after his execution, Peter Manuel's name continues to evoke fascination and morbid curiosity. The enduring appeal of his story can be attributed to several factors:

Psychological Intrigue

Psychologists and criminologists are drawn to Manuel's case because it provides a window into the mind of a psychopath. His ability to compartmentalize his actions, feign normalcy, and manipulate those around him raises questions about the nature of psychopathy and the psychology of serial killers.

Unresolved Mysteries

Despite Manuel's conviction and execution, some aspects of his crimes remain shrouded in mystery. Not all of his victims were definitively linked to him, leaving room for speculation about the extent of his violence. The motives behind some of his murders also remain enigmatic.

The Impact on Scottish Society

Peter Manuel's reign of terror left an indelible mark on Scottish society. The trauma inflicted on the communities he targeted and the collective fear that gripped the nation left scars that endure to this day. His case has become a part of Scotland's true crime lore, a cautionary tale that serves as a reminder of the capacity for evil that can lurk within seemingly ordinary individuals.

Legal and Ethical Questions

The trial and execution of Peter Manuel raised profound legal and ethical questions. The debate over the death penalty, the use of the insanity defence, and the limits of criminal responsibility continue to resonate in contemporary discussions of criminal justice.

Conclusion: A Chilling Enigma

The story of Peter Manuel is a chilling enigma, a complex narrative that challenges our understanding of human nature, criminal behaviour, and the capacity for evil. As we continue to explore the enduring fascination with his crimes, we will also confront the unresolved mysteries that continue to surround his case. Peter Manuel's legacy is not merely one of terror but also a testament to the enduring quest for answers in the face of unfathomable darkness.

Chapter 14

The Legacy of Peter Manuel

The story of Peter Manuel, the infamous Scottish serial killer, does not conclude with his execution in 1958. Instead, it reverberates through time, leaving a lasting legacy that touches on various aspects of society, criminology, and culture. In this chapter, we will delve into the enduring legacy of Peter Manuel, exploring the impact of his crimes on the criminal justice system, popular culture, and the broader societal consciousness.

1. Criminal Profiling and Serial Killers

Peter Manuel's case played a pivotal role in the development of criminal profiling, a technique used by law enforcement to identify and apprehend criminals based on behavioural patterns and psychological traits. Manuel's ability to evade capture and his cunning manipulation of victims and authorities forced investigators to reassess their methods.

The Birth of Criminal Profiling

In the midst of the manhunt for Manuel, detectives sought the expertise of forensic psychiatrist Dr. David Abbot. Dr. Abbot's work on the case contributed to the emerging field of criminal profiling, helping law enforcement better understand the psychological motivations and patterns of serial killers.

Serial Killers in Popular Culture

The fascination with serial killers, exemplified by cases like Peter Manuel's, has permeated popular culture. Books, movies, and television series often draw inspiration from real-life serial killers, shaping public perceptions and sparking discussions about the psychology of criminal behaviour.

2. The Insanity Defence and Mental Health

Manuel's trial raised significant questions about the insanity defence and the intersection of mental health and criminal responsibility.

The Debate over Mental Illness

Manuel's defence team argued that he was not in control of his actions due to severe mental illness, a claim that stirred debate about the role of mental health in criminal cases. The trial highlighted the complexities of assessing an individual's mental state at the time of the crime and the challenges of balancing justice and mental health treatment.

Reforms in the Legal System

In the wake of Manuel's trial, there were discussions about potential reforms in the legal system, particularly regarding the use of the insanity defence. The case prompted a re-evaluation of how the legal system should handle defendants with mental health issues, a topic that remains relevant in modern criminal justice discourse.

3. The Death Penalty Debate

Peter Manuel's death sentence reignited the debate over capital punishment in Scotland and the United Kingdom. The ethical and moral questions surrounding the death penalty were brought to the forefront of public consciousness.

Abolition Movements

Manuel's execution was part of a broader context of declining support for the death penalty in the UK. His case, along with others, contributed to the eventual abolition of the death penalty for murder in the United Kingdom in 1965.

Continued Debate

While the death penalty is no longer in practice in the UK, the ethical debate persists in many countries worldwide. Peter Manuel's case serves as a historical marker in this ongoing conversation about the ultimate punishment.

4. True Crime and Public Fascination

The enduring fascination with true crime, exemplified by cases like Peter Manuel's, has grown exponentially in the modern era. Television documentaries, podcasts, and books dedicated to true crime stories attract a dedicated and ever-expanding audience.

Exploring the Dark Side

The allure of true crime lies in its exploration of the darkest aspects of human behaviour. Audiences are drawn to the mysteries, the psychology of criminals, and the intricacies of investigations.

Ethical Questions

However, the fascination with true crime also raises ethical questions about the glorification of criminals and the impact on victims' families. It underscores society's complex relationship with crime narratives.

5. Victim Advocacy and Support

The legacy of Peter Manuel extends to the realm of victim advocacy and support. The traumatic impact of his crimes on the victims' families and survivors led to a greater recognition of the need for victim-centred approaches in the criminal justice system.

The Emergence of Victim Support Services

In the aftermath of Manuel's reign of terror, support services for victims and their families began to emerge. These organizations provided counselling, legal guidance, and emotional support to those affected by crime.

Policy Changes

Manuel's case also prompted policy changes aimed at better addressing the needs of victims within the criminal justice system. These changes sought to ensure that victims were not retraumatized during legal proceedings and that their voices were heard.

A Complex Legacy

The legacy of Peter Manuel is a complex one, encompassing a wide range of societal, legal, and cultural impacts. His case continues to be studied by criminologists, legal scholars, and psychologists, offering insights into the nature of psychopathy, criminal profiling, and the complexities of criminal justice.

Moreover, the enduring fascination with true crime and the ethical questions it raises remind us of society's enduring interest in the darkest aspects of human behaviour. Peter Manuel's crimes, trial, and execution have left an indelible mark on Scotland's history and the broader conversation about crime and justice.

As we conclude our exploration of the legacy of Peter Manuel, we reflect on the enduring questions raised by his case, the ongoing debates it has ignited, and the profound impact it has had on the lives of those touched by his reign of terror. Peter Manuel's story is not just a chapter in history; it is a reflection of the enduring complexity of the human experience.

Chapter 15

Unsolved Mysteries and Lingering Questions

The tale of Peter Manuel, the notorious serial killer whose reign of terror gripped Scotland in the 1950s, is one marked by horror, intrigue, and profound human tragedy. While the majority of his crimes were meticulously investigated, leading to his conviction and eventual execution, the story of Peter Manuel is far from straightforward. In this chapter, we explore the unsolved mysteries and lingering questions that continue to haunt the legacy of this enigmatic serial killer.

1. Unidentified Victims

One of the most perplexing aspects of Peter Manuel's crimes is the possibility that he may have had unidentified victims. While Manuel was convicted of several murders, some questions persist about additional potential victims who were never conclusively linked to him.

The Disappearance of Anna Watt

One such case is the disappearance of Anna Watt, the sister of one of Manuel's victims, Marion Watt. Anna was reported missing in December 1956, around the same time as her sister's murder. Although her body was never found, there have been speculations that Manuel may have been involved in her disappearance.

Other Unsolved Cases

In addition to Anna Watt, there were other unsolved murders and disappearances in the Lanarkshire region during the time of Manuel's crime spree. Some have suggested that Manuel's modus operandi and geographic proximity to these cases warrant further investigation, raising the possibility of additional victims who remain nameless.

The Murder of Sidney John Dunn:

On December 8, 1957, Sidney John Dunn was tragically murdered on a moorland road in Newcastle, England. He was shot dead, and the case remained unsolved for some time.

While there was suspicion surrounding Peter Manuel's involvement in the murder of Sidney John Dunn, it is crucial to note that he was not convicted or formally charged with this specific murder. Manuel's criminal activities and propensity for violence made him a suspect in various unsolved cases, but the evidence linking him to individual crimes was not always sufficient for prosecution.

In the case of Sidney John Dunn's murder, as with other unsolved cases linked to Manuel, the lack of conclusive evidence may have contributed to the case remaining open and unsolved. Manuel was eventually arrested, tried, and convicted for multiple other murders, leading to his execution in 1958.

The murder of Sidney John Dunn is a tragic part of the broader narrative of Peter Manuel's criminal activities during the 1950s. While Manuel's notoriety as a serial killer is well-documented, some individual cases, like that of Sidney John Dunn, may remain officially unsolved due to the challenges of gathering sufficient evidence and bringing a suspect to justice.

2. Motive and Methodology

The question of motive has always loomed large in the case of Peter Manuel. What drove him to commit such heinous acts, and what was the underlying psychology behind his crimes?

Sadistic Pleasure vs. Financial Gain

Manuel's motives appeared to be a complex mix of sadistic pleasure and financial gain. He often targeted women and families, subjecting them to horrific violence before robbing them. Yet, the extent to which he derived pleasure from their suffering, as opposed to seeing these acts as mere means to an end, remains unclear.

Sexual Motivation

Sexual violence was a recurring theme in Manuel's crimes. However, the true extent of his sexual motivation and whether it was the primary driving force behind his murders is a subject of debate among experts. Some argue that his sexual sadism played a central role, while others contend that his sexual acts were secondary to his desire for power and control.

3. The Accomplice Theory

One enduring mystery is the possibility of an accomplice or accomplices assisting Peter Manuel in his crimes. Some aspects of the murders, such as the apparent absence of struggle from some victims, raised questions about whether Manuel acted alone.

The Sudden Change in MO

During his crime spree, Manuel's modus operandi appeared to shift abruptly. The earlier murders involved more violence and overt sexual acts, while later ones were marked by a greater degree of restraint. Some have speculated that this change in behaviour could be attributed to the involvement of an accomplice who exerted influence over him.

Inconsistencies in Statements

Manuel made various conflicting statements during his interactions with law enforcement, often offering contradictory accounts of his actions and motivations. These inconsistencies have fuelled suspicions that he may have been protecting someone else or concealing the involvement of others in his crimes.

4. The Influence of Mental Illness

The role of mental illness in Peter Manuel's crimes remains a topic of debate and speculation. His defence team argued that he was driven by severe mental illness, while the prosecution contended that he was fully aware of his actions.

The Validity of the Insanity Defence

The success of Manuel's insanity defence raises questions about the validity of such claims in criminal cases. Did Manuel genuinely suffer from a mental illness that rendered him unable to control his actions, or was his behaviour calculated and driven by psychopathy?

The Continuum of Responsibility

The case of Peter Manuel highlights the complexities of criminal responsibility in cases involving mental illness. It raises broader questions about where the line should be drawn between mental illness as a mitigating factor and personal responsibility for one's actions.

5. The Last Confession

In the days leading up to his execution, Peter Manuel reportedly made a cryptic last confession to a prison chaplain. While the details of this confession have remained largely undisclosed, it has fuelled speculation about what Manuel may have revealed about his crimes in his final moments.

The Unanswered Questions

The last confession, shrouded in secrecy, leaves us with a host of unanswered questions. What did Manuel choose to disclose in his final hours, and did he provide any closure to the families of his victims? The content and implications of this confession continue to be a subject of intrigue and mystery.

6. The Ongoing Fascination

The enduring fascination with Peter Manuel's crimes, trial, and legacy is a testament to the enduring allure of true crime stories. His case has been the subject of books, documentaries, and debates, as well as a source of inspiration for writers and filmmakers.

A Complex Tapestry

Peter Manuel's story is a complex tapestry woven from threads of horror, psychology, and mystery. His crimes continue to captivate the imaginations of those who seek to understand the darkest corners of the human psyche and the enduring questions of justice, motive, and responsibility.

The Shadows of the Past

The case of Peter Manuel is a haunting reminder that some mysteries may never be fully unravelled. His crimes, motivations, and potential accomplices remain shrouded in shadows, leaving us with enduring questions that defy easy answers. As we reflect on the enigma of Peter Manuel, we are reminded that some stories are destined to remain cloaked in darkness, forever challenging our understanding of the human capacity for both cruelty and fascination.

Chapter 16

Peter Manuel's Personality, Mental health, Motivations and Behaviour

Personality Traits:

Peter Manuel's personality was marked by a complex interplay of traits, some of which appeared charming and charismatic on the surface, while others were deeply troubling and indicative of antisocial behaviour. Examining these traits provides insight into how he was able to manipulate and gain the trust of potential victims, as well as the darker aspects of his character:

Charm and Charisma: Peter Manuel was often described as charming and charismatic by those who encountered him. This charm served as a façade, allowing him to disarm potential victims and present himself as non-threatening. His ability to engage in casual conversations and put people at ease masked his true intentions.

Manipulation: Beneath the charm, Manuel possessed a remarkable talent for manipulation. He was adept at reading people and identifying their vulnerabilities, which he would then exploit to his advantage. He could convince others to lower their guard, making it easier for him to carry out his criminal acts.

Narcissism: Manuel displayed signs of narcissism, characterized by an excessive focus on himself and a belief in his superiority. His narcissistic traits likely contributed to his audacity in challenging law enforcement and taunting them during the investigation. This inflated self-image fuelled his belief that he could outwit authorities.

Aggression: Alongside his charm and manipulation, Manuel harboured a darker, more aggressive side. This aggression manifested in the brutal and sadistic manner in which he carried out his crimes. He derived satisfaction from exerting control and dominance over his victims, reflecting a deep-seated aggression.

Antisocial Behaviour: Manuel's actions were emblematic of antisocial behaviour, characterized by a disregard for the rights and well-being of others. His willingness to harm and kill without remorse, along with his history of theft and criminal activity, aligns with this trait. He operated outside the boundaries of societal norms.

Deceitfulness: A key component of Manuel's personality was deceitfulness. He would craft elaborate lies and fabricate stories to avoid suspicion and responsibility for his crimes. This deceit extended to his interactions with law enforcement and the justice system during his trials.

Lack of Empathy: Perhaps one of the most disturbing aspects of Manuel's personality was his apparent lack of empathy. He seemed incapable of experiencing genuine remorse for the suffering he inflicted on his victims and their families. This absence of empathy allowed him to continue his reign of terror without hesitation.

Intelligence and Cunning: Manuel possessed a sharp intellect and a cunning nature. He was able to plan and execute his crimes with a level of sophistication that kept him eluding capture for an extended period. This intelligence was, unfortunately, channelled into criminal pursuits.

In summary, Peter Manuel's personality was a complex amalgamation of traits that enabled him to manipulate and deceive those around him. His charming façade, combined with narcissism, aggression, and a lack of empathy, allowed him to gain the trust of unsuspecting victims before revealing his true, sinister nature. These traits, when taken together, paint a portrait of a deeply disturbed individual who posed a significant threat to society.

Psychological Profile:

Peter Manuel's psychological profile is marked by a range of behaviours and characteristics that suggest the presence of personality disorders, notably antisocial personality disorder (ASPD), and traits associated with psychopathy. While he may not have received an official diagnosis during his lifetime, a retrospective analysis of his actions and behaviours provides insights into his psychological makeup.

Antisocial Personality Disorder (ASPD):

ASPD is characterized by a pattern of disregard for the rights of others, impulsivity, manipulation, deceit, and a lack of remorse. Several aspects of Manuel's life and criminal behaviour align with this diagnosis:

Repeated Criminal Behaviour: Manuel's extensive criminal history, including thefts and burglaries, exemplifies a disregard for societal norms and the rights of others.

Lack of Remorse: He displayed a complete absence of remorse for his victims, even taunting law enforcement and their families during his trial.

Impulsivity: Manuel's impulsive nature was evident in his spontaneous acts of violence, often without any apparent provocation.

Manipulation: His ability to charm and manipulate individuals allowed him to gain their trust before betraying it, a hallmark trait of ASPD.

Psychopathy Traits:

Psychopathy is characterized by specific personality traits, including superficial charm, grandiosity, manipulativeness, and a lack of empathy. Manuel exhibited many of these traits:

Superficial Charm: He was often described as charming and charismatic, capable of presenting a likable exterior despite his sinister actions.

Manipulativeness: Manuel's ability to manipulate people, both victims and those in authority, demonstrates a keen understanding of human psychology and a capacity for manipulation.

Grandiosity: His belief in his own superiority, evident in his challenges to law enforcement and the justice system, aligns with a sense of grandiosity.

Lack of Empathy: Perhaps one of the most striking features of his psychological profile was a profound absence of empathy for the suffering he caused.

It's important to note that personality disorders, including ASPD and psychopathy, are complex and multifaceted. They often develop as a result of a combination of genetic, environmental, and neurological factors. While Manuel's psychological profile aligns with these disorders, a comprehensive assessment would require clinical evaluation, which is not possible posthumously.

These potential diagnoses likely played a significant role in Manuel's criminal behaviour, allowing him to rationalize his actions, manipulate others, and commit heinous crimes without experiencing the moral and emotional constraints that typically govern human behaviour. Manuel's psychological profile remains a chilling example of the destructive capacity of certain personality traits when they converge in an individual.

Fascination with Criminals:

Peter Manuel's fascination with other well-known criminals is a notable aspect of his personality and may have contributed to his own criminal aspirations. While it's challenging to pinpoint specific individuals he admired, as he did not leave extensive records or direct statements on this topic, certain elements of his life and behaviour suggest an affinity for notorious criminals. Here are some key points to consider:

Outlaw Image: Manuel often portrayed himself as a renegade and an outlaw. This image aligns with the romanticized view of criminals prevalent in popular culture, where outlaws like Jesse James or Billy the Kid are celebrated figures.

Evasion of Capture: Similar to famous criminals like John Dillinger or Bonnie and Clyde, Manuel took pride in his ability to elude the police and justice system. This may have appealed to his sense of invincibility and desire for notoriety.

Challenges to Authority: Manuel's repeated challenges to law enforcement and the legal system echo the rebellious attitude of certain legendary criminals. It suggests a desire to be seen as an adversary of authority.

Infamy and Media Attention: Manuel craved media attention and manipulated the press to amplify his crimes. Many infamous criminals, such as Ted Bundy or Richard Ramirez, also sought notoriety and revelled in the media's coverage of their deeds.

Emulating Criminal Tactics: Manuel's criminal techniques, such as breaking into homes and stalking victims, share commonalities with tactics used by other criminals. While not necessarily an indicator of admiration, it suggests a familiarity with criminal methods.

Psychological Profile: Manuel's psychopathic traits, including grandiosity and a lack of empathy, may have led him to view himself as a larger-than-life figure, akin to infamous criminals.

While it's challenging to identify specific criminals Manuel admired, his actions and behaviour reflect a broader fascination with the outlaw archetype and a desire for recognition and notoriety. This fascination may have fuelled his criminal aspirations, driving him to commit increasingly audacious and violent acts in pursuit of infamy and the thrill of eluding capture. Manuel's case serves as a chilling reminder of the complex interplay between personality traits, criminal behaviour, and the allure of criminal legends.

Motivations for Crimes:

Peter Manuel's motivations for his crimes were likely multifaceted, influenced by a complex interplay of psychological factors and personal desires. While it's challenging to definitively pinpoint his motivations,

Power and Control: Manuel exhibited a strong desire for power and control over his victims. His crimes often involved acts of dominance, such as sexual assault and murder. This need for control may have been a primary motivator, allowing him to assert his authority and inflict fear upon others.

Sadistic Tendencies: There are indications that Manuel derived sadistic pleasure from the suffering of his victims. This sadism could have been a significant motivating factor in his violent crimes, as he relished the pain and terror he inflicted.

Financial Gain: While Manuel's crimes often involved theft and robbery, financial gain may not have been his primary motivation. Instead, he seemed to prioritize the thrill of the crime and the psychological satisfaction of outsmarting law enforcement.

Psychopathy: Manuel exhibited traits consistent with psychopathy, such as a lack of empathy, shallow emotions, and manipulative behaviour. Psychopaths often commit crimes for personal gratification, disregarding the well-being of others.

Attention and Notoriety: Manuel's obsession with media attention and his manipulation of the press suggest a desire for notoriety. This may have been a motivating factor, driving him to commit increasingly audacious and publicized crimes.

Challenges to Authority: Manuel's repeated confrontations with law enforcement and the legal system indicate a desire to challenge authority figures. This could have motivated him to continue committing crimes to prove his invincibility.

Psychological Gratification: The act of stalking, intimidating, and ultimately killing his victims may have provided Manuel with psychological gratification. The sense of power and superiority he felt during these acts could have been a driving force.

In summary, Peter Manuel's motivations for his crimes likely stemmed from a complex interplay of power, control, sadism, and psychopathic traits. Financial gain may have been a secondary consideration compared to the psychological satisfaction he derived from his actions. His obsession with attention and notoriety, as well as his constant challenges to authority, further underscore the intricate motivations behind his heinous crimes.

Criminal Mindset:

Peter Manuel's criminal mindset was marked by a combination of cunning, premeditation, and manipulation. His strategies for avoiding detection were as calculated as they were chilling. Here's a closer look at his thought processes and criminal evolution:

Premeditation and Target Selection: Manuel's crimes were meticulously planned. He often selected victims who he believed would be vulnerable and less likely to resist or report the crimes. His choices included women walking alone at night or individuals he could easily overpower. This careful target selection demonstrated his ability to assess and exploit weaknesses.

Manipulation and Charisma: Manuel possessed a charm that he used to disarm his victims. He could appear friendly and non-threatening, gaining their trust before revealing his true intentions. This manipulation allowed him to approach potential victims without raising suspicion.

Escalation of Violence: Over time, Manuel's crimes escalated in both violence and brutality. Initially, he committed thefts and burglaries, but as he gained confidence and developed a taste for violence, he transitioned to sexual assault and murder. This escalation suggests a growing sadistic tendency and a desire for more power and control.

Cat-and-Mouse Game with Police: Manuel seemed to relish in taunting the police and playing a cat-and-mouse game with law enforcement. He left cryptic clues and messages, even contacting the media to boast about his crimes. This behaviour reflected his need for attention and a belief in his own invincibility.

Audacity and Public Crimes: Manuel's audacity reached its peak when he committed murders in public places, such as parks and golf courses. These public crimes were not only intended to maximize fear but also to challenge the authorities publicly. He seemed to derive satisfaction from demonstrating his ability to commit crimes with impunity.

Forensic Awareness: Manuel displayed a degree of forensic awareness. He took measures to avoid leaving behind incriminating evidence, which posed challenges for the police and investigators. This awareness likely contributed to his ability to evade capture for a considerable period.

Psychopathic Traits: Manuel exhibited psychopathic traits, including a lack of empathy and remorse. These traits allowed him to rationalize his actions and view his victims as mere objects for his gratification.

In summary, Peter Manuel's criminal mindset was marked by a disturbing blend of premeditation, manipulation, and escalating violence. His ability to carefully select and approach victims, coupled with his audacity and forensic awareness, made him a formidable and elusive criminal. His psychopathic traits further enabled him to rationalize his actions and continue his reign of terror.

Impact of Childhood and Family:

Peter Manuel's upbringing and family background indeed played a significant role in shaping his personality and potentially contributing to his criminal tendencies. Several aspects of his childhood and family dynamics may have influenced his behaviour:

Immigrant Experience: Manuel's family immigrated to Scotland from the United States when he was a child. This immigrant experience could have contributed to feelings of displacement and alienation, as they struggled to fit into a predominantly Scottish community. This sense of being an outsider might have fuelled his desire for attention and recognition.

Troubled Family Life: The Manuel family faced challenges that likely had a profound impact on young Peter. His parents' marriage was tumultuous, marked by frequent arguments and instability. Witnessing this strife could have left emotional scars and a distorted perception of relationships.

Financial Struggles: The family also experienced financial difficulties. The pressure of financial instability can cause emotional distress and potentially lead individuals to seek unconventional means of financial gain, such as criminal activities.

Psychological Vulnerability: There are suggestions that Manuel may have experienced emotional and psychological difficulties during his childhood. Some reports indicate that he exhibited unusual behaviour as a child, such as setting fires, which could be indicative of deeper psychological issues. These vulnerabilities might have made him more susceptible to criminal influences.

Early Criminal Activity: Manuel's involvement in criminal activities during his adolescence, which led to his incarceration in borstals, is a significant factor. His exposure to the criminal justice system at a young age could have hardened his criminal tendencies and introduced him to a network of fellow offenders.

Lack of Parental Guidance: The absence of strong parental guidance may have contributed to Manuel's lack of moral compass. With his parents occupied with their own issues, he may not have received the guidance and structure necessary for healthy emotional and moral development.

In sum, Peter Manuel's upbringing was marked by a combination of factors, including the immigrant experience, family strife, financial difficulties, psychological vulnerabilities, and early exposure to criminal influences. While these factors alone do not explain his criminal behaviour, they likely contributed to shaping his personality and may have created a fertile ground for his later criminal tendencies to emerge and thrive.

Interaction with Law Enforcement:

Peter Manuel's interactions with law enforcement during his criminal activities were marked by a complex interplay of arrogance, manipulation, and a penchant for taunting the police. These interactions offer insight into the psychological aspects of his criminal persona:

Taunting and Arrogance: Manuel exhibited a brazen and arrogant demeanour when dealing with the police. He often taunted investigators, leaving cryptic messages at crime scenes and sending letters that boasted about his crimes. His taunts were calculated to provoke law enforcement and demonstrate his superiority.

Game of Cat and Mouse: Manuel engaged in a dangerous game of cat and mouse with the police. He seemed to relish the challenge of evading capture and outsmarting law enforcement. This behaviour could be indicative of narcissism and a need for constant validation of his intellect and cunning.

Psychological Warfare: Manuel's taunting and cryptic messages can be seen as a form of psychological warfare. By keeping the police on edge and drawing media attention to his crimes, he exerted a level of control and power over the investigation.

Challenging Authority: His interactions with the police also reflected a deep-seated resistance to authority figures. This resistance might have been rooted in a desire for autonomy and a rejection of societal norms and rules.

Psychological Thrill: Manuel appeared to derive a psychological thrill from his interactions with law enforcement. The ongoing cat-and-mouse game likely provided him with a sense of excitement and purpose, further fuelling his criminal behaviour.

Need for Recognition: Manuel's taunts and cryptic messages also suggest a need for recognition and infamy. He wanted to be known as a formidable criminal and sought acknowledgment for his crimes, adding another layer to his complex psychology.

In summary, Manuel's interactions with law enforcement were characterized by a combination of arrogance, manipulation, and a desire for recognition. His behaviour indicated a need for psychological validation, a challenge to authority, and a propensity for psychological gamesmanship that made him a particularly enigmatic and dangerous criminal. These aspects of his personality contributed to the difficulty law enforcement faced in apprehending him.

Chapter 17

Detective Inspector William Muncie

The police officer detective in charge of the Peter Manuel investigation was Detective Inspector William Muncie. He played a pivotal role in pursuing and apprehending Manuel.

It was Detective Inspector Muncie who arrested Peter Manuel on January 2, 1958. Manuel had been acting suspiciously in a Glasgow neighbourhood, which led to his arrest. During the encounter with the police, a firearm was discovered in Manuel's possession, which later became crucial evidence in the case against him. This arrest marked a significant breakthrough in the investigation into Manuel's crimes and eventually led to his trial and conviction.

Detective Inspector William Muncie played a crucial role in the investigation and arrest of Peter Manuel, making him a notable figure in the Peter Manuel case. Here are some additional details and context that you can include in your book:

Background and Experience: Detective Inspector Muncie was an experienced and respected officer within the Lanarkshire Police force. He had worked on numerous criminal cases throughout his career, which prepared him for the complexities of the Manuel investigation.

The Enigmatic Suspect: Muncie was faced with the formidable task of apprehending a highly intelligent and elusive suspect in Peter Manuel. Manuel's ability to blend into the community and his cunning manipulation of evidence presented a unique challenge. Muncie's dedication and determination were evident as he led the pursuit of Manuel.

Coordination of Resources: Muncie recognized the need for a specialized task force to handle the Manuel case effectively. This led to the formation of the "Manuel Squad," comprised of seasoned detectives and investigators who worked tirelessly to unravel the web of darkness that Manuel had cast over the region.

Public Pressure: As the lead investigator, Muncie faced immense public pressure to solve the case. The fear and hysteria that had gripped Glasgow and its surrounding areas during Manuel's reign of terror added to the urgency of his mission.

Trial Testimony: Muncie likely played a significant role as a witness during Manuel's trial, providing insights into the investigation and the challenges faced by law enforcement in capturing the serial killer.

Legacy: Detective Inspector Muncie's role in the Manuel case contributed to his legacy as a dedicated and skilled detective. His successful pursuit and arrest of Peter Manuel demonstrated the commitment of law enforcement to bringing dangerous criminals to justice.

By incorporating these details, you can provide a more comprehensive and nuanced portrayal of Detective Inspector William Muncie's involvement in the Peter Manuel case in your book.

Chapter 18

Samuel and Bridget Manuel

Peter Manuel's parents, Samuel and Bridget Manuel, had their own legal troubles separate from their infamous son. Samuel and Bridget were immigrants from the United States, and their legal issues in Scotland were unrelated to Peter's crimes but were significant in their own right.

1. Samuel Manuel's Court Appearance: Fraudulent Activities

In the early 1950s, Samuel Manuel faced legal troubles related to fraudulent activities. He was accused of various offenses, including theft and fraud, which were unrelated to Peter's later crimes. Samuel's legal issues stemmed from his involvement in a scheme to steal and sell goods through fraudulent means.

His court appearance would have been a significant event within the community, especially considering that his son, Peter, would later become one of Scotland's most notorious criminals. It's worth noting that Samuel's legal issues did not have a direct connection to Peter's actions.

2. Bridget Manuel's Court Appearance: Handling of Stolen Goods

Bridget Manuel, Peter's mother, also had her own legal problems. She faced charges related to the handling of stolen goods, which involved receiving and possessing items that had been stolen. This legal issue was separate from Peter's criminal activities but contributed to the family's troubled reputation.

The court appearances of both Samuel and Bridget Manuel would have undoubtedly attracted attention within their community. These legal troubles added to the family's notoriety, and the Manuel family became associated with criminal activities in the public's perception.

It's important to note that while Peter Manuel's crimes would later eclipse his parents' legal issues, the family's encounters with the law were a part of their complex history in Scotland.

During the trial of Peter Manuel, a dramatic and unusual event unfolded when he cross-examined his own mother, Bridget Manuel, about a police invitation for her to accompany them to prison to hear him allegedly confess to the murders. This event added to the sensational nature of the trial.

Context:

Peter Manuel was conducting his own defence during the trial, a highly unusual and controversial decision. He sought to undermine the credibility of the police and cast doubt on the integrity of the investigation. One of his strategies was to raise questions about the police's treatment of his parents, suggesting that they had been coerced or manipulated into making statements that incriminated him.

The Cross-Examination:

During the trial, Peter Manuel questioned his mother, Bridget Manuel, about the police inviting her to accompany them to prison. He implied that the police had attempted to pressure her into attending the meeting with the intention of extracting a confession from him. The implication was that the police were willing to use a mother's presence to manipulate him into admitting to the murders.

Outcome:

It's essential to note that this event was part of Peter Manuel's overall strategy to cast doubt on the police investigation. While it added a sensational element to the trial, it did not ultimately change the outcome. Peter Manuel was found guilty of multiple murders and sentenced to death, regardless of this dramatic moment in the courtroom.

This incident served as an example of the highly unusual and theatrical nature of the trial, with Peter Manuel conducting his defence and using various tactics to create reasonable doubt. However, the weight of evidence against him, including eyewitness testimonies and forensic evidence, led to his conviction and eventual execution.

Chapter 19

William Watt

The case of William Watt, who was wrongly arrested for the murders of his wife, daughter, and sister-in-law in Burnside, Glasgow, is a tragic and harrowing tale of justice gone awry. Peter Manuel's involvement in the case and eventual arrest played a pivotal role in exonerating William Watt. Here's an expanded account of this story:

The Murders:

In September 1956, a gruesome triple murder shocked the quiet suburb of Burnside in Glasgow, Scotland. Marion Watt, her daughter Vivienne, and her sister Margaret Brown were brutally killed in their home. The crime scene was marked by extreme violence, and the killer left behind few clues.

Wrongful Arrest of William Watt:

Suspicion quickly fell on Marion Watt's husband, William Watt. The authorities believed that he might have had a motive, possibly financial, for the murders. William Watt was subsequently arrested and charged with the murders of his wife, daughter, and sister-in-law.

Despite the lack of concrete evidence linking him to the crime, Watt found himself in a precarious legal situation. The case against him relied heavily on circumstantial evidence and his alleged suspicious behaviour.

Peter Manuel's Involvement:

Around the same time, Peter Manuel had already gained notoriety as a serial killer and was known for committing a series of murders and other violent crimes. He had been arrested for various offenses but was not yet charged with the murders that would eventually lead to his execution.

While in custody, Manuel realized that the police were pursuing the wrong man in the Burnside murders. He saw an opportunity to manipulate the situation to his advantage. In a cunning move, he sent a letter to Watt's lawyer, George Murphy, confessing to the murders and providing details of the crime scene that had not been publicly disclosed.

Manuel's Confession and Legal Strategy:

Manuel's confession letter to George Murphy shocked both the defence and the prosecution. He claimed that he had killed Marion, Vivienne, and Margaret, and he provided accurate details about the crime scene that only the real killer could have known.

This revelation led to William Watt's release from prison after spending 67 days behind bars. It became clear that Watt had been wrongly accused and that the true perpetrator was Peter Manuel. Manuel's confession served as a crucial piece of evidence in exonerating Watt.

Subsequent Arrest and Trial of Peter Manuel:

With his confession, Peter Manuel effectively cleared William Watt's name. However, it led to his own arrest and eventual trial for the Burnside murders, as well as several other murders and crimes he had committed during his crime spree.

At trial, Peter Manuel attempted to act as his own defence attorney, a move reminiscent of his later trial in Glasgow. He used the proceedings to further manipulate and taunt the authorities and the victims' families.

Manuel was eventually found guilty of multiple murders, including those of Marion Watt, Vivienne Watt, and Margaret Brown, and he was sentenced to death. He was executed by hanging in 1958.

The Burnside murders and the wrongful arrest of William Watt serve as a stark reminder of the complexities and challenges of criminal investigations. In this case, it was ultimately the cunning of a serial killer, Peter Manuel, that exposed the wrongful arrest and helped bring justice to the true victims of the heinous crimes.

Epilogue

The Shadow of Darkness Lifted

In the spellbinding conclusion to "Dark Confessions: The Beast of Birkenshaw - The Peter Manuel Story," we've embarked on a harrowing odyssey through a world of crime, justice, and the intricacies of the human psyche. Peter Manuel's twisted life, from the crucible of early struggles to the abyss of darkness, has left an indelible mark on Scotland and the world. As we conclude this gripping narrative, we peer into the multifaceted legacy of this notorious figure and explore the enigmatic questions that continue to haunt us.

A Legacy of Infamy: Peter Manuel, the infamous "Beast of Birkenshaw," etched his name into Scotland's annals of infamy. His reign of terror, spanning from petty thefts to heinous murders, cast a long, menacing shadow over the nation. His cunning evasion of authorities and audacious taunting of law enforcement added a spine-tingling layer of intrigue and fear to his story.

Unanswered Enigmas: Despite exhaustive investigations, courtroom dramas, and Manuel's eventual execution, mysteries and riddles persist. Some of his crimes remain shrouded in darkness, leaving victims' families bereft of closure. The motivations behind his macabre acts and the depths of his criminal network remain elusive, locked in the labyrinth of his psyche.

A Complex Psyche: In Chapter 16, we ventured deep into Peter Manuel's psyche, exploring his twisted personality, mental health, motivations, and behaviour. His aptitude for manipulation, his morbid fascination with criminality, and his chilling psychopathic tendencies create a disconcerting mosaic. Experts have dissected his mind, yet we're left with a disquieting comprehension of the abyss that consumed him.

The Unyielding Pursuit of Justice: Chapter 17 delves into the indomitable role of Detective Inspector William Muncie, whose unwavering commitment and dedication brought Peter Manuel to justice. Muncie's unwavering resolve is a testament to the core principles guiding those sworn to shield society from its most perilous threats.

Bridget Manuel's Anguish: In Chapter 18, we caught a glimpse into the life of Bridget Manuel, Peter's mother, who watched helplessly as her son descended into darkness. Her courtroom appearance and the emotional turmoil she endured underscore the profound impact of Manuel's crimes on his own family, reminding us that the ripples of his malevolence reached far and wide.

As we draw the curtains on Peter Manuel's life and malevolence, we're left with a persistent sense of disquiet and fascination. The echoes of his dark confessions still resonate through the annals of history. His legacy serves as an eerie reminder of the unfathomable depths humanity can plunge into and the ceaseless quest for justice that society demands.

"The Beast of Birkenshaw" may have been extinguished, but his story endures as a chilling cautionary tale—a stark reminder that malevolence can fester in the most unsuspecting corners of society and that the pursuit of truth and justice is an unwavering odyssey in the face of unrelenting darkness.